PRAISE FOR KIKI SWINSON

"After reading *Candy Shop*, all I could say was scandalous!"
—K'wan, *Essence* bestselling author of *Still Hood*

"*I'm Still Wifey* is the truth! Swinson has done it again. This book pulls you from the first page."
—Treasure E. Blue, *Essence* bestselling author of *A Street Girl Named Desire*

"Kiki has written a gripping, 'reality-based' story about living life married to a drug kingpin—which isn't glamorous . . ."
—Crystal Lacey Winslow, *Essence* bestselling author, on *Wifey*

"The eagerly awaited sequel from the author of the bestseller *Wifey*, Kiki Swinson continues to thrill with excitement . . ."
—Anthony Whyte, author of the Ghetto Girls trilogy

Also by Kiki Swinson

Wifey

I'm Still Wifey

Sleeping with the Enemy (with Wahida Clark)

Life After Wifey

KIKI SWINSON

Dafina
Books

Kensington Publishing Corp.

http://www.kensingtonbooks.com

DAFINA BOOKS are published by

Kensington Publishing Corp.
850 Third Avenue
New York, NY 10022

All Kensington Titles, Imprints, and Distributed Lines are
available at special quantity discounts for bulk purchases for
sales promotions, premiums, fund-raising, and educational
or institutional use. Special book excerpts or customized
printings can also be created to fit specific needs. For details,
write or phone the office of the Kensington special sales
manager: Kensington Publishing Corp., 850 Third Avenue,
New York, NY 10022, attn: Special Sales Department,
Phone: 1-800-221-2647.

Dafina and the Dafina logo Reg. U.S. Pat. & TM Off.

ISBN-13: 978-0-7582-2903-8
ISBN-10: 0-7582-2903-8

First Dafina mass market printing: March 2009

10 9 8

Printed in the United States of America

Dedication:

In spite of all the obstacles & the people who have inter-fered in my life and tried to tear my world apart, I have to thank my Father in heaven, for interceding & giving me the strength to keep moving on.

&

Shaquira, Lil John & Kamryn, thanks for showing mommy what true love is. You know I'm gonna always have y'all back, right?

Acknowledgments:

To my Publisher/Agent *Crystal Lacey Winslow*, you have always made sound business decisions for me and you never let me down, so I want to thank you for it.

To all my family & friends, I love you all! To the book clubs like: *The Beauty Shop* out of Virginia Beach, VA (Trina, April, Kim & Tiggy), *Chapter II Chapter* out of N.C. (Charisma, Kesha & the rest of the ladies), & *OOSA* online book club (Nardsbaby & Toni), thanks ladies for the love, but most importantly your constructive criticism. Also to the *D.C. Bookman* (I carry your words with me all the time, *"It's not a game!"*)

To my new family over at *Kensington/Dafina*, watch out because I'm coming! And when I come, I'm coming hard! (smile). And last but not least, to all my peoples on lock: *Charles "Silk" Dunn* (FCI Elkton), *Leonard "Bolo" Marshall, Andrew King, Reggie "Lee" Spears, Leshawn Pullie & Kevin "Ron" Jones*. Keep your heads up!

To everyone else I didn't mention, just know that I do love you & respect the hell outta' ya!

A note from the author:

I want to thank all my readers for their love and support. You guys mean everything to me. The loyalty y'all have for me is amazing. I never really knew what that word meant until it was displayed by all of you. I must also add that I got some mixed reviews on my novel *"The Candy Shop."* While most were saying that they enjoyed it & can't wait for the sequel, I was also told by a lot of you that you loved my *"Wifey"* series more because you can't relate to the whole heroin addict scene. So I say, it's really entertaining to read about a ***ride or die chick*** & her ***baller husband*** and how they live their lives driving hot whips and spending thousands of dollars on expensive diamonds and furs. But what about the people who suffer & lose everything so that the ballers and their wives can have that glamorous life? Being a drug addict is no joke. So I wrote that story for one purpose: to let you see what heroin does to these people. It rips their lives apart and it doesn't take very long to do it. So, if you know anyone who has an addiction, pick up *"The Candy Shop."* It's both informative and entertaining. I guarantee it!

Thanks a bunch,

Kiki Swinson

Prologue

Barely a second after I walked through the front door of my apartment, my cell phone started ringing. I threw all of my things down on the floor and retrieved my phone from my handbag.

"Hello," I said.

"Hey, where you at?" Nikki asked me.

"At home. Why?" I asked and then I took a seat on my living room sofa.

"I'm on my way over there."

"Why? What's wrong?"

"Syncere did it!"

"Did what?"

"I just found out he was involved with Mark getting killed."

"How did you find that out?"

"Because when he was in the shower this morning, I went through his Sidekick to see if he had any messages from any chicks and that's when I ran across an old message he had received the same night you and Mark got shot."

"What did the text message say?" I asked as my heart sunk into the pit of my stomach.

"It said, 'Squad leader was with his broad, so we had to plug both of them. We got his heat, his jewels and his dough, so holla at me when you want me to make the drop.'"

"Oh, my God," I screamed. "We gotta call the police."

"I know, but what are we going to tell 'em?"

"We are going to tell them that muthafucka had my man killed," I screamed at the top of my lungs.

"But, we have no proof."

"Where is his Sidekick?"

"He has it."

"Well, it doesn't matter, 'cause I'm gon' call the police anyway. Ain't no way I'm going to let that bastard walk the streets as a free man after today!"

"Will you wait until I get there?"

"You better hurry up."

"I will. Give me about thirty minutes, 'cause I'm way out here in Newport News."

"Well, I'm going to jump in the shower, so you better come on."

"Okay," she replied and then we both hung up.

I was pissed off once again and hurt that Syncere was the one who had Mark killed. What was I going to do? How were we going to prove the allegations? We had no murder weapon or motive, as the police would say. Our best bet was to get that T-Mobile Sidekick away from him, which is going to be very hard to do. But I guess we would figure something out. I owed Mark at least that.

I got undressed and hopped in the shower because my body needed it badly. The hot water piercing the tender parts of my muscles felt great, so I took my time and bathed every inch of my body.

When I was done, I turned off the water and flung back the shower curtain.

There, was a man pointing his gun directly at me. I

wanted to scream. But before I could let out a single cry, he said, "Don't say a fucking word." There was no expression in his voice at all.

"Okay," I said, my voice barely audible, with my hands partially covering my mouth.

"Here, take this," the guy told me as he handed me a newspaper clipping.

I reached and grabbed it like he instructed me. He said, "Papí wanted me to give you that, so you can see that he took care of Russ."

Hearing this man tell me that this article was about Russ made me want to read it.

The article was printed in black ink in the *Washington Post*'s Metro section. It was about the execution-style murder of a Russell Hastings. He was found in his bed at one o'clock in the morning, shot in the head three times. Police detectives had no suspects at the time.

"This is Russ?" I asked the guy.

"Yes, that's him."

"So, can I ask you why you got that gun pointed at me?"

"Because my job isn't finished."

"Wh-wh-what do you mean?" I began to stutter, trying to figure out what this man was talking about.

"I heard you talking on the telephone about calling the police and that's not good."

"But it was about something else, " I tried to reassure him.

"I heard you. I know you were talking about your husband's murder."

"No, I wasn't. I swear."

"Why are you lying to me when I already heard everything you said?"

"Listen, it's not what you think. I promise you that I wasn't talking about my husband's murder. I could care less about that muthafucka."

"Well, it wouldn't matter anyway because you took money from Papí."

"But I didn't ask for it. He just gave it to me."

"You took it though. When you did that, you let him know that you were weak and could be bought at any price. So, now you got to go, too."

"Wait," I screamed because I wanted to explain myself. But it was too late because he had already pulled the trigger. That meant that my life as I knew it was running on empty and my soul began to emerge from my body.

1

Choosing Sides

Nikki Speaks

From the time I jumped into my car and left Syncere's house until the time I pulled in front of Kira's apartment building, I wrecked the hell out of my brain trying to rationalize and make sense of the text message I had just read on Syncere's T-Mobile.

The message was clear but I could not bring myself to believe that my man had something to do with Mark's murder, not to mention the fact that Kira had gotten caught up in the crossfire and lost her baby. I didn't want to sound stupid or naïve, but there had to be an explanation behind this whole thing. I needed to find out what it was and how involved Syncere was before Kira blew the whistle on him because whether she realized it or not, I needed my man. So, I was not letting him go that easy.

Immediately after I got out of my car I stood there on the sidewalk and took a deep breath. After I exhaled, I put one foot forward and proceeded toward Kira's apartment to confront the inevitable. Knowing she was going to bite my head off the moment I jumped to Syncere's defense was something I had prepared myself for. As I made my way down the entryway to her building, this fine-ass, older-looking Hispanic guy wearing a dark blue painter's cap and overalls came rushing toward me, so I didn't hesitate to move out of his way. But, what was really odd about him was when I tried to make eye contact and say 'hello' he totally brushed me off and looked the other way. Being the chick I am, I threw my hand up at him and said, "Well, fuck you too! You ol' rude muthafucka!" I kept it moving.

Patting my right thigh, with my hand, to a rhythmic beat as I walked up the last step to Kira's floor, I let out a long sigh and proceeded toward Kira's front door. Upon my arrival, I noticed that her door was slightly ajar so I reached over and pushed it open. "Girl, did you know that your door was open?" I yelled as I walked into the apartment. I didn't get an answer, so I closed the front door behind me and proceeded down the hallway toward her bedroom. When I entered into her room and saw that she was nowhere in sight, I immediately called her name again and I turned to walk toward the master bathroom. "Kira, where you at?" I turned the doorknob and pushed the door open.

"Oh, my God," I screamed at the top of my lungs the second my mind registered the gruesome sight of Kira's body slumped over the edge of the bathtub, while her head lay in a pool of her own blood. I couldn't see her face because of the way her body was positioned. I rushed over to her side, got down on my knees and crawled over next to her. My heart was racing at the speed of light and my emotions were spiraling out of control as I grabbed her body and pulled her toward me.

"Kira, please wake up!" I begged her and began to cry hysterically. She didn't move so, I started shaking her frantically. "Kira, please wake up!" I screamed once again. "Don't die on me like this," I pleaded. Out of nowhere, her eyes fluttered and slowly opened. Overwhelmed by her sudden reaction, my heart skipped a beat and I pulled her body even closer. "Oh my God, thank you," I said in a joyful manner and cradled her head in my lap. "I almost thought I lost you," I told her and wiped the tears away from my eyes. Meanwhile, Kira struggled a bit to swallow the blood in her throat and then she tried to speak. I immediately leaned forward and positioned my ear about two inches away from her mouth so I could hear what it was she had to say.

When she finally moved her lips, the few words she uttered were just above a whisper and barely audible. I was about to ask her to repeat herself and she started choking. I panicked. "Ahh shit! Don't do this to me. Take a deep breath," I instructed her as I began to massage her chest. Then it suddenly hit me that I needed to call an ambulance. I retrieved my cellular phone from the holster on my right side and dialed 911.

"911, what's your emergency?"

"My cousin's been shot," I answered with urgency.

"What's your cousin's name?"

"Her name is Kira Walters."

"And what is your name?"

"My name is Nicole Simpson."

"Okay Nicole, I need for you to stay calm. Can you tell me if Kira is conscious?"

"Yes, she's conscious. I've got her lying in my arms."

"Okay, tell me exactly where Kira's been shot."

"In the left side of her head, right above her temple."

"Is that the only place she's been shot?"

"Yes ma'am."

"Nicole, I'm gonna need you to give me the address to where you are located. In the meantime, I'm gonna need you to remain calm and grab something like a sheet or a towel and press it against Kira's head to stop some of the bleeding. Has she lost a lot of blood?"

"Yes, she has," I assured the woman. Shortly thereafter I gave her the address.

The operator stayed on the phone with me until the police and the paramedics arrived. Covered from the waist down in Kira's blood, I was ushered out of the bathroom and into the kitchen by this short, white, female police officer who had a ton of questions for me. I only answered the questions I knew the answers to. Once our little session was over, another detective—this time a white male—came in and asked me almost the exact same questions as the female officer did. I found myself repeating everything over again.

My back was turned when the paramedics took Kira out on the stretcher. By the time I realized that she had been taken away, she was already in the ambulance, headed to the nearest emergency room. The white, male detective informed me where they were taking her so I immediately called my family, told them Kira had gotten shot and that they needed to meet me at Bayside Memorial. After they assured me they were on their way, I hung up with them. On my way out, I noticed at least a dozen detectives and forensics investigators combing every inch of the apartment to collect evidence so there was no doubt in my mind that they were going to find her killer.

I got to the hospital in no time at all and to my surprise my mother, my father and my grandmother arrived shortly afterward. We all sat and waited patiently for one of the doctors performing the emergency surgery to come out and give us an update on Kira's condition. In the meantime, my grandmother had a few questions for me to answer.

"Nikki, are you sure Kira was conscious when she left with the paramedics?" she asked as if she was making a desperate attempt to find the answer in my eyes.

"Yes, she was," I replied in a reassuring manner. "She even tried to say something, but I didn't understand her. When I asked her to say it again she started choking and that's when I called the paramedics."

"Well, how was she breathing when they took her out of the house?"

"I don't know, Grandma. I was in the kitchen when they carried her out," I told her and then I put my head down in despair. Knowing that my cousin was in surgery fighting for her life and I couldn't do anything to help her put a huge strain on my heart. Not to mention the fact that if I would've gotten to her apartment a little sooner this probably would not have happened to her. In a sense I felt like her getting shot was partially my fault. Which was why I was feeling so terrible right now.

"What in the world do y'all got going on?" my father interjected as if the sight of me made him cringe.

"What are you talking about?" I looked at him with an expression of uncertainty.

"What kind of people are y'all mixed up with?"

"Come on now, honey, I know you're upset but this is not the time or the place," my mother spoke up.

"Yes, your wife is right," my grandmother agreed trying to keep the peace.

But my father wasn't trying to hear them. Their comments went in one ear and right out the other. "Whatcha trying to do, end up like your cousin in there?"

"What kind of question is that?" I snapped.

"Just answer the question," he commanded.

"No, I'm not," I replied, irritated with his questions.

"It's hard to tell," my father snapped back. "Because

every time I turn around, somebody's either getting shot or killed. And if you keep walking around here like you ain't got the sense you were born with, then you're gonna end up just like your cousin back there."

"Alright now, that's enough! I don't want to hear another word," my grandmother whispered harshly with tears in her eyes. Her tone sent a clear message to my father that she was sincerely pissed and he'd better not utter another word.

But, knowing how much my father loathed when people told him what to do, the chances of that happening were slim to none. The moment she closed her mouth and rolled her eyes at him, he parted his lips and said, "You know what, Mama . . ."

But fortunately for us, he couldn't finish the thought because we were interrupted by an Asian doctor dressed in green hospital-issued scrubs, walking toward us. "Are you the family for Kira Walters?"

"Yes, we are," I eagerly replied.

"I'm Dr. Ming and I was called in to perform emergency surgery on Miss Walters."

"How is she?" my grandmother asked.

"Yeah, how is she? Can we go in and see her?" my mother asked.

"I'm sorry to inform you but Miss Walters didn't make it."

"What do you mean, she 'didn't make it?'" I screamed in disbelief.

"Ma'am," the doctor began in the most apologetic manner, "believe me, we did everything in our power but she was nonresponsive."

Hearing this man tell me that my cousin just died hit me like a ton of bricks. I couldn't believe it. I mean, there had to be some kind of mistake. Kira couldn't be dead.

I just had her wrapped up in my arms back at her apartment a couple of hours ago. Whatever this man was talking was pure nonsense and I couldn't accept that.

Meanwhile, as the thoughts of living my life without her started consuming me, my grandmother walked off in another direction, crying her poor little heart out. My parents got a little more in-depth with the complications Kira had and why they could not save her. I, on the other hand, just sat there in a daze.

My family and I left the hospital shortly after the doctor broke the news to us. Unfortunately, no one was able to see Kira's body except my grandmother. A nurse escorted her down to the morgue to ID her and get her belongings. My parents and I were cornered in a small room by the same two detectives from Kira's apartment. They didn't have much to say this time, so our little chat went by quickly.

When we arrived back at my grandmother's house I went off into a room by myself while my parents sat around in the living room with my grandmother. I heard bits and pieces of their conversations. But when they started talking about making Kira's funeral arrangements, I immediately turned a deaf ear to them because I wasn't ready to accept the fact that my home girl was dead. As it turned out, they ended up handling everything and I was truly fine with it because it took the burden off me.

2

Just Another Funeral Service

Nikki Speaks

Immediately after the burial everybody, including my family and Kira's friends, gathered around my grandmother's house to pay their last respects. I had to admit that this whole thing had been one emotional ride for me and it would not be over until the niggas who had done this to my cousin got dealt with. I had been crying myself to death from the moment I laid eyes on Kira lying in a pool of her own blood. And what was bugging me the fuck out is that I believe I walked by the grimy-ass bastard who murdered her. I mean, who else could it have been? This guy, whom I'd never seen in this area, was running from the direction of her apartment building right before I found her body. And even though I couldn't give the homicide detectives an accurate description of how that man looked, I do remember him being an older guy of Hispanic descent. I would be able to pick his ass out in a lineup if I had a chance to. I just wish I had gotten there sooner.

Maybe I could have done something and she would be still alive. Sitting there watching everybody grieve her death was becoming unbearable and I needed to excuse myself and get a breath of fresh air.

On my way toward the exit that led to the patio, Kira's hair salon partner, Rhonda, approached me and asked me if I was all right. As badly as I wanted to respond, I couldn't. I got choked up and my eyes welled up with tears. Feeling my pain, she embraced me and led me onto the patio.

"Go ahead and let it out," she told me, rubbing her hand across my back in a circular motion.

"I just can't believe she's gone," I said, burying my face deep in Rhonda's shoulder.

"I can't believe it either," Rhonda replied, letting out a long sigh. "What's really upsetting me is that she couldn't have an open-casket funeral so we couldn't really bid our farewells."

"I know. I felt the same way," I said to Rhonda. "But her face was so disfigured that the funeral director advised us to have a closed-casket ceremony."

"Have those detectives contacted you again?" Rhonda asked.

"Yeah. They came by my apartment last night right after Syncere left," I told her immediately after releasing myself from her embrace.

"Do they have any suspects yet?"

"Nope," I said and then I let out a long sigh.

"Girl, don't worry. They will."

"Yeah, I'll believe it when I see it. I mean, look how they're dragging their feet with finding the niggas who shot her outside her apartment and killed that new guy, Mark, she was fucking with."

"Oh yeah, I see what you're saying. Somebody's definitely not doing their damn job."

"You got that right! But, I'll be damned if I sit back and let this shit right here go unsolved," I yelled. I became enraged by the thought of my cousin's killer going unpunished and tears began to fall rapidly from my eyes.

Rhonda told me to calm down and assured me that somebody would pay for what they did to Kira. She put her arm around my 5'3, 125-lb. frame and held me tight. The sheer, black, spaghetti-strapped dress I was wearing got tangled up in Rhonda's gold-plated costume jewelry bracelet, creating a small rip in the lower back part of my dress, right above my huge-ass butt.

"They sure will," I told her and tried to fix my dress by camouflaging the hole with the stained lining.

"I am so sorry about your dress," Rhonda expressed, looking directly at the rip.

"It's okay. It ain't nothing but a dress," I assured her, my half-breed–looking complexion becoming even more flushed with the redness of my eyes. I walked back into the house leaving Rhonda standing out on the patio.

I went directly upstairs into my grandmother's bedroom to be alone and collect my thoughts. I was beginning to feel like I was on the verge of having a nervous breakdown. Then I figured, what good would that do? I needed to do some soul searching and figure out what I was going to do about everything that was going on. I could not let Kira's killer go unpunished. I didn't care who it was.

It could have been Syncere and I would have felt the same way. He was public enemy number one right now for arousing suspicion of his involvement in Mark's murder through a text message he got from one of his hit men. So believe me, whoever was involved would pay for all the pain my family was feeling right now. I couldn't see it any other way.

* * *

The last person left around eight-thirty. I locked the front door and I went to accompany my grandmother, who was standing over the kitchen sink, washing dishes.

She was very quiet and I could tell she was in deep thought, so I broke the silence by asking her what was on her mind.

She sighed heavily, "Oh, I'm just thinking about how things are going to be without Kira. She's going to truly be missed around here."

I let out a long sigh and replied, "She sure is, grandma." I took a seat at the kitchen table.

"Have you decided whether you were going to hire a professional moving crew or are you going to move her things out of her place yourself?"

"I'm going to hire a crew to move the big things. But me and Rhonda are going to pack up and move the small stuff ourselves. Speaking of which, do you know I overheard Cousin Maxine and Aunt Brenda squabbling over who was going to get Kira's clothes and furs?"

"Now, I know they ain't done no mess like that," my grandmother replied with an expression of disbelief.

"Oh, yes they did. And you should've heard Aunt Brenda ranting and raving about how Kira was her favorite niece so she knows she's going to get a couple pieces of her diamond jewelry and a few pairs of her designer shoes."

"Well, since Kira was the favorite niece, where was she when Kira was going through all those problems with her husband and needed somebody to talk to? Because if my memory serves me correctly, every time Kira picked up the phone to call Brenda, she would always be short with her or tell her she was going to call her back."

"Oh yeah, I remember that. It use to hurt Kira's feelings too, because she felt like Aunt Brenda was the only person in the family she could talk to."

"Yes, I know. But, we are not going to continue to dwell on that. We are going to look forward and make sure we handle all of Kira's affairs in a proper fashion."

"I second that."

"That sounds good, Nikki, but do you think you're ready to go back into that place?"

"I've been fighting with it, but yeah, I'm ready. And besides, the thought of one of those guys stealing any of Kira's valuable things just does not sit right with me."

"What kind of valuable things does she have?" my grandmother asked while rinsing her hands off under the running water from the faucet and turning around in my direction.

"Well, for one, she's got some really expensive jewelry and fur coats in there. I know she's got three expensive wall paintings and a set of oriental vases she inherited from her mom after she passed away. We've got to make sure that stuff stays in safekeeping."

"What do you plan to do with those things?" my grandmother asked.

"I was going to take some of it to my apartment and bring the rest of it here."

"I ain't got any room for no more furniture around here," she protested.

"I know that, Grandma. That's why I'm going to take Kira's furniture and bring whatever I can't fit into my place over here and store it upstairs in the attic."

"That's fine. So, what do you plan to do with her car?"

"I'm gonna sell it."

"But why, Nikki? It's a brand new vehicle."

"I know. But I'm beginning to feel like every time I get behind the wheel there will be a black cloud looming over me and I don't want to feel like that."

"Well, just pray to the good Lord and He'll give you that

peace you need to endure what you're gonna come up against," she replied as she took a seat at the table next to me.

"I know," I said, burying my face in the palms of my hands. The thought of Kira's death was becoming impossible to deal with. Plus I was riddled with anxiety, knowing that her killer was still out there. Not to mention that my life could be in danger, which was even scarier. How do I even attempt to deal with that? I mean, it wasn't like I had a couple of bodyguards around to protect me. I was alone now.

Kira was all I had. She was like my big sister and my best friend. Plus, she took care of me, made sure I was straight and always had my back. That's why I could not let her down. I would die before I let those bastards get away with taking her from me. Believe me, the muthafuckers who were responsible for shooting and causing her to miscarry and then shooting her again—but this time killing her— would suffer. That was my word!

"Have you talked to those detectives again?" My grand-mother's voice broke into my thoughts.

"Yeah, last night."

"What did they say?"

"They just wanted to know if there was information I could think of that would help them come closer to solving the case."

"What did you tell 'em?"

"I told them exactly what I told them the first time."

"Do you think they have some good leads?"

"I'm not sure, Grandma," I said, my voice screeching as an attempt to cry out for help. I wanted so badly to let out everything I had bottled up in me. But I realized that my grandmother would not be able to handle it. She wouldn't understand the game and how it worked. She really wouldn't understand it if I told her Kira had something to do with her husband Ricky getting murdered.

Oh my God! She would lose her mind and fall apart. Then she would have those same detectives breathing down my neck with a long list of questions. Who knew? I'd probably be behind bars a few hours later, charged with conspiracy to commit murder.

And I could not have that. My place was out here on these streets. My best bet was to keep my mouth closed.

"Are you okay, Nikki?"

"Nah, Grandma, but I'll be okay. I'm gonna head on home and get some rest." I got up from the kitchen chair and pushed the chair under the table.

"Are you sure you can drive in your condition?"

"Yes, Grandma, I can."

"Okay, baby. Well, drive carefully and call me as soon as you reach home."

"I will, " I said and kissed her on the cheek.

3

Sleeping With Da Enemy

Nikki Speaks

When I reached my apartment, I walked straight into my bedroom and found Syncere lying on my bed, shirtless, with a sheet draped across the bottom half of him. His chest muscles looked like they were about to pop while he relaxed against the bedpost watching a porno flick. His hand was wrapped around his big, thick dick, pumping it for dear life. On a good day I would've wanted to join in on the action since it was one of our norms to watch a flick together; but today I was too busy mourning my cousin. I turned around to walk back out of the room when he stopped me.

"Hey, where you going? Come on over here so I can shoot this bullet up in you."

"Come on, Syncere, you know I am not in the mood for that right now," I told him and proceeded toward the living room.

"Wait!"

I ignored him and kept right on walking. I sat on the

sofa in my living room and buried my face in my hands as I thought about taking on the challenge of going into Kira's apartment to pack up her things. Five minutes later, Syncere joined me.

"Damn, Ma, you sure missed that explosion!"

I lifted my head up from my hands and said, "Please baby, not right now."

"Ahh, cheer up!" he insisted as he wrapped his arm around my shoulder.

"I wish it was that simple," I responded and then sighed heavily.

"But, it can be."

"How Syncere? Especially after knowing the nigga who murdered Kira is still out there. I mean, come on. It could be anybody. And for all I know this nigga could've been hiding out somewhere in the neighborhood, saw me when I went into her apartment and is waiting for a chance to knock me off."

"Yo, trust me, ain't nobody gon' fuck wit' you," he said in a cocky manner.

"How you know? I mean, how can you be so sure?" I asked in a suspicious tone.

"Because I am, that's all!"

"Well, why do I feel like you're keeping something from me?" I boldly asked, sitting straight up as I turned my body to face him head on.

In an abrupt manner, he became very defensive and replied, "What the fuck could I be keeping from you?"

"That's what I'm trying to figure out."

"Yo, Nikki, I don't know what you're trying to insinuate but my gut feeling is telling me that whatever it is, I ain't gon' like it."

"It's probably your guilty conscience messing with you," I responded sarcastically.

"What the fuck you mean by that?" he snapped at me as he swung a powerful punch in my direction. When I saw his fist coming toward me with much force, my reflexes kicked in and allowed me to react by using my arms to shield my head.

Immediately after his fist landed into my arms, I somehow jumped to my feet.

"What the fuck is wrong with you? Don't no niggas be putting their hands on me! I don't play that Tina Turner shit!" I was bobbing my head like I was ready to go toe to toe with this nigga.

"Shut the fuck up, bitch!" he retaliated and lunged back at me, grabbing me around my neck. The moment his hand locked around my throat my air passage began to tighten up. I found myself gasping for air.

"Get off me," I managed to utter as I feverishly tried removing his hand from around my neck. But it seemed like the harder I tried, the tighter his grip got.

"Just shut the fuck up," he yelled with rage, adding more pressure to his grip.

Seeing how belligerent he had become after the accusation, I promptly tried a different approach. I honestly wanted nothing more than for him to release his hand from around my neck. I began to display no resistance at all and just stood still there before him with a helpless expression, as my eyes began to tear up. Once my actions were in full force, I found that my tactics were beginning to work because about twenty seconds later Syncere took his hand from around my throat and, without warning, pushed me back onto the living room sofa.

"Owww!" I said, after stumbling back onto the couch.

"Yo, didn't I just say shut the fuck up?" he said, pointing his finger in my face as he stood over me.

Filled up to my neck in fear, I nodded my head as I

massaged my neck. Seeing him act this way was a first-time experience. I was treading on new territory and I did not like it one bit. I was beginning to feel terrified and unsure of what to do next, so I sat back calmly and waited patiently for him to make the next move. I felt I had to let him believe that he had full control of the situation.

"Don't say another word until I tell you to. 'Cause I see you don't know what the fuck to say outta your mouth!" he replied, as he moved closer to me. "Do you know what I do to women who call themselves trying to disrespect me?"

I shook my head no.

He continued by saying, "I rip their fucking tongues outta their mouths and put them to sleep!"

Hearing his response sent my heart racing out of the front door. I just couldn't get up the gumption to get my feet to follow.

"So, the next time you want to come out of your face like you did a few minutes ago, you better think about it first. 'Cause I ain't gon' be responsible for what happens to you once my mind goes blank. You feel me?"

I nodded my head yes.

"Good! Don't ever question me again about any bodies 'cause whether you believe it or not, your cousin had that shit coming to her. Anybody in their right mind could see that that was a direct mob hit from the niggas who her husband probably owed some dough to. Quincy ran shit down to me about the Russians her husband was fucking with. Yeah, I heard them cats were about their business! And when they figured out that they wasn't gon' get their dough once the Feds shut down their shop, I guess they felt the need to cut their losses altogether. Now, am I right or wrong?"

"I really don't know, to be honest. But, there is something in the back of my mind that's telling me that whoever killed Mark had something to do with Kira's murder," I replied in a very cautious manner and waited for Syncere's facial expression or body language to change.

And it did when he responded aggressively by saying, "Tell me who the fuck put that stupid shit in your head!" He roughed me up by placing his right hand on the side of my mouth, gesturing for me to talk.

"Nobody!" I finally got up the nerve to say.

"You lying to me?"

"No, I'm not lying."

"So, where is all this shit coming from?" He released his grip on my face.

"It's been on my mind since Kira got killed. And for the life of me, I can't figure out who could be responsible for her death other than the guys who shot her the first time. That's all!"

"You sure them detectives ain't put that shit in your head?" he asked suspiciously.

"No, they didn't. But the question did come up."

"Who brought it up?"

"They did."

"What did they say?"

"They asked me if I believed the two incidents were connected."

"So, what did you tell 'em?"

"I told 'em I didn't know. But . . ." I began to say but I stopped mid-sentence.

"But what?"

I sighed and said, "But, there's a huge possibility that they could be."

"And what did they say?"

"Syncere, we've already been through this. Why are you making me repeat everything over again?"

"Because I want to make sure you didn't leave anything

out. Now, tell me what they said," he replied like he was getting aggravated.

Noticing that his behavior pattern was about to do another 180-degree turn, I realized that it would not be a smart move to step back out of my circle. If I gave him a chance to grab me around my neck again, he might not let me go until I was flat lining. So, I took a deep breath and said, "They asked me if Kira ever mentioned to me if she knew the guys who might have had something to do with her and Mark's shooting."

"And?"

"And I told 'em no. I said she was just as curious to know, as we all are."

"So, what did they say?"

"They believed what I told them and gave me their cards in case I remembered something else."

"Well, the next time they come to you with a whole bunch of fucking questions tell 'em to contact your lawyer."

"But, I don't have one."

"You will after tomorrow."

"But, why would I need one? I mean, it's not like I'm their number-one suspect or something."

"Don't question me, a'ight? Just do what I tell you to do and we gon' be all right. But if you don't then there's going to be some serious fucking problems."

"Why do you always have to threaten me?"

"Bitch, just shut up before I go upside your muthafucking head again."

I barely recognized the man in front of me. "Can you tell me what happened to the Syncere I fell in love with six months ago?"

"Oh bitch, cut it out! You ain't in love with me. You're in love with the fact that I got money and I can take care of your ass."

"So whatchu trying to say?"

"Come on now, don't be stupid. Because if I wasn't paying all these bills around here and giving you two grand a week allowance, you wouldn't of fucked with me."

"Yes, I would've."

"No, you wouldn't," he said pointing directly at me. "You did it so you could show Kira that you could get somebody to take care of you too. It wasn't nothing but a competition thing and you know it. Because as soon as I started lacing you with all that Jean Paul Gaultier and that Marc Jacobs shit you got in your closet, you started acting all big headed like you wasn't use to shit. But, it was cool. I didn't care if you wanted to flaunt and get your shit off around her since you didn't have to work as her shampoo girl anymore. But, when you come at me like you run shit over here, then I'm gonna have to carry you a little different than your friends do. So, know that the next time you try to come at me like you did earlier, I'm telling you now that it's gonna get real ugly. And I ain't gon' say it again."

Hearing the tone of his comment and watching him as he turned to walk out of the room, sent chills through my entire body. This man was fucking nuts. I was sleeping with the enemy. I mean, what man in their right mind would come off on me like this bastard just did? And for me to sit here and take it like I am a damned fool showed him how weak I was. But I got a trick for his ass. I had never ever been in a relationship with a nigga who put his hands on me, so the ball dropped here. And if he thought I was going to tell those detectives to back off me with the questions just to get the heat off him, he was mad. It would not happen in this lifetime. Ol' psycho muthafucka!

4

True Story

Syncere Speaks

After that stunt I just pulled on Nikki, I know she was probably sitting back in the crib thinking that I was some bugged-out-ass nigga. But, it wasn't like that for real. I am just a regular ol' cat who is stressed the fuck out right now because of all that heat I've got on me. And then to have her questioning me about her cousin's murder kind of fucked my head up. I mean, come on. Nikki should've known better than to come at me like that. For a minute I thought she was trying to trick me into doing some confessing type shit. But, then again, she couldn't be that fucking stupid. I mean, what street nigga you know would confess to a body? Not Syncere. Shit, I'm from Newark, New Jersey, where niggas in my hood run around like beasts. Cats from my way wouldn't confess to a body if they were caught butchering a nigga in broad daylight. So, what part of the game was she playing? Whatever it was, she'd better slow her roll, before she ended up like Kira. And I just might be the muthafucka to do it.

Don't get me wrong, I liked fucking around wit' her, 'cause she was cool to be with most of the time, plus she's got some good pussy. The only thing about her I didn't like was that she was green as hell. She wasn't hip to the streets at all, which was why I kept her as far away as I could from my business. A chick like her would getcha life in prison if you messed around and put her down with your grind. She would bitch up and tell those crackers everything they wanted to hear and I couldn't have that. So, the best place for her is to continue riding this dick every time this muthafucka rock up. Other than that, she needed to stay out of my way or she was gonna find herself sleeping next to her cousin. And believe me, I ain't gon' lose no sleep behind it, either. She'd be just another funeral service I contributed to because life is too short for the larceny.

I'm a brown-skinned, handsome, 30-year-old cat with chiseled features and a build of 5'11, 220 lbs. who loved to make plenty of dough and fuck plenty of pussy. Niggas tell me I remind them of that rich-ass nigga 50 Cent. And I know they ain't lying because he's all about his business and I am too. So if a day goes by and I can't acquire one or the other, shit just ain't gon' be right. And whoever was in my circle at the end of the day would feel the repercussions from it. Take, for instance, the shit that went down with Mark's murder. Yeah, I had that nigga done up. And I had a good reason for doing it, too. See first of all, I didn't give a fuck who you were, you ain't gon' disrespect me, which was what that nigga did. Okay granted, I tricked up a lot of his dough and stepped on his packages more times than he wanted me to and brought the quality of it down, but that was still no reason for him to scream on me in front of my soldiers. Calling me out and asking me in front of my homeboys if I was hanging out in the dope spots, getting blazed with the fiends, was the most disrespectful thing he could've ever said. And what set the whole shit off was how he came off on me. This muthafucka screamed on me like I was his hoe. So, you can imagine how my homeboys was looking at me. I felt like a little bitch standing there, high as gas and looking stupid than a mu'fucka. And since I didn't want to fuck up my high, I went on and let him get his shit off his chest. But everybody, including him, knew that I was gon' straighten his ass out later. The game was built on principle, so he should've pulled me to the side and stepped to me in a better way. But nah! He wanted everybody around us to know that he was the big man and that he was the nigga frontin' me all the dope I was getting, which was the wrong move. It didn't matter to me that I was working for him. What mattered was the fact that he fronted on me like I was a fucking crackhead. And to keep him from trying that bullshit again, I got my boys to eliminate his ass. Shit, I've got a reputation to protect.

Niggas respected me 'cause they knew I was a loose cannon. So, I couldn't let that shit he did slide. That's why I had to deal with it. Too bad Kira got shot and lost her baby in the crossfire. She shouldn't have been at the wrong place at the wrong time. I mean, hey, shit happened. And now that Mark was out of the equation, I had a truckload of free dope and a whole lot of customers who want to buy. My only problem was that I had to get those homicide detectives from off my back. And if Nikki didn't stick to her guns and do like I told her, she was gonna end up on the side of a milk carton. Bottom line! Anyway, I was gonna head on down to Norfolk, to my car wash, so I could clear my head. Maybe then I could get a better sense of why Nikki came off on me like she did. Luckily for her, I wasn't in the mood to put her in a body bag. But I wasn't gonna lie: If this shit kept up, it was gonna happen sooner than later. And that was my word!

The parking lot of my car wash was empty except for my man Quincy's whip and a white 2007 LS 460 that belonged to dis nigga named Lloyd. Lloyd was a big, black, flamboyant type of nigga from P-Town. Hoes be going crazy over his ugly ass because he looked like Biggie Smalls and he had a little bit of dough. Seeing this nigga's car parked out here this time of the night sent a clear message to me that there was a serious dice game going on inside. And if they were throwing around the type of money I liked, then I'd have to get in on the fun, too.

"Ay yo, niggas, what's good," I said the moment I unlocked the door to my office and walked through it. But to my surprise, these niggas weren't rolling dice. Quincy was sitting in the lounge chair just a few feet away from my desk, playing *Madden 2007* on the PlayStation 3 we copped two days ago from this dope fiend. And that nigga Lloyd was sitting in the other chair across from him, talking on his cell phone. His loud and ignorant ass was telling some chick that he wasn't gon' stop by and see her if she wasn't gon' let him get his dick wet. Me and Quincy both laughed at his crazy ass. He found himself to be amusing too, 'cause as soon as he hung up with the chick, he smiled at me and said, "Yeah nigga, I got dem hoes trained!"

I threw my hand in the air and waved him off. "Yo, man, dem hoes ain't thinking about your ass, for real!"

"Shiiid! I betcha I can take your girl," Lloyd fired back at me and then he laughed.

"Oh nah, son! You can't take nothing I got, especially if it's a chick. So, you need to get that outcha mind!"

"You wanna put some money on it?" Lloyd retaliated in a cocky manner, simultaneously pulling a wad of money from his pants pocket.

I took a seat in the chair behind my desk and said, "Yo,

nigga, you better put that li'l bit of money back in your pocket before you fuck around and lose it, for real."

"Yeah, whatever, nigga," Lloyd replied as he pushed the money back down into his pocket.

Quincy burst into laughter as he continued to play the game and said, "Y'all niggas is funny!"

"Nah, that's your boy Lloyd over there, acting like a clown."

"Oh trust me, I'm far from being a clown. But I am killer at heart," Lloyd struck back in a condescending manner and then he laughed it off.

"Shiiid, nigga, you ain't the only cat 'round here who'll bust a gun," I told him.

"Damn sure ain't," Quincy interjected, never taking his eyes off his game.

Lloyd chuckled and said, "Y'all niggas think y'all really tough, huh?"

"Throw some heat my way and see what happens," I fired back.

"Nigga, you always ready to get into a damn gun fight," Lloyd blurted out.

"Damn right, nigga! I'm trained to go," I told him, getting hyped by my words.

"A'ight, since you trained to go, suit up one of dem pits you got and meet me at the spot in P-Town, so I can get some of that car wash money I seen Quincy counting earlier."

"Oh nah, you'll never see none of that dough 'cause dem bitches I got back at my kennel are beasts."

"Well, pull 'em out and bring 'em on down to the spot. 'Cause I got this vicious, all-black pit who's a straight killer. And when I blow this special whistle I got for him, he goes crazy and tears shit apart."

"How many fights has he been in?" I asked.

"Just two. Because I just recruited him from this cat who breeds my pits."

"How much money you laying down?" I asked him.

"Twenty grand."

"Oh shit!" Quincy stopped playing and looked at us. "That nigga ain't playing!"

"You sure you wanna lay down that type of dough?" I questioned Lloyd.

"Yeah, I'm sure. So, what's up? Can you match it?"

"Come on now, son, don't try to play me!"

"I ain't trying to play you, Syncere. But if you feel like I'm putting up too much dough, then I can lower the count to ten or fifteen."

Getting pissed off by this nigga's sly-ass remarks, I stood up from my chair, dug in my pockets and pulled out all the dough I had and said, "Nigga, I got twenty grand right here and got more where this came from. So, what's up?"

"Oh, I'm ready."

"Well, what time are you trying to get down?" I asked.

"That nigga Mike is opening up the ring tonight after eleven. So, you can meet me up there at midnight," he replied and got up from his chair.

"A'ight! Well, let's do this, then," I said. I looked over at Quincy and told him to get Rameek on the phone and tell him to get my fighters up and ready.

"A'ight," he said and got on his cell phone to make the call.

Meanwhile, Lloyd made a few more slick-ass comments, but he did it in a joking manner as he headed for the exit. So I let him live.

Quincy followed me down to the spot in P-Town and, as expected, the joint was packed. I recognized a lot of the cars parked outside so I knew right off the bat that this was going to be a good night. After me, Rameek and Quincy rounded my bitches up and locked them up 'round back in the storage shed to keep 'em away from the other dogs, I went back 'round front to sign in and place my bet. Quincy caught up with me a few minutes later while Rameek stayed behind to keep a close eye on my investment.

In this game, it was very important not to leave your dogs unattended. Niggas in this business will do everything in their power to sabotage your chances of walking away with all their dough. I remember a while back, some niggas poisoned three pits that belonged to this cat named Big Hank. And boy, when that nigga found out about it, he shot this place up because he knew that once he placed his bet, he wasn't going to get his dough back, regardless if his dogs got killed or not. So, homeboy lost out all across the board. But, lucky for him, he busted his shots into the ceiling and nobody got hurt.

Because I believe if he would've pointed his gun anywhere else, he would've been taken out of here in the same body bag with all three of his pits. That's why you had to stay on guard at spots like this, because it was crazy and these other niggas didn't give a fuck aboutchu.

Right before my beasts had their face-off with Lloyd's pits, I stepped to him to make sure he had already laid down his dough. He was standing in a huddle with a crew of niggas he fucked with from P-Town. Two of the cats I knew from coming to the car wash; the other two I'd never seen before. So when I approached Lloyd, they gritted on me like they were his bodyguards or something. But it didn't stop me from stepping to him. "Yo, nigga, you ready?"

"You ready?" he struck back in a way like he was trying to show off in front of his homeboys.

"Oh, no question," I assured him.

"Put that twenty grand down yet?" he asked me in a sarcastic kind of fashion.

"Got my ticket right here," I told him and flashed it in front of him.

"I got mines, too," he assured me by patting his right pants pocket.

"Yeah, well, I hope it was for that same twenty large you was talking about earlier."

"Don't worry about it. I gotcha covered."

"Well, that's what's up, den. So, we got the next fight, right?"

"That's what I was told."

"A'ight. Well, I'mma holler at you in a few."

"A'ight," he replied and turned his back to me as I walked off.

I headed back over to where Quincy was standing and said, "I can't wait to see that fat nigga's face when I take his dough tonight!"

"What he say?" Quincy asked.

"The nigga ain't say shit! But he was over there showing off, like he's got some serious paper."

Quincy started laughing and said, "Come on now, you know that nigga is known for trying to shine in front of his peoples."

"Yeah, I know. But, sometimes he be taking that shit to another level and I don't like it."

"Yo, man, don't sweat that shit he be talking. 'Cause he ain't nothing but a pussy-ass nigga anyway."

"Yeah, that's probably why he got dem whack-ass niggas over there surrounding him, like they're his bodyguards or something."

"That's how that nigga roll when he's got a certain amount of dough on the line."

"Well, if he knows like I know, he needs to get rid of

dem crab-ass niggas and recruit some real soldiers that look like they trained to go!"

"Lloyd ain't getting rid of none of them niggas 'cause two of 'em is his cousins and the other two are his flunkies."

"Yeah, well, we gon' see how loyal dem niggas are when the heat is coming at 'em."

Quincy burst into laughter again and said, "I would sure love to see that."

I looked at Quincy with a grim expression and said, "If shit don't go the way I plan, you might see it sooner than you think."

"Well, you know you gon' have to kill every last one of them, right?"

"Yeah, I know that," I responded in a nonchalant way. Instead of Quincy responding, he just looked at me with an expression that said he was down for whatever. I gave him a nod to let him know that I was feeling his loyalty and we left it just like that.

A few minutes later, I sent word for Rameek to bring out my Brindle pit named Coco, because the fight was about to start. That fat nigga Lloyd stood on the other side of the ring with his pit on the leash. And I ain't gon' lie, that muthafucker he had standing beside him was a beast. His head was big as a muthafucker, but the frame of his body was a little smaller than Coco, so he might be able to lock onto her neck and cripple her ability to breathe. But hopefully Coco wouldn't let that happen and would just rip his ass apart from the door. Rameek entered the ring with Coco, Lloyd came in from the other side with his pit and the crowd started going crazy. Both Rameek and Lloyd stayed in their corners so they could finish prepping both dogs. Not too long after, the judge entered the ring and instructed Rameek and Lloyd to bring the dogs to their scratch lines. Seconds later, the short, old, gray-haired man yelled, "Let 'em go!"

Immediately after those words left his mouth, the adrenaline inside me started pumping like crazy. Niggas all over the spot started going wild when Coco and Lloyd's pit charged at each other. And like two Mack trucks, they slammed into each other hard with their teeth flashing as they tried desperately to find a vulnerable spot to tear into. "Get him Coco! Get 'em!" I roared into the ring. Listening to my command, Coco stretched open her mouth and leaped head first and grabbed the pit's right front leg, tearing into the coat and ripping open the flesh. Blood shot out all over the floor and into Coco's face. All of a sudden, you heard a *snap*, and the other pit got flipped onto its back. And from that point, I knew my girl had broken one or two of that pit's bones because he couldn't get back onto his feet. Coco released his leg and went straight for his throat and tried to lock onto it, but the judge hurried up and ordered Rameek and Lloyd to break them up.

Rameek rushed in and grabbed Coco while one of Lloyd's homeboys walked into the ring with a blanket and picked up his pit. While this was going on I watched Lloyd's facial expression the entire time. And boy, was he pissed. "Dump that muthafucker outside 'round back," he told Rameek.

"That nigga Gaza ain't gon' let us leave him here," Lloyd's homeboy said as he struggled to hold the pit in his arms.

"Well, do something wit' 'em, 'cause he ain't going back to the crib wit' me," Lloyd fired back.

"Want me to get the vet 'round back to set his leg?" the guy asked like he was pleading for the pit's life.

"Shiiid, nigga, is you crazy? I ain't paying no vet two grand to set his leg. Just throw his ass in the back of the truck and get rid of 'em," Lloyd snapped back and then he walked off.

Now you know I wasn't gonna let that nigga walk out of here without me saying something, so I caught up with him. "Ay yo, nigga, you 'bout to leave?"

"Yeah, why?" he asked in a frustrated manner.

"Oh, because I didn't want you to leave without me saying thanks for that easy money!"

"That wasn't no easy money. That was just luck. Because if they would've let me use my drill whistle, your bitch would've been done from the gate."

"Nah, homeboy. I don't think so, because Coco is a Presa Canario and they go harder than any other pit 'round here."

"Nigga, I don't give a fuck what kind of pit you got," Lloyd fired back. "Cause, that pit I got is a Blue Nose and he's a monster and if these ol' sucker-ass niggas would've let me use my joint, you wouldn't be smiling right now."

"Yeah, nigga! Whatever," I replied with a smile as I waved him off with my hand and walked off. I mean, it wasn't making any sense for me to keep talking to the moron. He wasn't trying to hear me anyway. I bounced and headed over to the bookies to collect my dough. When that mission was completed I put my dough away in a safe place and hopped back in my whip.

After that twenty-grand victory, I camped out in my hideaway spot in Chesapeake. It was a nice, plush, four-bedroom lake house, sitting on two acres of land, overlooking the Garden Ridge Lake off Battlefield Boulevard. I picked up this pretty, red chick named Sasha on the way here since I was in the mood to get my dick sucked. Quincy called her up for me and told her to meet me up at the car wash.

He fucked her a few times himself and told me that she

was about her work and I wouldn't have to pay much for her services. All I had to do is promise the hoe breakfast and a shopping spree in the morning and I would get the royal treatment. It worked every time. When it comes to dem' other hoes like Nikki's cousin Kira, you had come at them from a different angle. Believe me, they were hip to the game and they could smell bullshit from the gate. So, I handled Nikki the way I would've handled Kira, if I would've met her first. She was one clever chick and she knew how to manipulate niggas to do what she wanted. I'm sure Nikki mastered some of her tricks so I would be keeping my eyes on her and always make sure I watched my steps around her. Hoes like that can't be trusted, which was another reason why Nikki ain't never been here. And I intend to keep it like that too. Because if anything were to ever go down, I could come here and lay low without worrying about if she was gonna tell muthafuckers where to find me. And that was a good feeling to have. But, what's going to be even better was right after I bang Sasha's back out, I was gon' catch me some shut eye. What a way to end the night!

5

Three hours later

Me and Sasha were lying in the bed knocked out when we heard a loud bang. That shit scared the hell out of us.

"What was that?" she asked, sitting straight up in the bed clutching the sheet against her chest.

"I don't know. But it sounded like somebody just kicked in my front door."

"Whatchu want me to do?"

"Get underneath the bed and hide," I instructed her as I jumped to my feet and grabbed my .40-caliber Glock from underneath my pillow.

While Sasha was climbing underneath my bed, I tiptoed over to my bedroom door. After I closed and locked it, I stood there butt naked, dick hanging, pistol in my hand and one hollow point bullet in the chamber ready to bust it at the first thing moving. Now as I began to stand there, I couldn't help but wonder who in the hell could be in my house. The only muthafuckers who knew about this spot were Quincy, home girl underneath the bed and Mark. And Mark's dead. I know my boy Quincy wouldn't sell me out. So, to be in the dark about what's going on the other side of this door was killing me. And I ain't gon' lie, I want so badly to open up that door and just start blazing everything moving. But, I know that would be a bad move on my part so I was just gonna sit tight and wait to see what happened next.

Twenty seconds later, I heard a couple sets of footsteps creeping up the stairs to the second floor, which was where my bedroom was, and my mind started racing faster than my heart. And without even giving it a second thought, I took a couple steps backwards and aimed my burner directly at the door because I didn't know what was about to happen. And judging from them foot steps I just heard, it had to be at least two or three niggas out there, so I had to be ready to go for what I know. And that was some real shit!

While I was standing there, a whole bunch of emotions were running through my entire body. But the one that was overpowering 'em all was the feeling of uncertainty.

And I didn't like feeling like this. It was not a good thing. But hey, what could I do?

Sasha was hiding underneath the bed and so it was like I was on my own. While I was trying to contemplate my next move, one of them niggas grabbed a hold of the doorknob and turned it. As soon as he figured out that it was locked, three bullets tore right through the door, leaving huge holes around the lock area of the doorknob. Sasha screamed, as I jumped back and started busting my gun.

"Boom! Boom! Boom! Boom! Boom! Boom!" I let off six shots. "Die you muthafuckers," I screamed, and then continued to empty out the entire fifteen round magazine, while shells were popping out all over the place. My bedroom door looked like Swiss cheese and was barely hanging on its hinges because I wasn't the only one busting off rounds. Immediately after I sent the first slugs through the door, dem' niggas started returning heat too. And at that point, I knew I needed to take cover so I dove on the other side of my bed and landed next to my jeans.

Hiding there with thoughts of me lying in my own casket wasn't something I wanted to think about and immediately erased that thought. I also knew that in order for that *not* to happen, I was gonna have to find a way to get out of this place. I knew going out of the bedroom door would be out of the question and since the window was my only other option, I knew that was the exit I was gonna take. I peeped underneath the bed skirt and noticed that Sasha had her face buried in the floor. She looked as if she was scared to death. I know she was beating herself up on the inside for hopping in the truck with me tonight. And I honestly couldn't blame her for feeling that way. Because the way shit looked right now, I ain't gon' be able to help her. It was too many mutha-fucking bullets flying around here for me. The best thing for her to do was to stay where she was and hope them niggas don't find her because as soon as I get the right opportunity, I'm gonna be ghost. And I ain't gon' look back either. In the meantime, I also needed to figure out how the hell I was gonna get into my safe that's hidden in the back of my closet. There was $200,000 in it so if I didn't get to it before them cats busted up in here, then I might as well forget it.

The very second that I got up the nerve to crawl over to my closet, the shooting stopped, which either meant that dem' niggas were reloading or they were standing out there waiting to hear any sign of movement. Either way they were going to be coming in here and I didn't want to be around. Without giving it a second thought, I snatched up my jeans and put them on and slightly opened the window. "Psst, Sasha," I whispered. "Come on we gotta bounce."

Her stupid ass began to make all type of noise as she tried to climb from underneath the bed.

"Shoot 'em! He's trying to get away!" one nigga yelled as he kicked open the door and stormed into the room.

Seeing this muthafucker dressed in all black and a mask covering his face sent me straight in panic mode. And when he aimed his burner at me and started busting dem' caps, I knew this nigga wanted to take my life. I did a Superman stunt and dove right through the partially opened window. When I hit the ground I could feel my skin burning in my right shoulder so I knew that I had been hit. Not only that, I believe that I had either sprung my ankle or broken it because after I hit the ground and tried to get back up, my leg couldn't stand the pressure, so I just laid there and pretended as if I was dead.

"You think he's dead?" one voice asked as he peered out the window.

"He should be because I hit him with at least two or three joints when he was going through the window," the second voice replied.

"Want me to go down there and make sure?" the first voice asked.

"Nah, we ain't got time for that," the second voice said. "Now, let's get what we came here for."

Hearing the second guy's decision to leave me alone made me happy as hell. But, I knew that I wasn't in the clear until they broke camp.

Meanwhile, I was lying face down in the semi-wet grass and the burning sensation of my bullet wound was starting to torture the hell out of me. The shit was becoming really unbearable and I was pissed that I couldn't stand up on my feet and make a run for it. Man, if I wouldn't have fucked up my ankle I would've been gone. But, since I had to play it safe and thug it out right here, then that's what I was gonna do.

While I lay there feeling helpless and stupid, I heard one of them niggas fire two shots.

"Pop! Pop!"

I ain't gon' lie; that scared the shit out of me. I knew that it was Sasha's body that took them two slugs. At that point I was really feeling fucked up behind that. I mean, I really liked shorty. She was cool as hell and her fuck game was on the money. So, she would be missed.

As I continued to lay face down in this fucked up condition, I heard the doors to a car slam shut and then I heard the tires squeal as they peeled off. Immediately I felt a sense of relief. At that point, I knew that I was going to live. But, that feeling of joy came to an abrupt end when I heard the sound of someone walking on the broken pieces of glass in my bedroom surrounding my window. And boy, was my heart on the verge of jumping out of my chest, as I laid there, my back facing the window and my eyes closed tightly. As I waited for whoever it was to make their next move, something unexpectedly happened.

"Oh my God, they killed him," a woman cried out softly.

I wanted to believe that I just heard Sasha's voice and that my mind wasn't playing tricks on me, but I continued to lie there. Then something in my mind convinced me otherwise and I opened up my eyes, lifted my head up and turned it around as far as my neck would allow me to and then I said, "Nah, Sasha I ain't dead. But, I'm fucked up pretty bad."

"Can you get up?" she asked.

"Nah, I think I broke my ankle."

"All right. Well keep still and I'll be right down," she assured me and before I could blink my eyes twice, home girl was fully dressed, ready to do whatever I needed her to do.

"You know I thought dem' niggas put two slugs in you, right?"

"You talking about when one of them shot their gun twice?"

"Yeah."

"Nah, they weren't shooting at me. They shot at that safe they found in the back of your closet."

"How do you know?"

"Because I saw them when they pulled it out and tried to open it. And when they saw that they couldn't get in it, they opened fire on it."

"What happened after they shot it?"

"Nothing. It still wouldn't open so, both of them picked it up and carried it with them."

"Ahhhh shit! Nah, don't tell me dem' niggas got my dough."

"Well, I'm sorry but they did. And the way that they went straight to it, lead me to believe that they knew exactly where to find it."

"Please tell me that they slipped up and dropped some names," I begged.

She shook her head and said, "Nope."

"Well, did you get to see what kind of whip they were driving?"

"No. I didn't come from underneath the bed until after I heard their car drive off."

Frustrated, I screamed out, "Damn!" And then I shook my head in disbelief.

It took Sasha some time to get me off the ground and back into my house. But, she did it and I was truly grateful for that. We ended up going to the downstairs bathroom since I couldn't make it back upstairs. When we got in there I could see all the damage that was done to my body.

"How bad is it?" I asked.

Sasha sighed and then she said, "All I'm gon' say is that you need to get on your knees and thank God."

"Why? Whatcha' talking about?"

"First of all, out of all those bullets that were ringing all around that room, you only got a flesh wound."

Surprised by what she had just told me, I said, "What."

"Don't say 'what'. Say thank you God," she instructed. Then she said, "And not only that, your ankle doesn't seem like it's broke. It looks like its sprained."

"For real!"

"Yes, I'm for real. But, you still need to go to the emergency room to have everything checked out."

"A'ight. But, do me a favor first."

"What's that?"

"Go upstairs and get my cell phone off my nightstand."

"They took it."

"Are you fucking serious?"

"Yeah."

"But, for what? I mean, why in the hell they need my muthafucking cell phone?"

"I don't know, but they took it. And they took your watch, wallet and chain."

"Come on, you're joking, right."

Sasha shook her head again.

Out of anger and frustration, I grabbed the soap from the soap dish near the sink and threw it against the wall as hard as I could. I knew my sudden act of rage scared the hell out of her, but I couldn't be concerned about that. I was trying to figure out how I was going to deal with the cats that robbed me at the house nobody was supposed to know existed.

I ended up using my house phone to make the call to Quincy. I knew I couldn't say much, out of fear that someone could be listening on the other line, so I kept my conversation short and sweet. He got the message loud and clear because when I got to the hospital, he was already there standing by the payphone at the front entrance of the emergency room area.

We couldn't really talk because two nurses grabbed me as soon as I walked through the sliding doors. I did manage to tell him to stick around until they got through with bandaging me up. I also instructed Sasha to stay back with him so she could tell him what went down.

While I was in back, the doctor and dem' two nurses had a lot of fucking questions for me. They claimed they needed to alert the police that I had a bullet wound and wanted to know how it happened. So, I made up a bogus ass story about how I had just left my girlfriend's apartment to go home and when I was getting into my truck, two guys came up from behind me wearing masks, put a gun up to my head and told me to run my shit. Then I told them that when they guys started acting all crazy like they wanted to put me to sleep, I took off running. Somehow they managed to pump one in me.

The doctor asked me how I managed to sprain my ankle and get the small cuts all over my arms and chest. I told him that I got it from tripping and falling down in a filthy ass alley. Now, I don't know if they believed me, but at this point I didn't care. My main thing was not to get the police involved over at my crib. I got enough heat on me as it was. Not only that, I wanna deal with this matter on my own. The police ain't gon' be able to serve justice to dem' niggas like I'm gon' do when I found out who they were.

And that's some real shit!

After they bandaged up my gunshot wound and wrapped my ankle, they gave me a set of crutches and sent me out the door. On my way to the parking lot, I told Sasha that I was going to hop in the car with Quincy so she was going to need to follow us to the Hilton Hotel in Virginia Beach right across the street from Pembroke Mall.

The drive from Chesapeake General Hospital to Virginia Beach was about 20 minutes, so I had enough time to talk to Quincy about a few things.

"Man, you wouldn't believe how that doctor and dem' nurses was grilling my ass back in that emergency room," I said.

"What they say?"

"They wanted to know how I got fucked up like this and who did it."

"What did you tell 'em?"

"I just gave 'em some ol' bogus ass story about a couple of niggas wearing masks sneaking up behind me while I was trying to get in my truck. Then I told them they robbed and shot me," I replied and then I looked into the side mirror to see if Sasha was still following us.

"You think they believed you?"

"They probably didn't but who gives a fuck?" I responded sarcastically and then I looked away from the mirror.

"So, what's your next move?" Quincy asked.

"Yo dawg, I don't know what I'm gon' do. But I do know that I wanna kill someone."

"Man, I know how you feel. Because I had a couple niggas run up on me like that a few years back. But, instead of 'em gunning me down, they pistol whipped me and left me to bleed to death behind an abandoned building. And still to this day, I can't tell you who did it."

"Well, I'm gon' find out who ran up in my crib. Because believe me, somebody is gonna slip up and say something about it. And when they do, I'm gon' be right there."

"Look man, I know you're upset, but right now you are not in no condition to go running up on niggas."

"I ain't gon' do nothing now," I told him. I wasn't really trying to convince him.

"But, as soon as I get right, I'm gon' murder everybody who sounds like dem' niggas."

"Come on now dawg, you know you can't go around killing every nigga who talks like them cats. Look, this is what we gon' do," he explained making a right turn to get on Highway 64. "Since dem' cats who robbed and shot you think you're dead, then you're gonna have to let them keeping thinking that by staying out of sight for a little while. And in the meantime, I'm gon' poke my head out there and see what the word is."

"How long is a little while?"

"Like a week or so. But not only that, it would also be wise for you not to show your face around the spot either. Because dem' same niggas might wanna camp out somewhere in the vicinity or even get their car washed so they can watch everything moving in and out of there."

"That makes sense. But damn, Q, you trying to kill me!"

"Nah, man I ain't trying to kill you. I just want you to chill so I can be able to make the right moves and bring dem' niggas back to you on a silver platter."

"But what if I need to make some moves of my own?"

"What kind of moves you talking about?" Quincy questioned.

"Like personal shit!"

"Well a'ight, I'll tell you what; if you gotta' go out, make sure somebody is driving you and it's at night."

"A'ight, I can do that. But, I'm gon' need you to do something for me."

"What's good?"

"I want you to keep an eye out on that nigga Lloyd and dem' nigga's he fuck wit', 'cause my gut is telling me that they had something to do with this whole shit. I mean, who else knew I had a lot of cash on me?"

"But, how did they know where to find you?"

"He must've had dem' follow me."

"A'ight. Well, I'm on it then," Quincy assured me.

Right before he dropped me off at the hotel, I told him I needed him to go on a few errands for me since I was in dire need of some clothes, a cell phone, a rental car and some dough. He didn't have a problem with it and made it happen. When I got situated in the room, I sat Sasha down and told her I was gon' need her company for a few days. She gave me one of her cute little smiles and told me that she would stick around for as long as I needed her. Boy, was I happy to hear that because that meant I had a chauffeur, a maid and a whore all packed up in one chick.

Later on that evening, I sent Sasha on a dinner run, so I could have some time alone to make a phone call to Nikki. When I first got her on the phone she acted like she was preoccupied doing something else. But when I told her the same story I told that doctor and dem' nurses, whatever it was she was doing went right out of the window.

"Where you at, Syncere?"

"I'm chilling."

"Chilling where?" she demanded.

"A couple of my niggas got me hiding out in this spot until everything's resolved."

"Where at?"

"Look Nikki, I can't tell you all that right now. But, I will say that I'm not that far from you."

"So, when am I gonna see you?"

"In a couple of days."

"How badly are you hurt?"

"I just got a flesh wound and a sprained ankle."

"Well, can I call you?"

"Nah, because dem' niggas got my cell phone."

"How am I going to get in touch with you?"

"Don't worry about that. I'mma call you. A'ight."

"A'ight," she replied and then she sighed as if she was forced to agree with me. "But, what am I going to do while you're away?"

"Do whatchu been doing."

"But, what if somebody asks me about you?"

"Just tell 'em we broke up or something. Shit, I don't know!"

"Have you talked to Q?"

"Yeah, he just dropped me off. So, go to him if you need anything, a'ight."

"Yeah, a'ight," she replied.

By the end of our conversation, I had to reassure her at least five times that she would be seeing me in the next couple of days. And by then I had had enough of her whining, so I hurried up and got her ass off the phone. I know she meant well, but I wasn't really in the mood to hear all that crying bullshit. I've got more important things to think about. Trying to find out who robbed and shot me were at the top of my list.

6

Shit Just Ain't Addin' Up

Rhonda Speaks

"Yo, where you going?" Tony asked me the moment I grabbed my purse from off the kitchen table.

"I'm gonna go and meet Nikki at Kira's apartment so I can help her pack up Kira's stuff."

Not at all happy by my response, Tony sat up in the recliner facing their 36-inch HDTV. "Nah, Rhonda, that ain't gon' work!"

"Whatcha talking about?" I asked him.

"You know I don't want you going 'round there."

"Yeah, I know. But I can't let Nikki go in Kira's place by herself."

"And why not?"

"Because she ain't gon' be able to handle seeing all that dried-up blood splattered around in the bathroom."

"But, that's not your problem."

"That may be true. But I'm doing this for Kira."

"And that's all well and good. But I don't like you being around that chick Nikki. That hoe is poison!"

"Boy, shut up! That girl is not poison."

"Yeah, a'ight! Then, tell me how in the hell she got out of jail after getting caught with all Ricky's shit?"

"She had a good lawyer," I replied, jumping to Nikki's defense.

"Good lawyer, my ass! You know that bitch was snitching her ass off. That's why Ricky and his whole crew got bagged up."

"Nah, I don't believe that."

"I don't know why. Everybody on the streets is talking about it."

"Well, if that's the case and knowing how demented Ricky was, don'tcha think he would've had her ass killed?"

"It's obvious that he didn't know. But let's say he did; he was probably too wrapped up in all that shit his crew gave to the Feds."

"But that doesn't make any sense. I mean, if she did snitch on him, don'tcha think they would've made her testify against him."

"Not necessarily. 'Cause see, these days all the Feds need is two people to say the same thing about a nigga in the streets and they can indict you on conspiracy charges. So, when they finally get the mu'fucka they indicted inside of a cold-ass room and threaten to put their ass away for life if they try to fight the charges, trust and believe, a nigga is gon' bitch up and plead out real quick. And to kill two niggas with the same slug, they gon' sing their ass off; which is going to make them crackers' job easier, save the taxpayers dough and the snitcher's time from testifying. And that's how they walk away from it."

I shook my head in disbelief because I was still not convinced that Nikki would do that.

"Nah," I said. "Kira wouldn't have let it go down like that."

"Shiiid! You and I both know Kira didn't give a fuck about Ricky, for real! 'Cause remember, she signed over the salon to you one day and planned to bounce out of town the next, which was the same day Ricky and his boys got locked up. Now, tell me that shit didn't sound suspect to you?"

"Nah, Kira wasn't that type of chick. And even though Ricky dogged her out, she was still loyal to him."

"Well, since she was so loyal, then why was she about to haul ass on the brother?"

"Because she was tired of his shit. And not only that, she had just found out that the chick named Sunshine, who used to work at the salon with us, was fucking Ricky behind her back. So, I guess she felt like the only way to deal with that situation was to leave town and start over somewhere else."

"Did she tell you why she changed her mind all of a sudden?"

"Not until later," I told him, lying through my teeth. I didn't want Tony knowing that Kira had planned to leave town with Ricky's partner, Russ, because he would call her a scandalous hoe. And then on top of that, he would've called her stupid for getting robbed by a nigga she was fucking.

"And what did she say?"

"She just said that she couldn't get up the nerve to leave her family behind, that's all." I continued to lie with much sincerity.

"Yeah, you'll tell me anything," Tony replied as he blew me off with a hand signal. Then he came out of left field and said, "But, I'll bet you all the dough in my pocket that the Feds stopped her ass from skating off and probably told her that if she left town, they was gon' lock her up."

I sucked my teeth with disgust because I was not at all pleased with how Tony was questioning Kira's motives for not leaving. Regardless of the real reason that she decided not to leave town, I knew for a fact that she was a good person. She was very forgiving and would give a person her last dime. So, all that salt he was trying to pour on her wasn't working for me. And to make it totally clear that he obviously didn't know what he was talking about, I told him to shut the fuck up!

"A'ight! I'mma shut the fuck up! But, don't call me when your stupid ass gets caught up in the crossfire."

"What crossfire?"

"Keep hanging 'round Nikki and you gon' feel them same hot balls that put Kira to sleep. 'Cause believe me, them same cats who murdered her is probably sitting around watching Nikki's every move so they can find a chance to knock her ass off too."

"Yeah, whatever," I retorted and then I threw my hand in the air right before I turned my back on him to leave. I attempted to close the front door behind me when Tony yelled out, "Don't be a dummy cause that nigga Syncere look like he can't be trusted either." Instead of feeding into his ridiculous comments, I shut the door and locked it. I figured, what the hell did he know, for real? He wasn't nothing but an ol' buster-ass nigga, waiting around for somebody to front him some dope so he could get all big headed and try to shine on me. But, the way his luck was going it wasn't gon' happen, which was why he was a typical hater!

As soon as I got into my car I called Nikki from my cellular phone and informed her that I was en route to meet her at Kira's place. She sounded a little sad, a little down but she did manage to say she would meet me there. After I hung up with her, I put my car in first gear and broke out.

7

A Few Minutes Later

Nikki Speaks

I decided to wait three days after we lay Kira to rest before I went back to her apartment. With Rhonda by my side, I figured I could handle anything I came upon. The temperature of her apartment was very cold, unlike the seventy-five degree weather outside, which altered my whole mood. I felt a sense of darkness looming over me. It was like Kira's soul was lingering throughout her apartment, crying out for help. The thought that her restless spirit could actually be here sent chills through my entire body, so I blocked it out and focused on what I had come here to do.

"So, where are we gonna start first?" I asked Rhonda, breaking the silence. barrier with the packing boxes in tow, simultaneously scanning the entire apartment from where I stood for a starting point.

"Let's start in the bedroom," Rhonda suggested.

"All right, let's do this," I replied and proceeded in that direction, as Rhonda followed.

Kira's bedroom was exactly the same way she left it. Nothing was out of place except for the items that were taken by the forensics team. However, there was a ton of fingerprint dust scattered across the place. I was almost afraid to touch anything. But I pressed forward and did what I had to do. Rhonda, on the other hand, went straight into work mode, which motivated me to do the same. We both tackled every inch of Kira's bedroom and we did it in less time than expected.

Just when I was about to haul two huge boxes out of the bedroom, Rhonda startled me by saying, "Girl, you will not believe what I just found."

I immediately stopped in my tracks and turned in her direction.

"What is it?" I wondered aloud, my heart skipping a beat.

Rhonda extended her left arm and resting in the palm of her hand, in plain view, was a black book.

"What is it?" I asked once again.

"It's Kira's diary," she finally replied.

"How do you know it's a diary?" I asked as I approached her.

"Because that's what it says on the front of it," Rhonda retorted as she held up the book, showing the big bold letters on the cover.

"Let me see it," I said and took the small, locked book out of her hand.

"How you gonna open it?" she asked me.

"With these scissors right here." I picked up a pair that lay on top of the dresser.

"Whatcha think is in there?"

"I don't know. But we're about to find out," I commented, taking a seat on the edge of the bed as my mind began to race full speed ahead.

My mind began to feed off of this anxiety-filled knot I

suddenly developed in the pit of my stomach as I craved for what was written between the pages of this diary.

Somehow, there was no doubt in my mind that Kira's black book would shed some light on a lot of unanswered questions. Maybe then I could get to the bottom of what led to her murder.

Rhonda sat on the bed next to me and watched in awe as I flipped to the first page. It was dated Friday, January 6, 2006, 11:30 p.m. In Kira's own words, it read:

The world has embarked on the 6th day of a new year. But, as I sit here, it seems like time is standing still. I'm laying here in my bed all alone, wondering where my husband is and what he's doing out there in those streets this time of the night. Probably making plans to make me a stepmother for the fourth time. You can never tell with him. Any and everything is possible when it comes to him. And since I know that I'll never be able to change him, I'm gonna have to shift my energy to someone who'll appreciate it, like my cousin Nikki, for instance. Right now, I know she's in desperate need of my help. So, I'm wondering how she's holding up while she awaits trial for making those drop-offs for Ricky; which, of course, has me sitting in limbo, trying to figure out what it is that I need to do? I'm completely torn between my family and a man who could care less about me.

This is the same man who also disrespects me on the regular. And when the damage is done, he is always coming back with extravagant gifts to pacify me. But when I follow my heart, I'm drawn back to the fact that Nikki needs me and has no one else in her corner but me. So, what am I to do? Violate the code of the streets and turn against my husband to help my

*cousin? Or follow suit and remain loyal to a mutha-
fucker who is going to one-day lead me to my grave?
I think not! Whether he knows it or not, shit is about
to get really wicked and as far as I see it, it's going to
be every man for himself. So, I'm going to make sure
Nikki and I come out on top. I put that on my life.*

After reading each word aloud and processing it in my
mind, I was beginning to understand what Kira was going
through. But I needed closure so I turned to the next page,
dated Sunday, January 7, 2006. It was unknown to me why
she waited an entire day to pour her feelings out, but I had
a hunch I would find out so I proceeded to read further.

*It's 7 o'clock in the morning and I'm just waking
up from an overdose of dick. Being all gung-hoe for
my man, I done let him talk me into fucking me in my
asshole with a gram of coke sprinkled down the crack
of my ass to numb it. It surprised the hell outta me
when he asked me to do it. And since I didn't want to
seem like a stiff, I happily obliged. I also did it because I wanted to put some excitement back into our
marriage. Shit has been really fucked up around here.
So, I said what the hell! You only live once. And besides, if I didn't do it then he would've probably gotten
another one of his chicken heads to do it. His hoes
are waiting in line to take my place. But it ain't gonna
happen. And because of my undying efforts of trying
to keep him happy, I am now suffering my ass off. My
butt hole is burning up! I think I'm gon' need to put
an ice pack down there in a minute, 'cause this shit is
becoming unbearable. Other than that, I talked to my
cousin last night and she sounds depressed like a
muthafucker. If only I could break her out of that joint*

and give her a one-way trip out of there. Damn, I am
gonna have to do something really fast, 'cause I don't
know how long she's going to hold up. To make mat-
ters worse, that nigga Brian ain't even doing his part.
Every time I try to get his raggedy ass on the phone
so Nikki can holler at him on three-way, he ain't
never available. But, I've got a trick for his flaky ass
and a one-way ticket to the big house. So when the
chips fall, he's going down right along with Ricky!
Believe that!

"Damn, I didn't know Kira was raw dog like that,"
Rhonda blurted out without hesitation the second I read
the last word from that page.

"Whatcha mean by that?" I asked, getting real defensive
and closing book.

"I'm just saying, I've never knew she had another side,
that's all."

"Well, she did. So, let's keep this between us, okay?"

"A'ight, let's get this done so we can bounce," she agreed
and stood up.

I stood up too and slid the diary into my right front pant
pocket. "And please don't tell anybody we found Kira's
diary."

"I won't."

"Not even the police."

"I'm not."

"You promise?"

"Come on now, Nikki, who do you take me for?"

"I'm not taking you for anything. I just want you to
promise me that this stays between us. That's all."

"Okay. Then, I promise."

"I'm talking about Tony, too."

"Whatcha mean?"

"I'm saying, you can't tell him either."

"I'm not. You've got my word."

"All right. Well, let's get back to work, then."

"So, when you gon' read the rest of her diary?"

"We can get together tomorrow after the shop closes and read it then."

"But, I can't wait that long," Rhonda protested.

"Well, you're gonna have to, girl, because we've got to get this stuff packed up in these boxes before the movers get here."

Rhonda sucked her teeth. "A'ight, then."

Once it was understood that we had to take a rain check on our diary-reading session, we got back on track and completed the mission we initially came here to do. By nightfall we had everything Kira owned packed up, sealed, and ready to be hauled off. The movers were scheduled to move all the big items the very next morning, so me and Rhonda carried the smaller and more valuable things ourselves.

Kira's seventeen-thousand-dollar Russian Sable fur coat came with me. I also confiscated that black, full-length Pelt Mink coat Ricky bought for her to wear on the trip to Amsterdam, that they never went on. Kira told me he paid a little over eight grand for the fur, so I'd be damned if I let anybody walk out of here with that. She had a couple of diamond bangles and earrings by David Yurman and a beautiful, platinum ten-carat diamond ring she bought from the Diamond District a few years ago while she was in New York on a shopping spree. I made sure I took the three and a half carat, diamond bezel Bvlgari wristwatch with a cream-colored alligator strap, a vintage Rolex and a gorgeous diamond necklace I only saw her wear when she rocked her fur coats. She also had a few other pieces like a tennis bracelet, a pair of diamond studded earrings and an iced-out ankle bracelet. So, after I took inventory of those things, I immediately slipped the entire jewelry box into my handbag. I saw Rhonda's jealous facial expression when she peeped the jewelry, but she kept it to herself. And good for her because the way I figured, she wasn't that damn cool with Kira to walk out of here with this type of stuff.

So, if she ever attempted to come out of her mouth and question me about it, then I would have to put that bitch in her place. And it wouldn't be pretty either.

On the other hand, I did give her Kira's eight-hundred-dollar Isabella Fiore handbag, a few pairs of sunshades by Gucci and Yves Saint Laurent, a gold and silver Chloé clutch handbag with a pair of Chloé sling back sandals to match and two beautiful Chanel scarves. She couldn't fit any of Kira's clothes, except for a Carolina Herrera cocktail dress. But, do you think I cared? Hell nah! That bad boy cost Kira every bit of two to three grand, so that was going with me too.

"Why you being so selfish, Nikki? You can't even fit the damn thing," she protested.

"I know I can't. But, I already promised to give it to my mother," I told her, lying through my teeth.

"Come on now, your mother hasn't even seen the damn dress."

"Yes, she has."

"When Nikki?"

"A while back when she saw Kira wearing it she told her that as soon as she got tired of it to send it right over to her. And Kira told her okay."

"Yeah, whatever, Nikki," Rhonda responded and stormed off like a big ass baby.

She went into the kitchen to finish packing up the remaining items of silverware as well as the seasonings and things. I stayed behind and good thing I did, because as soon as I cleared everything out of Kira's closet, I ran across her secret stash and found a huge sum of cash. It looked like it was about nine or ten grand but I wasn't really sure. However, I would find out when I got home because as far as I was concerned, Rhonda didn't need to know about the dough because there was just not enough to go around.

When I got back to my place I felt a sense of calmness fall over me, knowing that I was home alone. Luckily for me, Syncere was still hiding out with one of his homeboys trying to stay off the radar so he could find out who shot him. I didn't know how true all this shit was because I ain't seen him yet. But, you know what they say; you reap what you sow.

After I brought all of Kira's boxes into my apartment, I settled down in my bed and pulled out her diary. The sense of urgency to fulfill my curiosity was burning within me. I knew I would be lying to myself if I thought I could wait until tomorrow to get with Rhonda at the salon to sit down and read the contents of this diary. So I did what any other person in my shoes would do and plunged right back into the world of the unknown. I immediately picked up where I had left off. But, when I realized I had already read the contents of this page, I turned to the next dated Monday, January 8, 2006, and it read:

> *Dear Diary,*
>   *Here it is, two a.m. and I'm beginning to wonder where the hell my husband could be. He promised me earlier that he was going to be home by eleven, so we could finish our conversation from hours ago. But once again, he has made me out to be the fool that I am. I decided to call him with hopes of finding*

out his whereabouts. I dialed his cell phone number three times before he finally answered my calls. And when he said, "What's up, baby?", I hesitated before responding because I wanted a few seconds of silence so I could listen for clues that would indicate his whereabouts. But of course, he caught on to my tactics immediately and asked me why I was so quiet. So, I brought down the barrier with much attitude and asked him where the fuck he was. Of course, he went into his stash of lies and told me he was at one of his spots, taking care of business. So, I told him that I didn't believe him because it was too quiet. His explanation for the silence was that he was alone. So, I asked him where he was. He told me he was at the spot on B Avenue in Huntersville, but he was about to leave. So, I asked him why the hell I had to call three times before he answered his phone? His answer was that he was in the middle of counting some dough and that if he would've stopped in the middle of the count then he would've probably messed the numbers up. Yeah! 'What the fuck ever,' is what I yelled through the phone. And then before I hung up, I told him that he'd better have his ass beating down our front door in the next twenty minutes. But, I doubt it if he does. Because he rarely ever listened to me. He does whatever he wanted to do. And not only that, I heard him breathing heavy through the phone. So, I know he's probably at some chicken head's crib banging her back out; which is why his punk ass couldn't answer my first two calls. Yeah, knowing him, he probably either told her to be quiet or went into another room, so I couldn't hear anything. But, it's all good. Because my time is coming. And it won't be long either. Watch and see!

After reading the last word from that page, I flipped to the next page dated Wednesday, January 10, 2006, and it read:

> *Dear Diary,*
> *I talked to Nikki tonight and she was becoming a*
> *nervous wreck. The Feds were putting a lot of pressure*
> *on her to tell them whose drugs she was transporting.*
> *From the sound of her voice I could tell she wanted to*
> *spill the beans, which gave me a bad taste in my mouth.*
> *I warned her that talking was a very bad idea and that*
> *she would be putting herself, as well as me, in a com-*
> *promising position. Shit, I told her, I could go to jail too.*
> *So, she was gonna have to come up with another plan*
> *to get out of her predicament. Of course, she wasn't*
> *trying to hear me, but if she knows like I do, she'd better.*

Once again I found myself at the end of yet another one of Kira's well-thought-out passages. I could see that she really poured her feelings out onto these pages and it was a good thing that Ricky never stumbled across it. Instead of reading about Kira in the obituaries, she would've been reading about me. Thank God she had enough sense to hide it in an obscure place.

As I continued to sift through the next twenty-something pages, I realized Kira hadn't written about anything new and exciting. Every day up until January 22 consisted of nothing but Ricky being up to his old tricks, the drama she went through at the salon, and the latest news going on with my case. I elected to close the book for the night, since I was becoming restless. I figured it would be better if I got myself a good night's sleep and picked up from where I left off in the a.m. And even though I knew Rhonda was going to be upset that I read Kira's diary without her, she'd get over it. I'll just fill her in on what I've read thus far.

8

Making Power Moves

Syncere Speaks

I'd been hiding out for a little over a week now and I still hadn't heard a word in the streets about dem' nigga's running up in my spot. But, it was cool 'cause I already know that it was Lloyd and his henchmen. So, they were gonna pay and it was not gonna be very long before it happened because I ordered a hit on dem' niggas last night.

Since the robbery, I had a few of my home boys move all my shit out of that place and put it in a storage unit. I also switched hotel rooms. But, I still got Sasha riding my dick. Yeah, she's cool. Got some good pussy too. I know one thing and that is if she keeps up this ride or die chick image, I'm gon' let her take Nikki's place. And I'm talking some real shit too. Because I'm starting to jive like shorty wit' her freaky ass self. The bitch loves to keep my dick in her mouth and you know I love that. She knows how to control the muscles in her pussy too, that's why that shit is so good. Not only that, she's jive pretty as hell. She reminds me of Beyoncé, but with bigger titties. Yeah, she got B's complexion, long hair and her phat butt. That shit be looking good too when I be running up in it. Ol' good pussy bitch! 'Round here got me falling for her ass. But, I'll tell you one thing, she ain't gon' know it. No sir! A man of my status never tells a trick that he's in love with her, especially if she use to fuck around with your partner. That'll be really stupid and I'll definitely get clowned for it. And since I don't want that to happen, I'm gonna keep reminding myself that shorty ain't nothing but a temporary thing. Bottom line.

That shipment of dope I took off Mark's hands after I had his ass done in is a little on the light side; and the fact that I just got robbed for two hundred grand isn't making matters any better. But hey, I can't sit back and cry about because there's still a lot of money to be made. So, to keep things moving steady, I got my dog Quincy to make a few power moves for me because the cat me and Mark used to cop our shit from back in Jersey, Marocco, somehow vanished off the face of the earth. I don't know how true it is, but I heard some niggas from around my way robbed and kidnapped him and his wife while their kids were out with their nanny. They said them niggas walked away with over a million dollars in cash and five kilograms of coke. So, if that's true, then them niggas sure made off lovely. And believe me, a lot of cats with weight took notice to that shit too, which is why certain rules have changed. See, back in the day when cats like me wanted to buy or sell drugs, all we had to do was set up a time and a place so we could make the hand-to-hand exchange. Nowadays, it is mandatory to drop off your dough to the cat you're gonna make the trade with first. So, it's mad important that you know who you're fucking with because once you put your money in that person's hands, you are putting yourself in a vulnerable position. In this game, shit can go either way. And the fucked-up part is that you have to leave your dough behind and hope that that same nigga you just hit off call you back with the location to pick your shit up from. I know mad young cats who got jammed up like that.

And the niggas who stuck them up paid dearly for it too. That's why I try to stay connected with cats who are true businessmen. All them other counterfeits can suck my dick because I'm trying to come back up from that huge lose and no better way to do that than to get my hustle on with some good dope.

Now once Quincy made the call to his peoples in D.C., he got me back on the horn and told me to be ready because we're going to be hopping in his whip and heading in that direction later on tonight.

Happy as hell by the mere thought of me coming up from off this deal Quincy just made I jumped up from the bed and grabbed my cane. Sasha got it from the mall for me two days ago so I could leave them crutches alone. I was kind of hesitant to use it at first, but when she coached me on how to walk with it, shit fell into place. Yeah, she's still down for a nigga. I think I'm gon' keep her around for a while. But, for now, we're gonna have to check out of this room 'cause I've got things to do and money to make.

"Yo Sash'," I said cutting the 'A' off her name. "Something's come up, so I'm gon' have to leave for a while."

Stepping out of the bathroom, hair pulled back in a ponytail and wearing nothing but a towel, she looked at me and asked, "Is everything alright?"

"Yeah. Everything's cool. I just need to make a quick run out of town and I'm gon' be gone for a couple of days."

"So, is there anything you want me to do for you while you're gone?"

"Nah. I'm straight," I assured her as I began to gather up my things.

"So, are you going to call me when you get back?"

"Oh yeah. As a matter of fact, I'm gonna let you take the rental car since it's paid up for a month."

"Well, do you want me to go back to my sister's house and wait for you to call?" She searched my face for any signs that I wanted to get rid of her. So, I sat her down and told her that she could stay here at the room tonight since the day was already paid for. In the morning, though, she was gonna definitely have to go back to her sister's crib. When she gave me the long face, I told her that I wouldn't mind chilling with her some more but she was going to have to bring something more to the table besides some good pussy because I could get that from my other chick Nikki.

"Well, I betcha' Nikki can't suck your dick better than I can."

"Nah, she can't. But, I'm not concerned about shit like that. See, I like fucking with chicks that are smart and ambitious. You know, going to college and trying to get a degree in field that's gonna pay her a lot of dough."

She smiled and told me that she was tired of working dead end jobs and given the opportunity, would pay off the student loans she had and go back to school to become a registered nurse.

Surprised by what she had just told me I asked, "You've been to college?"

"Yeah, I've already completed two years."

"Oh okay, so that explains how you knew that my ankle wasn't broke."

She smiled and said, "Knowing whether or not the bones

in your feet are misaligned with the bones in your ankle was the first thing my professor taught."

"What school did you go to?"

"O.D.U."

"When did you stop going?"

"Last year."

"So, how much do you owe in student loans?"

"Well, I had a couple of federal grants so I probably owe about twelve or thirteen thousand."

"No way. Are you serious?"

"Oh yeah. You can ask anybody how expensive school is."

"I'll tell you what, find out exactly how much money you owe and I'll help you pay it if you go back to school."

"For real?"

"Yeah, I'm for real," I assured her. "Go get yourself together and make them calls because the way my life is going I might need you to take care of me one day."

"I'd do it too." She smiled and stood up from the bed.

"Well, it's settled. Now, get dressed," I instructed and smacked her on her ass as she walked away.

Before I walked out the hotel room, I handed Sasha a couple hundred dollars to hold her over until I got back. That was enough to get her some food and put some gas in the car. I also left specific instruction for her to go down to O.D.U so she could find out when the next semester started and pick up an apartment guidebook, so she could find herself a one-bedroom apartment. After she assured me that she was going to handle her business, I bounced.

9

Chasin' Dat Paper

Quincy ripped I-95 up to get to D.C. We got there one hour ahead of schedule so we checked in our hotel and then headed down to the strip club where the drop was suppose to be made. When we got there we still had about thirty minutes to burn so Quincy suggested that we go inside and get a few drinks while we waited for them niggas to show up. So, I said a'ight.

When we got out of the car, I let him walk ahead of me so I could make a quick phone call to Nikki. She said she was at home but it sounded like she was out in the fucking streets. I swear she was a lying ass bitch! And she wondered why I was always going upside her muthafucking head.

"You sure your ass ain't out in the streets Nikki?" I asked her.

"Yeah, I'm sure."

"Well, why does it sound like you're driving?"

"I don't know why but I'm not."

"What have you done since I talked to you earlier this morning?" I asked her, changing the subject.

"Well, I went to DMV first so I could register Kira's car in my name. And then I went to the shop and hung out."

"Oh, so you're keeping her car?"

"Yep, I sure am."

"Whatcha' gon' do with yours?"

"I gon' keep it and drive it sometimes."

"You think you're balling, huh?"

"Nah, I don't think I'm balling. I'm just being me."

"Yeah, a'ight. I'mma holler at you later."

"All right," she replied and then we ended the call.

Inside the strip club, Quincy was chilling in a corner watching some stripper chick on stage while he was sipping on a Corona so I walked over to his table and joined him. Minutes later a gorgeous, phat-butt freak named Sandy stepped up to me and asked me if I wanted a dance. Of course, I smiled and told her yes. Without hesitation, Shorty turned completely around, bent over and shoved every inch of her ass in my face.

"You think you can handle all dat ass?" Quincy asked me after he swallowed a mouthful of Henny, sitting in the chair next to me.

"Shiiid, you muthafucking right! I'll rip her ass apart," I commented and began to think of the many ways I could punish her ass. And the beauty of it all was that the way she was grinding on my dick kind of shifted my imagination into overdrive.

"Damn nigga, home girl gotcha drooling at the mouth," Quincy said, trying to clown me.

"That's because I wanna fuck the shit outta her," I yelled loud enough so he could hear me over the music.

"Holla at her den."

"Oh, you know I am," I assured him. So, right after my

lap dance was over, I pulled home girl by the arm and asked her if she had a man.

"Nah, I ain't got no man and, by the way, my name is Sandy," she replied as she stood up in front of me revealing dat phat hairy pussy she had connected to dem thick-ass thighs of hers. Her titties were kind of saggy but I could work with them.

"Well, Sandy, I guess it wouldn't be a problem if you hung out with me tonight then."

"Whatcha trying to get into?"

"I was hoping you could chill with me back at my hotel."

"Where is your hotel?"

"At the Grand Hyatt on H Street."

"And what we gon' do when we get there?"

"Yo, Shorty, I'm trying to fuck if you want to know the truth."

"Well, I hope you gotcha money right 'cause I don't be giving up the pussy for free."

"Okay, that's cool. But I don't want none of your pussy. I just want to fuck you in that phat ass of yours and feel your mouth around my dick."

"You got condoms?"

"Nah. Do you?"

"No. But I can get a few from one of my home girls in the back."

"A'ight. Well, go and handle that and be ready to bounce out of here in about twenty minutes."

"Okay," she said turning to leave. Me and Quincy both locked our eyes on this chick as she walked away from us. Watching her booty cheeks clap with every step she took was a sight to see. My dick was full blown.

"Yo, Syncere man, I don't think you gon' be able to handle all dat'. I mean, Shorty is working with one of dem donkey asses."

"Nah, Quincy ain't no need to worry about me. Sandy is the one you need to be concerned about. Because as soon as I get her back to the hotel, I'm gon' run deep in her ass, jack off in her mouth and then I'm gon' put her ass out."

Quincy burst into laughter and replied by saying, "How much you gon' hit her off with?"

"I ain't gon' give her shit but some cab fare." I couldn't believe he'd just asked me that question.

"Yo, dog, I don't think home girl is gonna let that shit go down. Trust me, chicks from D.C. be on the grind and they don't play about their paper."

"Yeah, a'ight. We'll see," I said with a smile and then I changed the subject because it suddenly hit me that the nigga we came here to meet hadn't showed up yet. I told Quincy to call his peoples and find out how much longer we had to wait. Of course, he did what I told him to do. But before he could whip his cell phone out, the nigga we were waiting for walked into the club. It was really dark throughout the whole place but I got a chance to get a good look at him. Even though this cat was a big, black, grizzly-looking muthafucka and looked like he was 6'1" and tipped the scale at 300 lbs., there was no doubt in my mind that I could take the breath from his body if he tried something stupid.

Right after Quincy motioned him to go into the men's bathroom, he got up to follow him. I stayed behind to watch Quincy's back. Believe me, I had my Ruger loaded and ready just in case somebody was lurking in the dark with plans to ambush us. But, luckily for everybody in the club, I didn't have to knock off two or three innocent bystanders because the second I noticed Quincy and that big, black, ugly nigga walking out of the bathroom about three minutes after they went in, I knew everything went smoothly.

"You ready?" Quincy asked me the moment he approached me.

"Hell yeah," I replied and stood up from my chair, holding the cane close to my side, trying to prevent putting a lot of weight on my foot.

"Well, go and snatch up your big-booty friend and tell her we got to bounce."

"Wait, here she comes right now," I told him.

"Are y'all waiting for me?" she asked, looking directly at me with her duffel bag thrown across her shoulder.

"Yeah. You ready?"

"I sure am."

"A'ight then, let's go," I said and began to walk in the direction of the front door to the club.

"What happened to your leg?" she inquired, walking along side of me.

"It's not my leg, it's my ankle."

"Oh, for real, what happened?"

"I sprained it about a week ago."

"How did you do that?" she asked, pressing the issue.

"I slipped and fell."

"Was it a pretty bad fall?"

"Nah, it wasn't that bad at all," I told her.

"Well, take your time and be careful 'cause there's like an incline at the entrance of the club. I would hate to see you miss your step and fall again."

"Yeah, me too," I replied and kept it moving.

Quincy walked out of the club first. Sandy walked out next and I followed, just to make sure dem niggas we had just scored from wasn't lurking behind one of these cars or in the nearby alley plotting to rob us. Lucky for them they weren't. I felt a little more at ease, especially when we got into the car and was able to pull off without busting off any shots.

When we reached the hotel, Quincy paid for another room. It was a wise decision on his part because we couldn't have the stripper and the drugs in the same room, just in case this bitch was looking to rob us. Too bad what would happen to her if she did try some bullshit like that. But, that's another story. While she got undressed to take a quick shower, I strolled up to Quincy's room, which was located on the fifth floor. At that time, there was nothing more important than to get a good look at the purchase I made. Needing to check out the quality of that half of a brick was something I couldn't put off until the morning.

After I knocked on Quincy's door one time, he opened up and let me in.

"Where's that bitch at?" he asked, taking a look down both ends of the hallway before closing the room door behind me.

"I left her ass in the room and told her to hop in the shower."

Quincy laughed at my comment as he pulled out the large zip lock bag from underneath the mattress. "Here take a look at this shit," he said, handing me the package.

I took the tightly wrapped zip lock bag out of his hand and sat on the edge of the bed so I could get a better look at it.

"Whatcha think?" Quincy asked.

"It's a'ight," I told him after I dipped my finger in the bag of the powder and licked it off with the tip of my tongue.

"My peoples said that shit is a missile."

"I hope so because if it is, we gon' be doing a lot of business with them," I assured Quincy as I folded the bag back up and handed it to him. "Here, put it back up."

"What time you wanna bounce in the morning?" he asked after he tucked the dope back between the mattress and box spring.

"Shit, I don't know. I guess when we get up."

"Well, I'm gonna get the front desk to give me a wake-up call for about eight o'clock. Is that a'ight?"

"Yeah, that'll be cool. Just call my room before you knock on the door," I told him as I made my way toward the door.

"A'ight," he replied and then I left.

* * *

Back at my room, Sandy was sprawled across the bed butt naked with her legs spread apart, exposing every inch of her phat pussy. My first thought was to dive in headfirst but I snapped back to reality and said, "Let me see you play with that pussy."

"Why don't you come a little closer so you can get a better look," she said as she began to rub her fingers across her clit in a circular motion.

Like any other nigga would've done, I took a seat on the edge of the bed facing her. At this angle, it felt like home girl was in 3-D mode and I had a front row seat to a freak show. And the fact that Shorty kind of looked like Lil' Kim in the face made it even better.

"You can't tell me you don't want none of this good, wet pussy," she commented like she was trying to entice me. But I wasn't going for that bullshit. Shit, I got more sense than that. That's how a lot of niggas get caught up with that AIDS shit. Don't get me wrong, if she was my girl, I would punish that pussy, especially 'cause of the way it is looking at me: all phat, juicy and wet. Trust me; it's only a mind control issue. But, since she ain't my girl, I am gon' have to settle for putting a hurting on her ass and her mouth. Instead of responding to her comment, I got up from the bed, stood up in front of her and unzipped my pants. "Slide over here and suck this dick." And like the whore she was, she took all 8½ inches of my dick into her hands and pushed it into her mouth. She started off doing her thing, but then her fucking teeth started getting in the way. So, I screamed on her silly ass and said, "Ay yo, what the fuck you doing?"

"I'm trying to please you, baby."

"It doesn't feel like it," I told her and then I took a step backward.

"Whatcha mean?" she asked me with a dumb-ass look on her face.

"Whatcha mean, what I mean? I know you felt your teeth scraping my meat up!"

"Oh, I'm sorry, baby. Come here and let me kiss it so I can make it feel better," she suggested as she grabbed my shirt.

"Nah. Nah. Nah. I ain't even in the mood for no more head. Just hand me a condom and turn around and get on your knees so I can get in that ass."

"All right. But, let me get the K-Y jelly out of my bag." She hopped up from the bed.

I stood there and watched her as she got off the bed and strutted by me. Once she got out the condoms and that white tube of K-Y jelly she suited up, cocked that phat ass of hers up in the air and I dug right in. But what bugged me out was that this chick's asshole was loose as a muthafucka. My dick slid in her joint with no problem. We didn't need that jelly shit at all. But, everything was still cool though. I was gon' let her stay in denial because even though the walls of her ass were somewhat chipped away, the feeling I was getting while I was fucking her wasn't that bad. Yeah, it wasn't secret that she could take dick like a champ. And now that I thought about it, if her booty hole was a little tighter, my shit would've probably gotten bruised up some more. So, I guess I couldn't complain. Right when I was about to cum, I pulled out, ripped the condom off and told her to turn around so I could dump this load off in her mouth.

"Don't waste a drop of it," she demanded and opened up her mouth wide as she could. Without gagging one bit, this chick swallowed all my juices like she loved it. There wasn't a drop left in her mouth. After she performed that disappearing act, she stood up from the bed and asked, "So, whatcha want to do now?"

Shit, I was weak as hell. I couldn't bust another nut right

now if I tried. "I don't know about you, but I'm gon' chill," I replied, tucking my dick back in my jeans.

"So, you telling me my job is done?"

"Do you want it to be? I mean, because that's really up to you, Shorty," I told her before I collapsed back onto the bed.

"Well, if I stay, will you take me home in the morning?"

"How far you stay from here?"

"About twenty-five or thirty minutes away."

"Nah, that's too far in the opposite direction me and my peoples heading in but I'll put you in a cab."

"Okay," she said and then lay down next to me.

What was really strange was that Sandy and I continued kicking it for about another two hours. I'm not really the talkative type but Shorty had some interesting shit to talk about which made me look at her in a different way. Come to find out, she was cool and funny as hell. I even ordered pizza for us. Can you believe that? I mean, I've never fed any of my tricks. But Sandy came off just a little bit different from all the other chicks I fucked and dipped on. So, if she played her cards right, I might come and holler at her again while I'm up here taking care of business. Shit, it wouldn't hurt me and she could probably come in handy at some point. Especially since it seemed like I was gonna be making a lot of trades with Quincy's peoples. But, we'd see. Anyway, by 2 a.m. I was digging in Sandy's pretty, red, phat ass again. Boy, did she know how to take dick. I rocked that ass hole until my dick got sore. What an experience that was.

Early in the morning, Quincy called my cell and told me he was on his way down to my room. I got up and got my shit together and told Sandy to do the same. By the time Quincy made it downstairs to my floor, me and Shorty was dressed and ready to bounce. But, before we stepped into the hallway of the hotel, I hit her off with one hundred and fifty dollars and told her to pay for her cab out of that.

"Oh, thanks baby," she said all excited.

"You're welcome. Now, put that dough up before we leave out of the room," I instructed her. Because on the real, I couldn't have that nigga Quincy know that I paid home girl for real. He'd clown me and tell all our peoples that I pay bitches to fuck me. And that ain't cool. I was too fly for some shit like that to get out. Not only that, he was gonna really trip out when he found out that I was gon' make Sasha my bitch and help her get back into college. But, if he knows like I know, he better keep that shit to himself.

"Yo, nigga, you ready?" Quincy asked me the second he saw me and Sandy come into the hallway.

"Damn right! Let's do this," I replied and we headed out.

When we walked outside, a cab was already waiting out front, so Quincy walked over to the parking garage while I walked Sandy to the cab.

"So, when am I going to see you again?"

"I don't know. But, I'm sure I'll hit you up when I come back up this way."

"Do you know when that's going to be?"

"I can't say. But, who knows? It could be in the next couple of days. It just all depends on my partner, Q."

"Well, here. Take my cell number and call me when you got time to come see me," she said as she handed me a piece of paper with a number written on it. I took the piece of paper and said, "Don't worry, shorty. You'll hear from me."

"Can't wait," she said with a smile and turned around to hop in the cab. But before she got a chance to get in, I smacked her on her ass and said, "Be careful."

"I will," she replied as she shut the door to the cab.

10

When It's Official

Nikki Speaks

I got the surprise of my life when I walked out of the front door of my apartment this morning. Watching Syncere pull up to my apartment building in a fucking rental car gave me an eerie feeling. I was honestly not looking forward to seeing this nigga. After I had time to think about it, I really didn't care that he'd gotten robbed and shot. All the shit he had done to people! Shit, it was just a matter of time before somebody wiped his ass off the face of this earth. And it was coming soon too. That's why I was gonna burn his pockets up and try to get everything I could from him. It was all he was good for. Trying to limit our time together, I locked my front door and began to walk in the direction of my car as if I had not noticed him. Once he realized that I was heading to my car and not toward him, he rolled down the passenger side window and yelled out my name.

"Ay yo, Nikki!"

I immediately turned in the direction he was calling me from and acted like I was totally surprised to see him.

"How long have you been sitting there?" I asked as I walked toward him.

"I just pulled up. I thought you saw me."

"No, I sure didn't," I lied. "Speaking of which, I thought you weren't going to be back for a couple of days."

"What, I caught you at a bad time or something?"

"No."

"So, where you on your way to?"

"To the shop so I can take care of some paperwork."

"Well, come on and hop in. I'll take you," he insisted.

"Nah, it's okay. I'm gonna take the Lexus because I've got an appointment to get it serviced later," I told him, lying to his face.

"Well, what time are you coming home?"

"Probably about six or seven o'clock. I mean, it all depends on how quickly I get through with everything I've got to do."

"You can't get off no sooner than that?"

"I probably can, Syncere, but I won't know that until I get there."

"Well, just call me and let me know."

"Okay," I said and eagerly turned to walk away.

I thought Syncere would get offended by how quickly I walked away from him without giving him a kiss. But this time, I was wrong. He sped off in his rental immediately when I turned to go to my car. Boy, what a relief that was.

Rhonda had just come from out of the bathroom when I walked through the front door of the salon. Even though the seventy-five-degree temperature outside voted against it, she was dressed in this expensive white, pink and blue

Ed Hardy T-shirt, blue jeans, and matching sneakers. So, I had to comment on it.

"Now, you know it's too hot for that," I joked.

"Hold up! Sounds like you're doing a little hating right now."

"Don't get it twisted, because I am not hating on you. I am only giving you the facts," I said, smiling. "And besides, why would I hate on you when I am rocking Chloé from head to toe." I placed my handbag down at an empty station and then I took a seat in the chair next to it.

"Yeah, whatever! You wouldn't have had any of that Chloé if Kira wasn't your cousin," Rhonda replied, giving me a fake smile as if she wasn't feeling my attitude.

"Well, she was so don't be mad. And anyway, you act like Syncere don't be buying me shit like this."

"I didn't say he didn't. All I'm saying is that as soon as Kira passed, you been trying to act like you run shit. And it's not cute."

"I don't know where you get that from because I've been acting the same since day one."

"Yeah, a'ight." Rhonda sighed and sat down in her stylist chair.

"So, what are we going to do about the shop?" I asked her, trying to change the subject. It was obvious that she was still mad at me about the way I divided up Kira's things. But who cared? She needed to get over it.

"What are you talking about?"

"Come on, you know I want to make some changes 'round here. You know, like take down this old wallpaper, get it painted and get some new furniture in here for the clients. I was figuring, if we did that, then how much do you think we should go up on everybody's booth rent?"

"I don't know. But, I do know that if we go up too much, Penny and 'em gon' have a fit."

"I don't care about them having a fit," I replied with the least bit of concern. "Because, for real, they can go somewhere else and do hair."

"Okay, so, how much are you trying to go up on the rent?"

"I don't know. That's why I was asking you."

"Well, let me think about it and then I'll get back with you," Rhonda told me and then she looked down at her watch.

"What time is your first client coming in?"

"The hoe was suppose to be here already."

"Who are you talking about?"

"Who's always trying to tell me how to curl and style that itty-bitty ball head of hers?"

I laughed, trying to break the monotony. "Who you be talking about?"

"Jasmine."

"Why can't she ever be on time? And always trying to rush us to get her stinking ass in and out of the shop because she's got somewhere to go."

"Because she thinks she's a fucking diva."

"Oh well, I'm sorry to hear that."

"Me too. Now, enough about that tramp. Pull out that damn diary 'cause I'm dying to read more of that juicy shit Kira got up in there."

Without hesitation, I whipped out the diary. Before I had it out, Rhonda grabbed the chair next to my station and sat in it. I opened up the diary to the section where I had the page folded, which was my way of knowing that was the last page I read.

Realizing I was a few pages past, Rhonda commented, "I see your nosey ass got a little busy last night too."

"Oh girl, hush. It's not that serious. Trust me, you didn't miss a thing. All Kira talked about in these last few pages was the constant bullshit Ricky put her through which I'm sure she already told you about."

"She probably did but I still wanna read it for myself."

"Okay, later. But first, let's start from this page."

"A'ight," she replied. Then she had the nerve to suck her teeth afterward.

I ignored her antics and proceeded to the page dated Saturday, January 21, 2006. It read:

> *Dear Diary,*
> *Late last night Ricky's cell phone started ringing off the hook while he was asleep, so I answered it. When I said hello, the person on the other end didn't respond, so I automatically knew it had to be one of his chicken heads. So, I said hello again and this time I got a response. Come to find out it was a chick by the name of Cinnamon. So, I immediately asked her why the hell was she calling my husband this time of the night and she fired back by telling me that he called her first—earlier that night, so she was returning his call. She also told me that they had been fucking around with each other for over a year and a half now. She even told me that she didn't mind him having a wife because there was enough of his money to go around. I cursed her stupid ass out for that smart-ass comment. But of course, it didn't matter to her because before we hung up, she assured me that she was going to continue to fuck around with him as long as he was hitting her off with his dough. Now, how could I compete with a hoe like that? She was the type of trick that would fuck her mother's husband if he paid her. So much for morals these days. I guess those characteristics went out the window a long time ago.*
> *And since it seemed like I was the only one left*

with some, I was seriously contemplating storing them away for a while so I could help my cousin get out of her jam. I mean, what the hell! Ricky had shown me over and over again that he was in it for himself. He didn't give a fuck about me or anybody else. So, was time to reciprocate what he shelled out to me. I couldn't see it no other way.

After reading the last word from that passage, I turned to the next page dated Sunday, January 22, 2006.

Dear Diary,

I'm just getting back home from one scary and bizarre night out. After leaving my hair salon late last night, I noticed that there was two white men parked outside in an unmarked Crown Victoria look-ing vehicle. I acted as if I didn't see them because I desperately wanted to know what their next move was going to be. When I got in my car and drove out of the parking lot, they started up their vehicle and began to follow me. Now, I ain't gon' lie; that shit scared the hell out of me and I knew right then and there that it had to be the Feds. My first thought was to call Ricky but I got a little hesitant because I wasn't sure if my car or my cell phone was bugged. I didn't know what to do so I figured I'd try to lose them. I waited for my exit to come up and at the last minute, I abruptly made a right turn. Luckily for me, those two white guys got caught up in the traffic and missed it. I ended up driving all the way to Chesa-peake and when I saw the first pay phone I stopped and tried to get Ricky on the line but I kept getting his voicemail on the first ring. I even tried to text him but that didn't work either. I decided to get a hotel

room. When I got up this morning, the son of a bitch
finally answered his cell phone and explained to me
that the guys who were following me were some
Russian cats who had fronted him some work. The
reason that they were all over me was because they
liked to keep an eye out on the people controlling
their investments. In layman's terms, they wanted to
keep an eye on my whereabouts just in case Ricky
fucked up their money. And that alone was some
scary shit! Especially knowing that my life could
come to an abrupt end at any given moment. What
a fucked-up life I was living. Something's got to give.
And it needed to be sooner than later.

Once again I found myself at the end of another one of
Kira's passages. Before I turned to the next page, Rhonda
said, "Oh my God, Nikki! I think the Russians killed her!"

"Nah, I don't think so, Rhonda."

"And why not? I mean, it's right there in black and white."

"Well, because I know for a fact that Ricky wasn't fucking wit' them Russians before he got locked up, so he could
not have owed them any money," I began to explain. "And I
remember Kira telling me he was fucking wit' some other
cats from out D.C. Not only that, the guy I saw leaving her
apartment that evening didn't look like he had a drop of
Russian blood in his body, so somebody else did it," I assured her and then turned the page.

"But what about. . . ." Rhonda was beginning to say, but
got distracted by two unexpected guests come into the salon.
My mouth dropped to the floor when I realized it was
Ricky's baby mama Frances, with her grown-ass daughter
Fredricka standing next to her. Before I could say something,
Rhonda beat me to the punch.

"May I help you?"

"Yeah, you sure can," Frances said. "Wait, aren't you Kira's cousin?" she asked, turning her attention to me.

"Yes, I am," I replied nonchalantly.

"Good, 'cause you the one I want to talk to." She started walking in my direction.

"What's going on?" I asked, my face expressionless.

"Well see, this is the thing. I was told by Ricky's other two baby mamas that they got a big lump sum of money from Kira's life insurance, since Ricky wasn't alive to collect it himself. So, I was wondering why my child didn't get her part."

"Oh, no this bitch didn't," Rhonda blurted, standing up like she was ready to fight.

"Oh yes, I did," Frances fired back.

"Wait a minute, sweetie," Rhonda snapped back. "You're barking up the wrong muthafucking tree!"

"Hold up, Rhonda," I said to her. "Let me handle this."

"Yeah, please let her handle this," Frances signified sarcastically.

Meanwhile, I stepped toward Frances and said, "Listen honey, I don't know why Ricky's other two baby mamas lied to you like that because they didn't get shit. As a matter of fact, Kira didn't even have a life insurance policy, as far as me and my family know. But if she did, trust and believe, y'all hoes would not have gotten a dime.

Especially after all the bullshit y'all took her through with them grown-ass kids y'all got."

"First of all, my daughter ain't grown and if she is, that's my damn business," Frances began saying, waving her index finger like she was trying to prove a point. "As far as the life insurance money is concerned, I ain't gon' believe it in a million years that your cousin didn't have a policy. That just don't sound right to me, especially since I know she used to own this place. You gotta' have insurance to own a business, so somebody is lying."

"Look, hoe!" Rhonda snapped at Frances as she jumped up from her seat. "Don't be coming up in here like somebody owes you something, because they don't. Now, if you need a handout 'cause your Section 8 voucher is about to run out and you ain't got a stitch of food in the refrigerator, then you need to act like you got some sense. Then, maybe we'll feel sorry for you and slide you a few dollars."

"For your information, I ain't on no muthafucking Section 8. But, if I was, that would've been my business too. Now, I don't need no handouts. All I need is what's due to my li'l girl."

"Frances, don't nobody owe you shit," I interjected. "The only nigga owed her something was her trifling-ass daddy and since he ain't here, you and your bastard child need to get lost."

"My daughter ain't no bastard child!"

"Bitch, I don't give a fuck what she is. Just get your broke ass out of my shop, please," Rhonda warned her.

"Yes, please carry your ghetto ass outta here before we call the police and get you for trespassing charges. 'Cause this sure ain't a soup kitchen!"

"You know what? Fuck y'all hoes, because I tried to be nice."

"Bitch, you ain't tried to be shit! Now carry your ass!"

"Yeah, whatever," Frances told us as she turned to leave. Then she stopped in her tracks and said, "That's why Kira got what the fuck she deserved."

"What the fuck you just say?" I asked Frances in shock as I started to charge into her direction. Rhonda grabbed me around my waist in a bear hug restraint and said, "She's not even worth it. Let her carry her stinking ass!"

"Yeah, you better listen to her. 'Cause I would hate to

whip your ass the same way I did Kira when I ran up on her prissy ass at the Taco Bell a while back."

"Keep talking, bitch," I roared.

"Sweetheart, if you really wanted to run up on me, your home girl wouldn't be able to hold you back, for real. So, sit your phony ass down and take a load off, 'cause you are wasting me and my baby's time."

"Frances, get the fuck out now! And I'm not going to say it again," Rhonda yelled with rage.

Frances heeded Rhonda's menacing tone and proceeded to leave. After her departure, I took a seat back in my chair and took some deep breaths. A flustered expression crossed my entire face. Rhonda took a seat back in her chair as well and said, "Can you believe that bold bitch came in here like that?"

"No, I sure can't. I mean, how dare that hoe come up in here and inquire about a damn insurance policy? And then on top of that, get all indignant and start talking about how Kira deserved to die. Boy, she's a lucky sister. 'Cause, if you wasn't in here to stop me, I would've pushed her ugly-ass daughter on the floor and beat the brakes off her ass!"

"Well, I'm glad I was here, even though I would've loved to see it," Rhonda commented and laughed.

Me and Rhonda continued to talk about the drama that had just unfolded before our eyes until clients started pouring in. We decided to take a break from reading Kira's dairy so we could get down to business.

11

Real Niggaz Do Real Things

Syncere Speaks

That dope I got Quincy to cop from his peoples in D.C. was pure garbage. I had my man Mario cook the shit up and most of it fizzled out, so I lost out big time. I couldn't even re-coup my re-up money so I called a meeting with Quincy. I told him to meet me at the car wash at 4 p.m. and he was there when I pulled up. I guess he heard the urgency in my voice so his bitch ass made it his business to be there. Ol' punk bitch!

"Yo, you know that shit we got from your peoples was real salty. I'm gon' need you to get on the phone and call dem niggas and tell 'em I want my dough back," I spit through my teeth as I tried to suppress the rage that was creeping up in me.

"Syncere, man, let's be serious! What cats you know in this game give niggas refunds on bad dope?"

"I can't see taking a loss like this so I guess they gon' be the first."

"Yo, man, I just don't see that happening. And I know

you ain't trying to hear this, but we are just going to have to take a loss."

"If I take a loss, somebody is going to get slaughtered!"

"Come on, Syncere, it ain't even got to go down like that!"

"So whatcha saying? It's all right for your peoples to take my money?"

"Nah, I ain't saying that," Quincy replied, trying to clarify himself.

"So, what is you saying? 'Cause it sure sounds like you taking up for these niggas when you supposed to be my partner."

"I ain't taking up for dem niggas! Fuck them! All I'm saying is that we don't need to start no unnecessary beefs!"

"What, you scared of dem niggas? You turning pussy on me?"

"Come on, dawg, you know me better than that!"

"Shiiid, you had me kind of worried there for a minute! Hmmm, I thought I was gon' have to put a slug in you my damn self!"

"Damn son, you carrying it like that over fourteen grand of bad dope?"

"You muthafucking right! I'd kill my girl if she took twenty dollars from me!"

Quincy threw his hands in the air out of frustration and said, "Yo, I'll make that call to my peoples on the strength of the loyalty I have for you. But, don't you ever step to me like I'm some kind of weak-ass chump again!"

I waved him off and said, "Yo, don't take it personal, it's just business! So, hit me up after you talk to them."

"Yeah, a'ight," Quincy uttered and turned his back on me.

I stood up, secured my burner back into my waistband of my jeans and began to head back out of the door when a thought came to mind. I turned back around and said,

"Oh yeah, I don't want that nigga Lloyd breathing no more after tonight. So, call Monty and dem' niggas and tell 'em I said be ready tonight."

"How you gon' do something to that nigga when your ankle is still fucked up?"

"I ain't gon' do shit! Monty gon' take care of everything. I just wanna be there when the shit gets done."

"Where you trying to make the hit?"

"In P-Town. After the dog fight."

"Nah dawg, that's gon' be too risky."

"You know where he stay at?"

"Yeah, him and his girl got a house out Suffolk."

"Do you know who she is or what she looks like?"

"Nah. But, it wouldn't be too hard to figure out who she is once we go inside their crib."

"Yeah, that's true. Well, tell Monty and 'em that's where we going."

"A'ight," Quincy replied and then I bounced.

And as soon as I got back into my rental car I got Nikki on the line.

"Hello," she said when she answered her cell phone.

"Where you at?"

"At the shop. Why?"

"Because I was gon' swing by there in the next hour or so, that's why," I replied sarcastically. Why was this bitch questioning me when I was trying to question her ass! That just didn't make sense to me. "So, are you gon' still be there or what?"

"Yeah, I'll be here," she replied and then she sighed.

"What's wrong wit' you, Nikki?"

"Nothing, I'm just tired," she answered nonchalantly.

"Yo, I know you ain't still mad with me from the other day?"

"Is that what you called me for?"

"Who you getting smart with?"

"Look, Syncere, I am not trying to argue with you. I've got too much shit on my mind right now for that nonsense."

"I didn't call to argue wit' your stupid ass! I just wanted to know if you was gon' be there, so I could come and scoop you up and take your silly ass out to lunch."

"Well, that sounds nice but I already ate."

"Yeah. A'ight, then. I'mma holler."

"Yeah, yeah, yeah," she replied and hung up.

I started to call her stupid ass back and curse her out, but I didn't have time to be fussing wit' her. The bitch is nutty as a fruit cake. And if she doesn't learn to watch her fucking mouth when she is talking to me, then she is gon' always have me smacking upside her muthafucking head. 'Cause see, I was taught that a man was suppose to be the ruler over his woman and that the woman was supposed to respect him. Ain't no talking-back shit allowed. And ain't no hanging out all times of the night, either. Trust me, I was gon' be the only mu'fucker doing the hanging out 'cause I was the one handling business and paying the bills. So, she was gonna either get with the program or keep getting the shit beat out of her. She could make a choice. Because I was not gonna have it no other way.

After I got off the phone with Nikki's simple ass, I started up the car and hopped on the road. I made a stop by one of my spots out in Huntersville to see if their supply was low. But, they were all right so I chilled out there for a hour or so just to make sure everything was running smoothly. Then, after I felt like I had seen enough, I got up and bounced. But before I left, I collected all the dough they made while I was there. The count was a little over eight grand which was a nice piece of change for me, so

I threw it in the glove compartment and hopped back on the road. I was gon' scoop Sasha up from her sister's spot in the Norview section of Norfolk.

I found out her sister wasn't there when I pulled up, so I went in the crib and got myself a quickie before she came back. The shit was good too. Ain't nothing like sneaking some pussy. That shit'll have your adrenaline pumping like a muthafucker.

On the flipside, I snatched her up and we went out. We rode around to a few apartment complexes to get applications and then we stopped at P.F. Chang on Virginia Beach Boulevard since we were in the mood for some Chinese food. After that pit stop, we decided to get a room at the Hilton around the corner. I wasn't in any condition to get my fuck on again. I really just wanted to chill since I had made plans to meet up with Monty and 'em later on. As soon as I walked into the suite, I took everything out of my pockets and climbed straight on the bed.

"Want me to take your pants and shoes off?" she asked.

"Nah. I'm cool."

"You sure?"

"Yeah," I assured her. "I gotta' go out later. So, I'm gonna take a quick nap."

"What time do you have to go out?"

"I wanna leave about ten o'clock, so wake me up."

"All right. But, when you leave out, I want you to drop me back off at my sister's house because I promised her that I would baby sit for her tonight."

"Why didn't you tell me that before I got the room?"

"Because I didn't remember until just now."

"Yeah, a'ight." I sighed, then I laid my head down on the pillow and closed my eyes.

* * *

Later on, around twelve midnight, I met Monty and his boy, Amir, at the Texaco gas station in downtown Portsmouth. Quincy was already in Suffolk. He called and told me that he was lying down on the ground behind a set of bushes one house over from Lloyd's crib. So, after I told them what the deal was, I hopped in their old beat up whip and left my rental parked on a street right around the corner from the gas station.

As soon as we touchdown in Suffolk, I got Quincy back on the phone and asked him his exact location.

"I'm on 6th Street, right off East Washington Avenue. So, park you car either on 3rd or 4th Street and walk to where I am," he instructed.

"A'ight," I said. But truly speaking, I wasn't in the mood to walk two muthafucking blocks. Did the nigga forget that I was walking with a fucking cane? Nah, see we're gonna have to come up with something better than that. So, I looked over at Monty and said, "Quincy just said that he was on 6th Street hiding out in some bushes, so we need to park the car on 4th Street and walk to where he is. But, I ain't gon' be able to do it with this cane. So, I'm gonna take this car, drop you and Amir off around the corner from Quincy and then I gonna park down the opposite end of 6th Street and wait for y'all to give me the signal."

"That's cool," Monty replied. From there the plan was executed.

Immediately after I dropped Monty and Amir off, I rode around the block and found a good hideout spot on the opposite end of 6th Street. Once I pulled into the lot, I saw that it was a small development site for contractors to build a new home.

There were huge piles of dirt all over the property with a bulldozer and a dumpster sitting along the curb. I parked the car directly behind the dumpster, reclined the chair and waited.

I think I listened to the entire T-Pain CD twice when I realized that I had been sitting in this tight ass car for over a hour and a half. You know I was beginning to lose my patience with this thing all together. And there was no better person to vent my frustrations to than Quincy.

"Man, what time is this nigga coming home?" I asked the moment he answered his phone.

"Shit, I don't know. But, I wish he hurry up 'cause I'm tired of hiding behind these fucking bushes," he complained. "And these bugs is tearing my ass apart."

"How are Monty and Amir holding up?"

"Ahh man, them niggas been ready to go."

"Look, if that nigga don't show up in the next thirty minutes, then we gon' go ahead bounce."

"A'ight," Quincy agreed.

Just as I was about to hang up my phone, Quincy said, "Hey yo', dawg, wait. Don't hang up."

"What's wrong?"

"Man you ain't gon' believe it, but your ship is pulling in right as we speak."

"You bullshitting!"

"No, I'm not. Check it out," he insisted.

I sat up in my seat, rolled down the driver side window and stuck my head outside of the window just enough so I could look around the dumpster. When I got a clear view of Lloyd's white, 2007-LS 460-Lexus creeping up the street, I started smiling. "Yeah, I see 'em. Just stay out of sight until I tell you when to rush 'em."

"But, I thought we were going to wait until he goes into his crib."

"I changed my mind; we ain't got time for all of that. Just hit 'em as soon as he gets out of his whip. And when he hits the ground, I want all three of you niggas to make sure he's dead first before you make a run for it. Oh yeah, and I want y'all to take everything that fat muthafucking got in his pockets too."

"Where you gon' pick us up at?"

"Meet me on 5th and I'll take you to your whip."

"A'ight," Quincy said and then he hung up.

I held my head out of the car window so I could see everything unfold. From the time Lloyd's whip pulled up in the driveway and stopped, everything seemed to go in slow motion. Just when everything seemed to be going according to plan, something unexpected happened. I immediately got Quincy back on the phone.

"What the fuck is going on? Where is this nigga at?" I asked the moment he answered.

"I don't know. But, that's gotta be his girl."

"What is she doing?" I asked, trying desperately to see her next move from where I was parked.

"She's on her way into the house. But, from the looks of it, she ain't gon' be in there long because she left the car running."

"Can you see in the car from where you at?"

"The tint is kind of dark but I can still see a little bit."

"Is anybody in there?"

"Nope."

"Do you think that nigga is already in the crib?"

"Nah man, ain't nobody in there. All the lights been off in the joint the whole time."

"Look, I want you and Amir to run up in there and rough her up until she tells y'all where that nigga is."

"Whatcha' want us to do with her after she tells us?"

"Call me first and then I'll let you know."

"A'ight. But, whatcha want Monty to do?"

"Nothing. I want him to stay put, so he can watch your back just in case somebody else decides to show up."

"A'ight," Quincy replied.

About sixty seconds after Quincy hung up with me, I saw him and Amir sprinting across the street like they were athletes. Less than ten seconds later, they were on the front porch and forcing their way into the house. I couldn't see anything beyond that, so you know it was killing me to know what was going on. But thanks to Quincy, I didn't have to wait that long to find out because that nigga called me less than three minutes later.

My adrenaline was pumping like crazy when my phone started ringing. The urge to know what was going on inside that house had an even greater effect. "Hey y'all all right?"

"A yo' dawg, you ain't gon' believe what I just ran into."

"What is it?" I asked anxiously.

"You gon' have to come down here and see it for yourself."

"Whatcha' mean I'm gon' have to come down there? Whatcha' trying to set me up or something?" I asked defensively.

"Come on now dawg, what kind of question is that? Man, you know I wouldn't carry you like that," Quincy replied, trying to reassure with me.

Trying to make sense of what he was saying, I hesitated. Then I asked, "Who else is in there besides the chick?"

"Nobody. It's just her and us."

"A'ight, well send Amir outside on the porch first and then I'll come."

"Man, you tripping! But, a'ight."

Moments later I saw Amir walk out on the front porch, close the door behind him and signal for me to come. I started up the ignition, drove the car half way up the block, got out and walked the rest of the way. Before I crossed over to the other side of the street, I walked by the set of bushes where Monty was and said, "A yo' nigga, I don't know what's going on in there, but if I don't come out in the next couple of minutes, I want you to run up in there blasting."

"I gotcha'," Monty replied in a low whisper.

By the time I got on the porch Amir was giving me this weird looking expression. So, I pulled my burner from my waist, pulled back on the chamber and asked, "What the fuck is going on? Y'all niggas trying to play me?"

Amir's red, short, stubby ass threw his hands up and took a couple steps backward and said, "Nah Syncere, we ain't trying to play you. You know we don't roll like that."

"Well, what's up with all the secrecy shit?"

"Ain't nobody trying to be all secretive. The only reason why Q wanted you to come in the house to see what's going on is because if he tried to explain it to you, you wouldn't believe it."

I hesitated once more and then I said, "A'ight, well, let's go on in before somebody comes up."

Since Amir was closest to the front door, he went in first and I followed. As I crossed the threshold into the living room, my eyes scanned the entire room and landed on something that caught me completely by surprise. I couldn't believe what I was actually seeing. And Quincy noticed it in my facial expression, but he kept his peace. He knew I was going to need time to soak everything in. But, it didn't take me long, because as soon as I walked completely in the house and Amir closed the door behind me, I walked directly over to Quincy standing over top of home girl with his pistol pointed directly at her head. "Sasha, what the fuck are you doing here?"

"She lives here," Quincy interjected. "This is Lloyd's girl."

"You fucking bitch," I roared as I lunged toward her and

hit her right across her left temple. The force behind the blow of the gun sent her dumb ass flying down to the floor.

"Owww," she screamed, grabbing her bleeding head.

"Shut the fuck up! You ol' snake ass bitch! Got me 'round here thinking you were down for me. Nursing me back to health and shit, but you was the one who had me set up to get robbed," I snapped and kicked her in her side. "I almost got killed behind your stinking ass!"

"I'm so sorry. Please don't kill me," Sasha begged after she managed to crawl onto her knees.

"Bitch, I ain't trying to hear that muthafucking shit! Just tell me where your fat ass boyfriend is?"

"He's at the gambling spot in Cypress Manor."

"Where the fuck is that?" I asked her feeling irritated and murderous.

"It's out here in Suffolk, off White Marsh Road."

"How far is it from here?"

"It's about five minutes away."

"How many niggas at the spot with 'em?"

"His home boy Spank is with him. Plus there's three other cats in there."

"Whatcha come in here for? 'Cause, I know he sent you here to get something?"

"When I walked in here she was pulling this dough out of the freezer," Quincy interjected as he retrieved a stack of money from his jacket pocket.

"Damn! I didn't know niggas were still hiding their dough in the back of the freezer. That's some ol' school shit!"

"Come on now, we're talking about some ol' country ass nigga from the back woods. So, he don't know nothing."

"He knew enough to get this bitch to set me up."

"True," Quincy replied.

"How much is it?" I asked.

"I don't know," Quincy said and then he looked down at Sasha. He asked her, "How much is it?"

"Ten grand."

"Anymore in there?" I asked Quincy.

"No," he replied.

"Well, where is all that muthafucking money y'all took from me?"

"I'm not sure."

"Whatcha' mean you're not sure?" I snapped.

"I don't know where he could've put it. Remember, I was with you." She continued to plead her case.

"Look, I ain't trying to hear that bullshit! 'Cause I know that nigga got some more dough hidden in here somewhere."

Before Sasha could respond, our attention shifted to a noise coming from the front porch. Me and Quincy jumped for cover while Amir took a look through the peep hole.

"What is it?" I whispered loud enough for him to hear me.

"Oh shit! Somebody's coming," he replied, as if he had saw a ghost.

Instantly, everybody pointed their burner toward the door. While we waited for the opportunity to unload, I snatched Sasha up from the floor and made her stand directly in front of me, just in case shit got out of control and I needed a human shield.

"Stop that muthafucking crying and ask who it is," I instructed her as I stuck my burner in her back.

She cleared her throat and asked, "Who is it?"

The person outside didn't respond so I sent Quincy out the back door to check things out. Within fifteen seconds that nigga was out the back door and around the front part of the house tapping on the living room window. "Open the front door. It ain't nobody but Monty," I heard him say.

Relieved to know that it was my nigga Monty out there

watching our back, I let out a sigh of relief and had Amir to open up the front door. "Damn nigga, you scared the hell out of us," I told him the moment he stepped into the house.

"Man, shiid, I thought y'all niggas was in trouble."

"Nah, we all right. We just trying to find out where Lloyd keeps his stash."

"A'ight. Well, handle y'all business," Monty said as he headed back out the door. But, then he turned back around and said, "Oh yeah, somebody needs to turn the car off outside before one of the neighbors get suspicious."

"Go ahead and handle that for me but make sure you don't leave no fingerprints."

"A'ight. But, whatcha' want me to do with the keys?" he asked.

"Leave 'em in the car 'cause we gon' be heading out of here in a few minutes."

"Want me to go back to my spot?"

"Nah," I said as I pulled the keys from my pockets and handed them to him. "Here, go and sit in the car and wait for us."

"A'ight," he said and headed back out the door.

Meanwhile, Quincy and I figured out a way to get Sasha to lure Lloyd out of the gambling spot, so we could take his fat ass out. But before we exited the crib, I made Sasha tell us where that nigga kept the rest of his stash. She led us to two central air vents located in the walls of their bedroom. Inside the vents we found close to one hundred thousand dollars. It wasn't close to the amount of dough they took from me, but it was better than nothing. So, once we had the money tightly secured on our bodies, we grabbed Sasha up and head back outside.

"Remember, Quincy, I want you and Amir to ride with Monty while I jump in the backseat of Lloyd's joint with Sasha. I want y'all to stay back some so that nigga won't notice y'all and try to make a run for it. Because remember, if we don't get him tonight, then we ain't gon' ever be able to get him."

"I gotcha," Quincy assured me and then we all pulled out.

Three minutes into the drive, Sasha's cell phone started ringing, so I pointed the gun directly at her and asked her who was calling.

"It's Lloyd," she replied after she picked up the phone and looked at the caller ID.

"How far are we away from him right now?"

"About two minutes."

"How far is that in walking distance?" I asked her.

"About another mile."

"All right, answer the phone and tell him somebody just hit you and drove off. When he asks you where you're at? Tell 'em you're right up the street from him. So, you'll need him to come where you are until the police gets here."

"Okay."

On the last ring, she answered her phone and told that nigga she was involved in a hit and run. "What! Somebody hit my muthafucking car!" I heard him screaming at her through the phone. She told him that she had already called the police. Right before she could tell him exactly where she was, he asked her where she was. "I'm about 3 blocks away from you, near the turn that takes you into Cypress Manor," she told him. I heard him sigh real loud and say, "Man shit! I just sent Spank ass on a run. But, a'ight. I'll be there."

Right after Sasha hung up with Lloyd I told her to pull the car over by the side of the road because it was a perfect spot to empty a few slugs in a muthafucker's head without being heard. There were no houses within a few walking blocks. However, there were a lot of tall trees and bushes on both sides of the street. It was the perfect place for somebody to hide because the only light was a dim street light and that was barely working properly. After she pulled over, I told her to turn the car off and hand me the keys and, of course, she did. While we sat back and waited, I got Quincy back on the phone and instructed him to tell Amir that I needed him to post up behind these trees to my right. I told him to tell Monty to turn the car around and park it on the opposite side of the street and to hang something out of the window like it's broke down. Right after I hung up with him, Sasha had the nerve to ask me something stupid.

"Are you going to kill me?"

"A yo', don't be asking me no muthafucking questions!" I snapped. "Especially after all that bullshit you popped to me."

"I wasn't popping no bullshit to you," she said, trying to explain.

"Bitch, shut up! Because nothing you say is gonna make me feel sorry for your stinky ass! And what's so fucked up about this whole shit is that I shared my muthafucking bed with you. I was gonna send your dumb ass back to college and make you my girl."

"I'm so sorry, Syncere," she cried out, tears welling from her eyes.

"Believe me, I wanted to tell you, especially after we started spending time together. I mean, I really started feeling you."

"Well, that's too muthafucking bad. 'Cause I'm gon' deal with you and that fat muthafucker as soon as he gets here."

Sasha's cries started getting louder. "Please give me another chance," she begged.

"You better shut the fuck up before I kill your ass right now!" I screamed, jamming the gun in the side of her head.

"Okay! Okay!"

When she did finally calm down, I took the gun away

from her head and sat back in the chair. A few minutes later, I saw Lloyd's fat, sloppy ass walking up the road toward us. The muthafucker looked like he was out of breath from that little ass hike he had to make, which I figured was less than a half a mile from the gambling spot, to where we were. So, I knew I had an edge on him. Not only that, this nigga didn't even have his burner out, so shit was going to go smoothly. "Put your phone up to your ear and act like you're talking to somebody," I told her as I braced myself for the confrontation with Lloyd.

My pistol already had a slug in the chamber, so I held it up and rested the barrel of it right over the passenger side head rest because as soon as that nigga opened the door, I was going to blast him. But, shit never goes the way you plan it.

Instead of him opening up the passenger side door to see what shape Sasha was in, he walked around the car to see what kind of damages he had. I ducked my head down so he couldn't see me. When he realized that nothing was wrong with his whip, he marched to the driver's side window with a puzzled expression and asked, "Where did you get hit at?" And as soon as Sasha rolled down her window, I sat up in my seat, aimed my joint right over her head and fired it. Boom! Boom! Boom! All three rounds went right through that nigga's chest and forced 'em on his back. I don't know if Sasha screamed from the loud roar of my burner or if it was because she just saw her man get oiled up.

Whatever it was, it really didn't matter because she had it coming to her too. I pointed my burner in the back of her head and fired two more rounds. Boom! Boom! Right before my eyes, her head exploded. Bloody brains and tiny pieces of bones of her skull splattered all over the fucking front seat of the car. A lot of that shit splattered in my face and got on my clothes too.

I didn't realize that Amir had come out of the bushes until after I jumped out of the car and saw him running toward Monty's car. That nigga wasn't wasting any time and neither was I. As soon as I closed the car door behind me and saw Lloyd lying there, I knew that I couldn't make the same mistake as he did by not making sure I was dead. So, to make sure there was no doubt, I shot him in his head too. Boom!

After I shot Lloyd in his head, Monty put his car in reverse and picked me up from where I was standing. Before I got in his car, I shoved my pistol down inside my waist, took my shirt off and tried to wipe as much of the blood off my face as I could.

"Come on dawg! We gotta go," Quincy insisted.

I got in the car and Monty sped off.

Later on that night, everybody huddled around in the kitchen of one of my drug spots so we could discuss some things. By the time I laid everything out for them, they understood the importance of keeping their muthafucking mouths closed. So, once everything was out in the air, I handed everybody a stack of cash. Amir and Monty got five grand and Quincy got ten. He finally straightened out that bullshit with his peoples in D.C. so he got more than them. That right there showed me loyalty.

12

You Reap What You Sow

A week had past since I murdered Lloyd and that bitch Sasha. Too bad I didn't get all my money back but it was cool. Taking their lives was an even and fair trade. Now that that part of my life is over, I could go ahead and take care of more important things.

For the past couple of nights I had been staying at Nikki's place. From time to time she'd give me a little bit of lip service, but it hasn't been enough for me to rip her fucking head off. When she finally left to go to the shop this morning, I hopped in my truck and headed down to the car wash since me and Quincy had some business to discuss.

The traffic was real bad on Virginia Beach Boulevard, so I jumped on I-264 from Rosemont Road. While I was driving and doing the speed limit, I saw a blue and white following me through my rearview mirror. Now, why were they on my ass like that? I sure hoped they wasn't getting ready to pull me over 'cause if they did, I was gon' be one sick nigga. Especially when they found out I was toting this burner. I couldn't let that happen, so if shit started to look funny, I was gon' have to push this gas pedal down to the floor and buck on dem crackers.

The adrenaline in my body was beginning to boil over but I knew I had to keep my cool after dem muthafuckas threw on their flashing lights. My first thought was to put the dip on them, but I figured I would have a better advantage if I caught 'em slipping outside of their car. But, the timing had to be right. Right after I pulled my truck over and came to a complete stop, I looked in my driver's side mirror and watched this tall, lanky-ass cracker walking toward my Rover with his hands on his burner. The other cracker got as far as the rear bumper of my truck and stopped, with his hand on his gun. As soon as the one on the driver's side got to my back door, I slammed my Timbs down hard on the accelerator and my shit took off! I think I almost ran over the cop's foot on my left. Oh well, fuck 'em! Before I knew it I was going over a 100 miles per hour in the rush hour traffic. I made a quick detour and got off on the Brambleton Avenue exit. But, guess what? Dem fucking crackers was still on my ass, plus they had another cop car trailing me, so I knew shit was about to get real ugly. I pressed down on my accelerator even harder. I even had to blow my horn at a few people trying to cross my path as I sped down the crowded two-way lane of Brambleton Avenue.

"Get the fuck outta the way," I yelled from my driver's side window 'cause I was trying to get outta some shit here and these stupid muthafuckers was trying to get me a hit-and-run charge. As the chase got more intense, I found myself dipping in and out of the traffic and then I turned down a one-way street laughing my ass off. All of a sudden, a little fucking shorty ran smack down in the middle of the street, chasing a goddamn basketball. To keep from running over his dumb ass, I turned, lost control of my steering wheel and ran dead into a mom-and-pop store. BOOM!!!!

I was blinded by the driver's seat air bag and the mutha-fucka almost smashed my face in. I was dazed as shit and tried to get my thoughts together. I hopped out of my truck but it was too late, 'cause as soon as I tried to turn and make a run for it, I found myself staring down the barrel of a 9mm glock.

"Freeze, you muthafucker!" dis cracker said. And then out of nowhere, this other cop came up and hit me right in the back of my head with his fucking police stick. Shiiid, I was out cold.

When I finally regained consciousness, I felt the dizziness from the blow of the police officer wearing off. When my eyes came into focus, reality began to set in and that's when I realized I was locked up in a cold-ass room the size of a closet. The room was sealed off by an iron door with every criminal's name carved in the walls like it was the fucking Wall of Fame.

I shook my head in disbelief and wondered how the fuck I was going to get out of this shit here.

13

Forty Bars & Running

Nikki Speaks

"Millennium Styles, Nikki speaking. How can I help you?"

"Ay yo, Nikki, this Quincy from the car wash."

"What's up, baby?"

"Yo, you ain't gon' believe this shit!"

"What happened?"

"I just got a call from Syncere, telling me he just got bagged up by the police!"

"Wait a minute, I just talked to him a couple of hours ago! What happened?"

"He didn't exactly tell me what went down 'cause he doesn't like doing the phone thing. But he did say he wrecked his truck and he got tore off with his burner."

"Oh my God! When did this happen?"

"He said it happened right after he left your crib this morning. He didn't even make it to the car wash."

Before I responded to Quincy's spin on the situation,

I looked down at my watch and realized that I had left my apartment around ten o'clock this morning. Now it was four o'clock. "Damn, he's been locked up for almost six hours! Why didn't he call me?"

"He said he tried to. But y'all got a block on the phone up there."

I sucked my teeth and said, "Oh yeah, I forgot all about that. But anyway, how much is his bond?"

"He didn't get one!"

"What do you mean, he didn't get one?"

"They denied him a bond."

"But why?"

"Since he's from New Jersey they say he's a flight risk."

"So, what is going to happen now?"

"We're gonna have to wait and see what happens in court tomorrow."

"Did he tell you what time he had to go before the judge?"

"Yeah, he said it was nine o'clock in courtroom number three."

"So, what do we do in the meantime?"

"We just sit back and wait."

I hesitated and sighed heavily. "All right, call me in the morning and I'll meet you down at the courthouse."

"Sorry *mami*, I don't do the courthouse scene because a nigga like me is on paper."

"Shit! I am too."

"Yeah, probably for failing to complete your community service," Quincy commented with a laugh.

"If you only knew!"

"Well, whatever it was, it can't be no worse than my shit! So, you're on your own with this one."

"What do you want me to do if the judge sets him a bail?"

"Call me or come by the car wash. I'll be here anytime after twelve."

"Will do," I told Quincy and then our conversation ended.

I slumped down in my stylist's chair, trying to get a handle on all the mixed emotions swarming around in my head. One part of me was happy as hell that this nigga was in jail because in the back of my mind, I was wrestling with the thought that he could've had something to do with my cousin's death. The other part of me was beginning to feel sorry for him because I knew how it felt to be behind bars without bail. I knew he was going crazy right now, especially since he couldn't contact me himself. Hopefully that would all wear off by tomorrow when he saw me stroll into the courtroom.

"Who just tore your world down that fast?" Rhonda asked, breaking my concentration.

"Girl, I just found out that Syncere got locked up on a gun charge."

"Was that him on the phone?"

"Nah, that was his partner Quincy from the car wash."

"When did it happen?"

"A couple of hours ago."

"Well, why ain't you down there trying to get him out?"

"Because his ass ain't got no bail yet! He does go before a judge in the morning, so hopefully he'll get one then. I'm gon' go down there around nine o'clock and see what's going on."

"Girl, I sure know what you're going through. Trust me, I done had my share of visits down to the Norfolk City Jail. Tony couldn't keep his ass out of there if his life depended on it! Shit, from all the cases that he had, you would've thought that nigga was a baller. Believe me when I tell you, he wasn't. And not only that, ask me who was paying his lawyer all that fucking money?"

"Who, you?"

"You damn right! That's why I told him to sit his

block-hustling ass down and get a real job. Because I was getting tired of using my money to bail his sorry ass out!"

"I'm glad Syncere has his own money, because if he had to depend on me to get out, he would be out of luck, especially on my salary."

"I'm feeling you."

"I'm glad somebody is, because my fucking head is spinning. Please tell me if I'm done for the day 'cause I am truly desperate to get home to my bed."

"Yeah girl, go home and take care of yourself. I ain't got nothing but two customers left. I'll be fine."

After Rhonda relieve me of my duties, I grabbed my purse and car keys and headed out the door.

"I'll call you in the morning before I come in," I told Rhonda before I closed the door behind me.

It took me forty minutes to get home because of the construction on Highway 264. Immediately after I entered my apartment, I checked my voicemail. I had one message from my grandmother and the other one was from Quincy, rehashing the incident that happened with Syncere. Coincidentally, after I erased the messages, I got a beep on the other line. When I clicked over it was the automated voice system from the jail indicating I had a collect call from the devil himself. I took a deep breath, accepted his call, and braced myself for the conversation ahead.

"Yo, why y'all got a block on the phones at the salon?"

"Because Rhonda wants it that way."

"Well, tell her to take that shit off!"

"I can't do that, Syncere, it's her shop."

"Well, you need to do something! 'Cause, I'm not gon' be able to call you collect on your cell phone."

"I'll see what I can do," I said just to shut his ass up.

"So, tell me what happened," I said, trying to move the conversation along.

"You ain't talked to Q?"

"Yeah, I talked to him."

"He didn't tell you what happened?" he asked sarcastically.

"He told me a little bit but he really didn't go into details."

"Well then, you know all you need to know!"

"No this muthafucka did not just get smart with me," I mumbled to myself, trying to fight the urge to curse his ass out. But, I held my tongue and continued the conversation. "Do you think you're going to need an attorney?"

"Hell yeah! What kind of question is that?"

"Syncere, I'm not going to be able to get you one by tomorrow morning."

"I know that. Just make sure you contact one after my court hearing tomorrow."

"Is there anyone in particular you want me to contact?"

"Yeah. I heard these niggas in here talking 'bout this lawyer name Taliaferro was good. So you might wanna call him first."

"All right, I'll do that. But tell me, how are you holding up?"

"You know me, I'm good. Kind of fucked up right now, but I'll bounce back."

"Have they taken you to a block yet?"

"Yeah, they put me in a block on the third floor with about twenty other niggas. And they got me sleeping on this cold-ass floor with this flimsy-ass cardboard mattress."

"They didn't give you a bunk?"

"Hell nah, 'cause this joint is overcrowded."

"You got money?"

"Yeah. I had about five hundred in my pockets when the police locked me up. The C.O. who processed me will put it on my books but I know they gon' keep that dough I had stashed away in my glove compartment."

"How much was it?"

"A little over eight grand."

"Did they give you a receipt for it?"

"Nah."

"Oh yeah, you can count that one a loss. 'Cause they gon' keep that, just as sure as my name is Nicole Simpson."

"Shiiid, I don't give a damn about that money. I just wanna get the hell outta here."

"You will, so don't worry about it. But, let me ask you this?"

"What's up?"

"If the judge gives you a bond tomorrow, where am I going to get the money to bail you out?"

"Q will handle that. Just give him a call."

"All right. Is there anything else you want me to do?"

"Nah, I got everything pretty much under control. Everybody on my payroll knows what they suppose to do while I'm off the scene. So, until they show me different, shit is all good!"

"What about your truck?"

"What about it?"

"Where is it? Do I need to have somebody go and pick it up?"

"No, that joint is a total loss."

"Whatcha mean? What happened?"

"I totaled it. It's smashed up!"

"Are you serious?" I asked with concern, as if I didn't already know.

"I'm dead serious. My shit is probably in somebody's garage being broken down into metal and scraps."

"Were you hurt?"

"Except for that airbag fucking up my neck, I'm straight."

"Do you think your insurance company will cover the damages?"

"That's a dumb ass question," he replied sarcastically. "Shit, I ain't had my driver's license long enough, but I do know that if you get a reckless driving charge, your insurance company will laugh yo' stupid ass out of their office if your try to get them to pay for your shit to get fixed."

"So, what cha' gonna do?"

"I'mma worry 'bout this case first 'cause I can always replace the Rover. Anyway, let me get off this phone, 'cause a whole line of niggas is trying to use it."

"All right. Are you gonna be able to call me back?"

"I'mma try but if I don't, I'll try to holla at you tomorrow before they take me to court."

"Okay. I love you!"

"A'ight."

My conversation with Syncere went pretty smooth. That nigga was so unpredictable, it's pathetic. The moment I answered the phone, I thought I was gonna get the tongue lashing of a lifetime, but I was wrong. Thank God, because I wasn't in the mood for his bullshit and now that I think about it, this nigga didn't tell me he loved me too. I wondered what kind of shit he was on. But, whatever it was, I was convinced it was something he had to work out on his own. Meanwhile, I was going to get comfy so that I could whip out Kira's diary and indulge myself in her madness. But, as I searched through the contents of my handbag, I realized that I must've left it back at the salon.

"Damn, how did I manage to leave it?" I asked myself, which made me realize that it was that damned phone call I got from Quincy that threw me off track. I called Rhonda on her cell phone to see if she had seen the diary once I left the salon.

"Hello," Rhonda said after the fourth ring.

"Hey girl, this is Nikki."

"Hey, what's up?"

"Where you at?"

"At home, laying in my bed. Why?"

"I was hoping you was still at the shop, because I left Kira's diary there. Did you happen to see it before you left?"

"Nope, I sure didn't. Where did you leave it?"

"I think I left it back in your office, because that was the last place I had it before I left."

"Well, you couldn't have left it in there because I straightened up the office right after you left."

"Oh well, I guess I must've left it over at my station."

"Yeah, you probably did. But, don't worry about it, ain't nobody gon' mess with it. Remember, I'm the only one with a key to the shop, so I'll see you in the a.m."

"All right."

14

Game Recognizes Game

Rhonda Speaks

My heart started racing fifty miles a minute the moment I heard Nikki's voice. I knew she was calling me about Kira's diary, that's why I already had a story ready for her ass. Yeah, I saw the diary. I picked it up and brought it home with me because I planned to read that bad boy tonight if it killed me. Shit, Kira was like my best friend. I wanted to know what she went through too. Now that she got off my phone, I was going to start off from where me and Nikki left off earlier today. The page from January 24, 2006, read:

> *Dear Diary,*
> *I met with Nikki's lawyer earlier today to go over the details of the interview I'm gonna have with the Feds on behalf of Nikki. I signed some documents that will give me immunity if I cooperated fully. I'm kind of having second thoughts about doing this, but hey, it's too late now. The damage is already done. I just hope*

the shit doesn't backfire on me because if Ricky were to ever find out what Nikki and I were doing to him, she and I both would come up missing for sure. The only thing that's left for me to do now is pray that everything works out the way that it's supposed to. Besides, who wants to go into protective custody if Ricky gets wind of what's going on? I sure don't. That's why I gotta' make sure the Feds do their part. After everything is over, I can go on about my life and live it in peace.

After reading this page of Kira's diary, my mouth fell open and I screamed at the top of my lungs. "Tony, come here!"

"What's wrong, baby?" he asked, startled by my scream.

"You are not going to believe this shit here," I told him, my chest heaving up and down.

"What is it?"

"Here, check this shit out! Read this page right here." I pointed to the page I had just read.

He took the diary out of my hand and slowly read every word from Kira's diary.

When he finally looked up at me, I immediately saw how the expression had changed on his face. "Where the fuck did you get this from?"

"Me and Nikki found it at Kira's house the day we went over there to pack her stuff up."

"The police didn't find this shit?"

"Evidently, they didn't. If they had, they would've used it for evidence in her murder trial."

"Didn't I tell you that them hoes was snitching?"

Instead of commenting, I nodded my head.

"You gon' start listening to me one of these days. I knew what I was talking about. And believe me when I tell you that if you keep reading her diary, you'll probably find out who killed her."

"I was thinking the same thing," I admitted.

"How long have you had the diary?"

"I just got it tonight. Nikki had it, but she left it at the shop today so I scooped it right on up and brought it home. She doesn't even know I have it, so I'mma read the whole thing tonight and put it back in the shop before she comes in the morning."

"What, she don't want you reading it?"

"I don't think she wanted me to have actual possession of it but she would read certain parts of it to me."

"Well, now you see why she didn't want you to have possession of it."

"Yep, I sure do."

"Good. Now, all you got to do is get that bitch Nikki out of that shop. If you don't, you gon' fuck around and catch a couple of strays dem niggas gon' be popping off at her ass!"

"But, how do we know somebody is after her? Remember, Ricky is dead."

"That didn't stop whoever killed Kira."

"You got a point there."

"Exactly. Whoever that nigga is has got to know Nikki was snitching too, which is why he's definitely coming back for her. It's just a matter of time."

"So, how am I supposed to tell her to leave when she done took over Kira's part of the ownership?"

"Is it in writing?"

"No."

"Then just tell her to carry her ass!"

"Come on Tony, she ain't gon' go for that shit. Especially the way she be carrying on now, parading 'round there wearing all of Kira's clothes and diamonds like she runs the whole shop."

"Look, I don't give a fuck what she's doing 'round there

because if she don't watch herself, she gon' be laid out somewhere."

Instead of responding to Tony's comment, I shook my head because I honestly didn't know what to say. My hands were tied with this situation and I wasn't gonna be able to do anything about it.

"Why you sitting there looking all crazy?" he asked.

"Because I don't know what to do."

"I just told you," he snapped.

"I ain't gon' be able to do it like that."

"Well, do you want me to do it? 'Cause you know I can't stand her ass! You know I'll make her feel the heat. Believe me, she won't ever show her face 'round the shop again."

Listening to Tony lay out his plan to get Nikki to leave the salon for good was becoming a little too unrealistic. His approach to the matter wasn't pleasant at all but, at the same time, I was beginning to understand his plan and decided to handled it myself.

"Don't worry about it," I told him. "I know what I'm gonna do."

"Yeah, a'ight! But, whatever it is, don't fuck around and drag your feet," he commented and then he walked back out of the bedroom, leaving me behind to come up with a plan of my own.

Before I put much thought into that plan, I buried my face back into the diary placed before me. My curiosity was beginning to get out of control. Before I knew it, it was four o'clock in the morning and I had read the entire diary. I was speechless and I honestly could not believe all the shit I had just read. From Kira dropping a dime on Ricky and robbing him of all his dough to her getting wrapped up with Russ and letting him take everything she worked so hard to get was kind of crazy, if you asked me. I mean, how fucking stupid could she have been? You don't tell the nigga you screwing around with that you'd been snitching on your husband to the Feds and expect him to be all right with it. That's a no-no! I don't give a fuck how good his dick was or how much he told you he loved you, all niggas were grimy. You couldn't trust none of them. All those bastards were vultures and fucking scavengers! They would never change. Then to read the part where Kira believed that Syncere had something to do with her and Mark getting shot outside her apartment was a complete shock. But, what got me was why didn't she tell the police this shit. What was going through her mind for her to keep something like that to herself? Was she on drugs or something? I mean, 'cause that was some weird shit! As far as Nikki was concerned, that was another issue. Whatever I decided to do about her would have to be played by ear. The bottom line was, she did have to go. This diary alone confirmed that.

I went to sleep a little after four a.m. this morning though part of me was still very much awake. It was a natural occurrence for me to listen to my children while they were fumbling around trying to get dressed every morning. Even though Tony was in charge of making sure they were properly dressed and fed, part of me was still on high alert, just in case the kids wanted to go about things their own way. But fortunately, I didn't have to go into Superwoman mode this morning because everything went smoothly. After I heard my last offspring head out the door, I turned over in my bed intending to fall back to sleep. But, for some odd reason, my body wouldn't let me. I lay there quietly for about fifteen minutes when I heard somebody knock on my front door. It was entirely too early for company, so who in the hell could it be this time of morning? On a good day, I would not have hesitated to get out of the bed to curse out this unexpected visitor. But why not let Tony handle it? Before I could yell out his name he yelled, "Who is it?"

For the life of me, I couldn't hear the other person's voice on the other side of the door. I couldn't figure out whether it was a man or a woman because the voice was so muffled. But then all that changed when he opened the door.

"Oh hey, how you doing?" I heard Tony say.

"I'm fine. Is Rhonda available?" I heard a woman ask which, of course, made me sit straight up in bed. Curiosity was beginning to get the best of me and I wanted to know who this woman was. I sat still and listened closely to her voice in hope of recognizing it. I figured if Tony knew her, then so should I.

"Oh, nah. She's asleep right now. Is there something I can help you with?"

"Well see, this is the thing—for the last three months, your rent has been late."

"Yeah, I know that," Tony told her.

"Well, she hasn't been including the late fees and now there's a $150 maintenance fee balance. It needs to be paid ASAP," I heard her stress to Tony.

"All right. When she gets up, I'll let her know."

"You do that and also let her know that I'll be expecting to see her by the end of the week."

"I sure will," Tony replied.

"Oh yeah, one other thing," she started to say.

"What's up?"

"Has the maintenance worker corrected y'all's water heater problem?"

"Nope, they sure didn't. As a matter of fact, one guy came through here about a week ago, unscrewed a couple of screws and said he'd be back later because he needed to get a special piece to fix it. But, he ain't never show back up."

"When was this?"

"About a week ago."

"Okay, I'll get on that and have someone else come out and have that fixed in no time."

"Thank you so much, Ms. Lady."

"Just call me Keisha."

"A'ight, thank you, Ms. Keisha." Tony continued to flirt which, of course, had my blood boiling over. But I remained cool and decided to wait for him to slip up again.

Being the person he was, it was bound to happen.

"You're quite welcome," she said and then I heard her giggle. But I couldn't figure out why was she giggling. I mean, it wasn't like he said something funny. As a matter of fact, I didn't hear Tony say another word. But I did hear her laugh again. I hopped out of the bed and went to see what the hell was so hilarious. When I reached the entrance to the front door I realized why I didn't hear Tony talking was because this muthafucka had a nerve to be whispering in her ear. This hoe was standing in front of my door in these tight-ass blue jeans showing off her pussy print, skinning and grinning like she's got some kind of schoolgirl crush for this broke-ass bastard. So, like any normal sister would do, wrapped up in a bathrobe but still ready to go for whatcha know, I opened my mouth as wide as I could and shut down their little flirting session.

"What the fuck is going on?" I yelled and scared the shit out of the both of those clowns.

"Whatcha' talking 'bout?" Tony asked, turned around stuttering.

"Just answer my damn question!"

"Ain't shit going on!"

"Well, why the hell are you out this muthafucker whispering like you don't want me to hear what you got to say to her?"

"I wasn't whispering," Tony said and that's when I got even louder.

"Don't try that lying shit on me, Tony! I ain't stupid, so please try to spare yourself the embarrassment because I'm about to show the fuck off in a few minutes if you don't tell me what the fuck you and her was talking about!"

"We were just talking about how lazy the maintenance guys are. That's all," the chick said, coming to his rescue.

"Oh, really," I said. And who are you?"

"My name is Keisha. I work at the rental office."

"Is that so?" I asked sarcastically.

"Yeah. But, to ease your mind, we weren't talking about anything else."

"Well, I can't tell! Because you were grinning your ass off out here before I rained on y'all little parade."

"Trust me, it wasn't nothing but a friendly conversation," she said, obviously trying to convince me.

"Yeah, that's what they all say! As for that $150 in late fees, I'll drop it off by the office before I leave and go to work this morning."

"Okay. That'll be fine."

"It's gon' have to be," I told her, watching Tony excusing himself from the conversation. I did give him the evil eye when he walked by me to come back into the house.

"Well, y'all have a nice day."

"We will," I said with the meanest grit I could muster up and then I slammed my door as hard as I could.

Tony got MIA, but I found his ass in the bathroom sitting down on the toilet with his pants down, like he was trying to shit. But, I wasn't going for that bullshit! And when I forced the door in with my right foot, he realized that I was ready to go for round two.

"Are you gon' let me shit in peace before you start screaming on me?"

"Fuck you, nigga! I'm so tired of your sneaky-ass ways, it's pathetic! What's so fucked up about you is that you're starting to get real bold with the shit too by standing outside of my damn house, skinning and grinning with some bitch that looks like her pussy stinks!"

"Why the fuck are you tripping? I wasn't trying to holler at that girl. And if I was, don'tcha think I would've had enough sense not to do it right in front of the crib?"

"Nigga, you think being in front of the crib matters? Hell nah, not when it comes to your sneaky ass. You'll do some slime ball shit in the same room with me, if you think I ain't looking!"

"Yo, Rhonda, stop bugging out! I don't even get down like that."

"Yeah, that's what your mouth say! But, I'll tell you what. If I catch that hoe in your face again, you better pack your shit up real quick 'cause if you don't, I'm gon' do it and you ain't gon' like it one bit."

"Yeah, whatever," Tony uttered real nonchalant like.

I smacked him upside his head and said, "Yeah, whatever, my ass! Now, try me and see what happens!"

"You need to keep your hands to yourself," he warned me.

"I ain't gon' do a muthafucking thing 'cause I'm really tired of your bullshit! Witcha broke ass you got a nerve to be smiling up in that bitch's face and don't even pay the damn rent 'round here," I screamed even louder. "If you wanna act like you doing something, step to her and get her to waive all them late fees and give us a discount on the muthafucking rent!"

"That girl ain't gon' be able to do that shit!"

"How you know? Did you have time to ask her that too?" I snapped and swung at his head.

He ducked and said, "Rhonda, you better go 'head before I get up from this stool and go the fuck off."

"Go 'head and get up, shitty!"

Tony sighed with frustration and said, "Look, will you please leave, so I can shit in peace?"

"Yeah, I'mma leave, 'cause you starting to stink. But trust me, I ain't through wit' your sorry ass!"

"Yeah, whatever," he mumbled underneath his breath.

As badly as I wanted to hit him across his head once again, I managed to restrain myself, knowing it was possible that he could jump up and knock the shit out of my ass at the drop of a dime. I did the next best thing and picked up the Dove from the soap dish and threw it at his ass. He tried to block it with his arms, but his reflexes were too slow. The soap popped him right across his forehead.

"Owww!" he yelled from the impact and that's when I stepped back out of the bathroom, smiling from ear to ear. "Try that shit again and see if I don't go upside your mutha-fucking head!" Rage spread throughout his entire face.

I ignored his idle threat and proceeded toward my bedroom to get dressed for work since I felt like I got my point across. Hopefully, for Keisha's sake, she got the same message.

15

Orange Jumpsuits

Syncere Speaks

Two C.O.s pulled me and some other cats out of the block to escort us to court. After they put my handcuffs and shackles on, I wasn't feeling how tight they had 'em on me so I had to let 'em know.

"Ay yo, C.O., can you loosen up these shackles a little bit? These joints is fucking my ankles up."

"You're a big man. I'm sure you can handle it, Mr. Jones. It's just a short walk to the courthouse," replied this big, black, ugly-ass C.O. Niggas in his joint called him Tiny because he wasn't nothing but a pussy, for real. But, I was gon' be cool and let him throw his weight right now because this was his spot. But, I'd hit his ass up later if I ever ran into him on the streets. And he wasn't gon' see it coming.

On the way to court, me and fifteen other niggas were all handcuffed and shackled together, walking in a line, playing Follow the Muthafucking Leader like we were in a fucking chain gang. The whole way there, we had to travel underground through a hollow-ass tunnel. The jail had it set up like that to keep niggas like us from escaping. Not only that, they wanted us to avoid the public at all costs. I just hoped I wouldn't have to make the trip down this road again after today, but I guess I'd just have to wait and see what the judge said.

Before court started they stuffed all our asses in this little-ass cell with one short, rusty-ass bench, so I took a seat on the floor next to the iron bars. A couple of niggas in here knew me or at least heard about me from the streets, so word got around real fast that I was nothing to play with.

"What's good?" This young'un, who kind of looked familiar, asked me. When he finally came face to face with me, I realized I had seen him at the car wash a few times. I stood up and gave him a proper handshake.

"Damn nigga, whatcha doing in here?" I asked him.

"On a fucking dope charge. The mu'fucking narcs ran up in my girl's crib where I keep my shit at and since I was the only person there, I had to wear the charge."

"That's fucked up! What's your name again?" I asked him.

"DeShawn, but everybody calls me Dee."

"Damn, Dee, how much did they catch you with?"

"A couple of rocked-up o.z.s."

"Did they pull a burner off of you too?"

"Nah, just the rock. So, I should be good when I go out there and ask the judge for a bond reduction."

"How much is your bond now?"

"Twenty-five grand."

"Damn nigga, you can't post that? Shit, all you need is ten percent."

"I got the dough, but my girl can't get a bondsman to pick it up. They trying to get her to give them collateral plus some money and we ain't got no collateral.

That's why I'ma ask the judge to lower my shit down to at least fifteen."

"Well shiiid, at least you got a bond. That stupid-ass cracker in the Magistrate's Office told me he wasn't giving me shit, talking about I'm a flight risk 'cause I'm from Jersey."

"You got a lawyer?" he asked me.

"Nah, but since my charge is a felony, they've got to give me a court-appointed attorney, right?"

"Oh yeah, they gon' definitely do that. Shit, all of us in here will probably get appointed the same state lawyer."

"I don't give a fuck what they do, just as long as I can get that lawyer to ask the judge to grant me a bail this morning."

"Oh, you'll be a'ight. Just tell the lawyer you got a job working at the car wash."

"Nigga, I run that joint," I commented in a cocky manner.

"I know that! But don't tell none of these judges that, especially if you go in front of Judge Brown. That mu'-fucka is crazy! He locks niggas up and give them ridiculous time for petty shit."

"Well, I'm definitely not trying to see him for this gun charge."

"You better keep your fingers crossed because it ain't nothing but two judges in this section and Judge Brown is one of them. What happens is, both judges will pick a file out of a box and call our asses at random, depending on how big their case load is. Once you go in front of the judge you see today, that will be the same judge you see until your case is over."

Before I could respond to Dee's comment, another C.O. called my name and told me to step out of the cell. Dee wished me luck as I walked in the direction of a side door with a sign taped to it that read, 'Quiet Please! Court In Session.' I entered into the courtroom with the C.O. walking by my side. I looked around the whole room to see if Nikki was there to give me her support and boom, there she was, sitting in the second row with a sad look on her face. I smiled at her which made her smile back.

The C.O. positioned me in the designated area for inmates and I found myself standing smack dead in front of the judge with his nameplate in clear view. The name on it read Judge L. Brown and I knew my chances for getting a bail were slim to none.

"Your Honor, this is case #0971-702, The Commonwealth of Virginia vs. Antonio Jones." The courtroom clerk, a little, old, white lady who looked to be every bit of seventy years old announced my charges. "Mr. Jones has been charged with possession of a firearm, reckless driving, and evading the police. He is also being held without bail as he's considered a flight risk." She handed Judge Brown the file. The judge took the folder from the clerk's hand, looked directly in my face, and asked if he needed to appoint me a lawyer or if I would be able to get one on my own.

"I would prefer to hire my own attorney, Your Honor. But right now, I was hoping I could get a bond hearing."

"Get yourself an attorney first and then you can have him or her petition the Clerk's Office for a bond hearing. I'm going to set your next court date for Tuesday, July 18, at ten a.m. Do you have any questions?"

"No, sir," I replied and allowed the C.O. to escort me back out of the courtroom. I refused to look in Nikki's direction for fear I would see her crying, so I held my head down the entire trip back to the cell.

16

Ride Or Die Chick

Nikki Speaks

After Syncere was taken back out of the courtroom with no damned bail the only option left for me to do was to get up and leave. I hopped into my car and headed toward Highway 264. While I was on the road I made two calls from my cell. One was to Rhonda to let her know I would be in the shop right after I made a quick stop by my P.O.'s office. She said okay. And my second call was to Quincy and boy, did he have a lot to say.

"I just left the court," I told him.

"What happened? Did he get a bond?"

"Hell no! The judge didn't give him shit! Today was just the arraignment process to determine whether or not he would be able to hire himself a lawyer."

"Did he get to see you?"

"Yes, he saw me. I was sitting in the second row."

"So, what are you going to do now?"

"I am going to hire him an attorney so he can get a bond hearing."

"Do you know who you're going to call?"

"Yeah, he told me to contact this lawyer name Taliaferro."

"Oh yeah, I've heard he was crucial. But, if he ain't available, you should holler at this cat name Broccoletti. I heard he was vicious in the courtroom. You can always catch him having lunch with judges, so you know he's got plenty of clout."

"Do you know where Broccoletti's office is?"

"Nah, but, I heard it's somewhere in Norfolk. Just look him up in the phone book."

"How long are you going to be at the car wash?"

"I'mma be here all day because I know your man is going to be giving me a call sometime soon."

"A'ight. Do me a favor."

"What's up?"

"When he does call you, tell him I'm at work but I'm going to be getting off early so I can meet with a few lawyers."

"A'ight! Call me later and let me know what the lawyers say and how much they gon' charge you to pick up his case."

"Okay, I will," I assured him and then we both hung up.

The waiting area of the probation office wasn't crowded so I was able to get a seat without any problems after I checked in with the receptionist. Sitting two seats over from me was this dark-skinned cutie with a low Caesar and dark sideburns. He looked like he was every bit of thirty-two or thirty-three years old with a well-maintained mustache and a work uniform. I could see every letter on his name tag from my position and it spelled out the name SETH. I was also able to make out the company's logo and realized that he had a gig with a Nissan dealership. Judging from the wear and tear on his uniform, he probably worked in the service department because a company like that wasn't about to let a convicted felon work anywhere else under their umbrella. You know, his paycheck would never exceed the required amount of revenue to live comfortably in this day and time, which was going to have home boy right back on the grind. And that quick hustle was going to buy him another trip back into the federal system. Then again, I could be wrong. They said never judge a book by its cover and for all I knew, this cat could be one of those reformed ex-cons who just got out of the joint from doing a fifteen-year stretch. Most niggas who done did all that time truly had enough of living with other niggas so they was gon' do everything they could to sleep next to some pussy every night, unless they preferred the former.

There was also another guy waiting around to see his P.O. He was an average-looking cat but he sure had the attention of this chick sitting across from him. She was one of your average-looking chicken heads with a head full of cornrows like she just stepped out of the joint less than twenty-four hours ago. She reminded me of Rosie Perez, but without the thick Hispanic accent. Speaking of which, her conversation was on zero and home boy used it to his advantage.

"How long you been home?" I heard him ask her.

"Almost a month now," she replied.

"You got kids?"

"Yep, I got three."

"How old are they?"

"My daughter Sara is seven and my twin boys, Juan and Antonio, are four."

"Who had them when you was away?"

"They was living wit' my sister."

"Do you have them wit' you now?"

"Yeah, I guess you can say that since I'm living at my sister's house too."

"So, when you gon' let me come see you?"

"Whenever you want to."

"Do you have your own bedroom?"

"No, unfortunately, me and my kids all sleep in the same room."

"So, where would me and you chill at if I was to come by there?"

"We could chill in the living room and watch TV, unless you want to take me out to a restaurant."

"I don't like going out to eat. Restaurant food ain't good for you. I'd rather have some of your home cooking."

"I can't cook. But my sister can."

"I need to be trying to holler at your sister then," I heard him utter under his breath.

"Whatcha say?" she asked and it was obvious she hadn't heard what he had said.

"I didn't say nothing," he told her and before I heard her reply, I heard my name being called.

When I looked up, my P.O., Maxine Shaw, was standing a few feet away from me. She was wearing a fly-ass, dark blue, two-piece pants suit with a pair of three-inch heels to match. She was not your typical sister. This Black chick was a beast. She was a smart and witty-ass lady plus she had the mentality that everybody had some kind of bullshit game up their sleeve. I'd done nothing but try to convince her otherwise, even though sometimes my tactics didn't work. Being affiliated with Kira's murder hadn't given me much favor with her either. As a matter of fact she'd been trying to ride my ass behind the police investigation more than the police themselves. So, I knew today's visit wasn't going to be any different from the last one.

"How is your family?" she asked the moment she closed her office door.

"Everybody's fine," I replied and took a seat in the chair placed in front of her desk.

"Are you still working at the hair salon?"

"Yes, ma'am."

"Have you turned in your monthly report for this month yet?"

"Yes, I left it at the front desk with the receptionist."

"How is the murder investigation going?"

"I'm not sure."

"What do you mean, you're not sure?"

"Well, I haven't heard anything."

"Has anyone in your family tried contacting the detectives who are conducting the investigation?"

"Yes, my grandmother and my dad have spoken with them a few times. But, all they keep saying is that when they have something concrete they will let us know."

"Have they tried to interview you since the last time?"

"No."

"Have you heard any buzz on the streets about who could have been responsible for her murder?"

"Nope, not a word."

"Well, what about you?"

"What about me?"

"How are you holding up?"

"Better than the day before but I still have my moments."

"I'm sure. So, is there anything new going on in your life?"

"No, everything is pretty much the same," I lied

"Have you come in contact with any convicted felons?"

"No, ma'am."

"Have you traveled outside the district without permission?

"No."

"Are you still living alone?"

"Yes."

"Do you possess or have access to a firearm?"

"No."

"Have you been questioned by any law enforcement officers, other than the two detectives investigating your cousin's murder?"

"No."

"Have you possessed any illegal drugs since our last visit?"

"No, I'm not that crazy!"

"Keep that same attitude and you'll stay on the streets."

"Believe me, I will."

"Good. Now, do you have any questions for me?"

"No, ma'am."

"Okay, this concludes our visit. Before you go, you'll need to give me a urine sample."

"Okay, no problem," I told her and then I stood to follow her to the restroom. And even though squatting over a toilet to piss in a plastic cup in front of another woman put me in a very awkward position, I was learning to find a way to live with it. Hey, what could I say? Shit like that would continue to happen as long as my ass was on paper.

Later on that night, while I was watching a movie I rented from Blockbuster, Syncere called. After his name played back from the record message, I pressed "0" and the call was connected.

"What's good, Nikki?"

"Nothing, what's up wit' you?" I asked after I turned the volume down on the TV.

"I'm just chilling. Waiting for y'all to get me a lawyer so I can get the hell outta here."

"Trust me, I'm working on it."

"You seen Q?"

"No, not today."

"Did you talk to him?"

"Briefly, why?"

"Because I've been trying to holler at him all day and he ain't been up at the spot."

"Want me to call him on three-way?" I asked.

"Yeah. Go 'head," he insisted.

"All right." I clicked over to the other line.

When I clicked back over, Syncere was blowing through the phone really loud, trying to mask the fact that I was attempting to connect him to a three-way call. If the jail's phone system detected it, they would disconnect our call immediately and block future calls. It was crazy how they got that shit rigged but what could you do?

"Syncere, I got Q on the phone," I told him.

"Ay yo, what's up dawg?" Quincy asked him.

"I'm a'ight, Q. What's up wit' you?"

"I'm just taking care of business. Why? What's up?"

"Did you holler at your peoples yet?"

"Yeah. I talked to 'em right after you left the car wash that day."

"What he talking about?"

"He said he's gon' take care of it," Quincy replied convincingly.

"So, when you gon' see 'em again?"

"I was gon' wait until you touched down first before I head back up there."

"So, he said he's gon' replace the whole joint?" Syncere questioned Quincy like he didn't believe him.

"Man, I don't know. But, I do know that he's gon' look out real decent."

"How long you been up at the car wash?"

"I was here earlier this morning but I dipped out for a few so I could take care of some business."

"Everything a'ight?"

Quincy sighed heavily and said, "Yeah, everything's cool. Just gotta clip a couple fingers before shit gets out of hand."

"Who ripping us off?"

"I'll tell you about it when you get out."

"Which spot is it?"

"The one you left right before you got bagged up."

"Oh nah, they ain't carrying it like that, is they?"

"Yeah, but I'mma handle it."

"Yeah, take care of that before shit starts getting good to 'em."

"Oh, I'm on it," Quincy assured him.

"So, how's business up there? We been getting plenty of cars coming through?"

"Nah, not really. It's been kind of slow these last few days. And I just had to get rid of that nigga Blake right before you called."

"What happened?"

"One of our customers caught him stealing quarters out of his cup holder."

"Ahhh man, no he didn't," I heard Syncere yell. "Do you know how that shit makes us look?"

"Yep, that's why I told him to get the fuck on!"

"You should've knocked his bitch ass out for doing that dumb-ass shit!"

"Come on now, you know I wasn't gon' let that nigga leave outta here without punishing his ass."

"Yeah, that's what's up," Syncere commented as if he was satisfied with how Quincy handled the situation.

"So, you say you holding up, right?"

"Yeah, I'm good for right now. But, as soon as I can get that lawyer to get me back in court so I can get outta here, I'm gon' be a lot better."

"Well, don't worry about it. We gon' take care of it."

"A'ight. Look, I'mma holler at you later so hold shit down!"

"You know I got it," Quincy assured him. "Yo Nikki, call me later."

"All right," I said and then I disconnected his line.

Immediately after I clicked Quincy off the line, Syncere changed his demeanor.

"Yo Nick, I wantcha to make a trip up to the car wash 'cause that shit he was talking 'bout just didn't sound right wit' me."

"Whatcha want me to do?"

"Just go up there and chill out with him for a while and see what kind of money coming through there."

"When you want me to do it?" I asked with little enthusiasm.

"Go up there tomorrow."

"All right, but I ain't gon' be able to chill up there for a long time because I've got a lot of clients to prep for Rhonda tomorrow."

"That's cool, but at least try to get up there between one and two o'clock, 'cause that's when we get the busiest."

"All right," I said. Then the pre-recorded voice message came on to let us know that we had one minute left before our call would be disconnected. Syncere told me that he was going to call me back in about thirty minutes after he took a shower. And as badly as I didn't want to, I told him I would be waiting.

17

Bad Company

Rhonda Speaks

Tabitha and I were the only two stylists in the shop, along with a handful of our customers, when Nikki walked through the front door. She smiled at me the moment our eyes connected plus she gave her usual greeting and, in unison, everybody in the shop spoke back. I knew she had just come from hearing Syncere's court case but her body language told a different story. As badly as I wanted to be nosey and ask her about the outcome, I elected not to because of the situation at hand and kept my guard up.

"Rhonda, what time did you get in this morning?" Nikki asked me.

"I got in here a little after nine," I replied, being really short and nonchalant.

"Did you happen to run across my little black book?"

"Girl, I forgot all about that book," I lied as I continued to curl my client's hair. And while I assumed Nikki would come at me with another question, she approached me with the exact same question as she began to search the drawers of her work station. But, before I got a chance to answer her, she found it.

"Good, here it is," she finally said with a sigh of relief and immediately she placed it inside her handbag.

I didn't acknowledge the fact that she found the diary because at this point, I could have cared less; I had already read the entire thing.

After a few hours had passed Nikki began to sense something was wrong with me because of the limited conversation between us. I played it off like I was just having a bad day and it was nothing personal toward her. But I could tell she wasn't buying it because the moment I stepped in the back office, she followed me and gave me the third degree.

"Are you sure I didn't do anything, Rhonda?" she asked me with concern.

"Yeah, I'm sure. It's not you. I'm just going through some shit right now."

"Is it Tony?"

"He has something to do with it but I'm dealing with something else too."

"Is there anything I can do? Do you want to talk about it because I don't like the vibe I'm getting from you today. It seems like there's a lot of tension in the air around here."

"Girl, ain't no tension around here."

"That's how it feels to me."

"Stop overreacting. It's not that serious."

"All right," Nikki said, giving me a nonchalant expression.

Ignoring her, I picked up the telephone and proceeded to make a phone call. I did this hoping she would catch the hint that I was going to need a little privacy. Honestly, I didn't have to use the phone at all. I used this tactic to get her out of my face because I felt the pressure mounting and, just as I had anticipated, it worked like a charm.

"Let me know when you're done, so I can come in here and go over the books," she said and then left the office.

Instead of replying, I nodded my head.

Nikki left the shop early today because she said she had to take care of some business for Syncere. I overheard her making a couple of phone calls to different lawyer's offices so I'm sure that was where she was going. Poor thang! She was about to run herself raggedy behind this nigga. They hadn't even been together a hot minute and he was making her play the wifey role. I didn't give a fuck how much money he had, how much dope he sold, or how many businesses he owned—he would have had to go. Not only that but by being on probation, she was jeopardizing her freedom by fucking with him. I sure hope she knew what the fuck she was doing because any way you looked at it, he wasn't worth it. And that was some real shit!

Before I closed down the shop for the night, I sat down and had a quick chat with my stylist Tabitha who was sitting down next to her station waiting for her ride to pick her up. She was a pretty girl with a close-cut, tapered hair style. She was also very petite like Jada Pinkett Smith but she was quiet and kept to herself so I knew that whatever I discussed with her tonight would remain between us.

"Tab, you've been working here for a while now. Be honest and tell me what you think about Nikki?"

"She was all right in the beginning but now she walks 'round here like her shit don't stink!"

"Oh, you noticed that too, huh?"

"Hell yeah! Everybody 'round here be talking about her

ass, saying she wants to be Kira so bad and that's why she drives her Lexus and wear all her clothes."

"Tell me how you felt about her raising the booth rent?"

"Shit! You knew how I felt about it. You saw how I pissed a bitch after she opened up her mouth at our meeting two weeks ago, talking about we gon' have to pay thirty dollars more a week. I mean, what kind of bullshit is that?"

"I know y'all were mad because I was too."

"Well, can't you do something about it? You are part owner, right?"

"Yeah, but Nikki is filling Kira's shoes so it's like she has more say so."

"Well, if you wanna know the truth, I wish we could figure out a way to get rid of that bitch! 'Cause I'm sick of her walking around here with her nose stuck up, trying to tell me what the hell to do. That shit just don't sit right with me."

Hearing Tabitha's true feelings about Nikki, gave me the urge to confide in her about what I read in Kira's diary. "If I tell you something, you promise you won't say anything?"

"Yeah, I promise," she replied with sincerity.

I took a deep breath and said, "I just found out she snitched on some niggas who were doing some major shit on the streets?"

"Are you serious?"

"Yes, I am. I also believe the same guys had something to do with Kira getting killed."

"Get the fuck out of here!" Tabitha's eyes nearly burst out of her head. "Do you know what that means?"

"Yeah, I know what it means and so does Tony."

"What did he say?" Tabitha asked.

"He just told me that if I didn't hurry up and get her out of here, the same niggas could run up in here and kill everybody in sight trying to get to her."

"Shit. She needs to go now because she's putting all our lives in danger."

"Yeah, I know. But, like I told Tony, I can't stop her from coming in here because the shop doesn't solely belong to me."

"So, what we gon' do?" Tabitha asked.

"I don't know. But, for right now, I want you to keep this conversation to yourself. Okay?"

"Okay," she assured me and then turned her attention to the front door when we heard someone tap on it. We both realized it was the person she was waiting for. Before she got up to leave, she looked back at me and wanted to know how I heard about Nikki supposedly snitching. I leaned forward and said, "I read Kira's diary and it was mentioned in there, along with a lot of other shit."

"Where did you find her diary?"

"Me and Nikki found it hidden between the drawers of her nightstand the day we went over there to move her things into storage."

"Where is her diary now?"

"Nikki has it. But between me and you, she doesn't know that I took it home last night and read it."

"Did Kira mention anything in her diary about me?"

"Nope. The only people she talked about in this shop was me and how much she couldn't stand the sight of Sunshine after finding out Ricky was fucking her behind her back. Other than that, she mainly talked about her and Nikki snitching on Ricky.

And then she mentioned how she ended up fucking around with Ricky's partner, Russ."

"Damn, I sure wish I would have read that because I could definitely use some entertainment in my life right now."

"Well, if entertainment is what you need, then her diary would have served its purpose."

"Damn! I guess I missed out on that one," Tabitha commented as she stood up from the chair. "But, do me this one favor," she said before she took a step to leave.

"What's that?" I asked her.

"Figure out what you're going to do before I walk through these doors tomorrow morning. Then call me and give me a heads up because if shit doesn't go according to plan, I might have to call in sick."

"You're serious, aren't you?"

"You damn right! So, holler at me," she replied and then she vanished into the night.

18

Street Certified

Nikki Speaks

I met with Quincy immediately after my last appointment ended with the second attorney. He told me to meet him at the car wash and when I pulled up into the parking lot of the service area, I found him posted up inside of his 2005 7-series BMW, looking like a true baller. When he saw my car approaching his, he motioned me to pull up beside him.

"Come get in my car," he yelled from his window.

It only took me a few seconds to step out of my vehicle and get into Quincy's car. The moment I sat down he smiled and said, "What's the word?"

I gave him a look of uncertainty and said, "The last lawyer I talked to, Broccoletti, said he would charge Syncere three grand for a bail hearing and fifteen grand to represent him on the gun charge."

"Damn! What the fuck can he guarantee for that type of dough?"

"He didn't say."

"Well, what did the other attorney say?"

"He said he would charge me fifteen hundred to get him a bail hearing and seven grand to pick up his case. But, if it goes to high court, his fee will go up another three grand."

"Which guy was this?"

"Taliaferro."

"Oh yeah, Syncere will be all right with him, 'cause he's a beast."

"So, do you think we should hire him?"

"Talk to Syncere first and see what he says. If he says okay, then let's go for it."

"All right," I said and grabbed the door handle, indicating that I was about to get out of the car. Quincy stopped me in my tracks by saying, "Why you in a rush? You got somewhere you got to go?"

"No, not really. I just wasn't trying to hold you up, just in case you had something to do. I mean, you were sitting in the car like you were getting ready to go on a mission."

"I ain't got nowhere to go. I'm just chilling."

"Yeah," I said sucking my teeth. "Okay, you're chilling now but as soon as one your women call, you're gonna be right back on the fast track."

"I don't have women like that. The chicks I fuck with are just my friends."

"Why all men say dumb shit like that?"

"I can't speak for the rest of the cats out here. I can only tell you about me and what I told you is some real shit!"

"Yeah, right! I remember when you used to fuck with my cousin Kira, so I know what type of nigga you are."

"You should never believe everything you hear."

"So you say," I commented sarcastically and smiled.

"Yo, you looked just like Kira when you just made that smile."

"You know, everybody tells me that," I replied and put my head down.

"You a'ight?"

"Yeah, I'm fine. I just get like this when somebody brings her name up."

"Did the police ever find out who killed her?"

"Nope, they're still investigating it."

"Do they have any suspects?"

"No."

"Damn, that's fucked up. But, I will say that whoever did it knew how to get in and out without leaving a mutha-fucking thing behind or without being seen."

"I'm almost positive I saw him."

"You did? When?"

"The day she got killed, I went to her house and when I was walking up to her apartment building, I noticed this Hispanic-looking guy who I had never seen before walking from the direction of her apartment wearing an old mainte-nance uniform. When I looked at him to say hello, he looked away from me. I didn't think much of it. I just brushed it off and thought that maybe he didn't speak any English."

"Did you tell the police this?"

"Yeah, I told 'em."

"What did they say?"

"That didn't say anything. But, they did find out that the apartment complex didn't have any Hispanic employees working in their maintenance department. He would be a suspect if they knew who he was."

"Did you see what kind of car he was driving?"

"Nope."

"Why not?"

"Because I didn't think to look."

Quincy shook his head in disbelief. "Damn, that sounds like whoever did it is going to get away with it."

"No they won't," I replied with certainty and changed the subject. "Let me get out of here before one of your chicks try to run up on us."

"I told you, it wasn't like that."

"Yeah! Yeah! Yeah!" I began to make my way out of the car.

"I told you to stop believing everything you hear."

"I'mma hold you to that," I told him and then I closed the door behind me.

"Where you on your way to now?" he asked me after rolling down his car window.

"Home to wait for Syncere's phone call."

"A'ight. Hit me up tomorrow and let me know which lawyer he wants to get, so I can get you the dough."

"Okay, I will."

The moment I left Quincy, I suddenly got up the urge to drive by Kira's old apartment. I don't know where this insane thought came from but I do know that I had been missing her like crazy. So, I went back to the place where she spent most of her time, hoping it would give me comfort and help me deal with the fact that she was gone.

Feelings of anxiety crept into my stomach the second I arrived inside the apartment complex. But as soon as I drove up to the building in which she had lived, my whole frame of mind changed. I could honestly say that a feeling of calmness overpowered me the instant I got out of my car. It felt like a breeze hit my face and took all the weight off my shoulders. What a feeling that was! As I moved toward her apartment, I started walking very slowly, giving my eyes a chance to look at the area surrounding the building. Everything on the outside looked quiet and normal. But just as I started walking down the sidewalk, I noticed that the yellow police tape was still taped across her door seal and around the entire entrance to her apartment. Seeing this quickly reminded me of how Kira was violated in her own house and that thought alone sent chills down my spine. I immediately turned around and headed back to my car.

Before I actually got a chance to open my car door, that worrisome detective decided to pull up and wreck my damn world. As badly as I wanted to haul ass out of there, I stood there and leaned against the driver's side door of my car, waiting patiently for him to get out of his car and ask me a whole bunch of questions. I knew his first question was going to be what was I doing there? I watched him open his door and exit his vehicle and I began to wonder why was he out here himself. It dawned on me that maybe he had been following me because Rhonda spilled the beans to him about me having Kira's diary and now he was here to confiscate it from me. But, I couldn't let that happen.

As the cracker detective approached me, he gave me this big ol' smile and asked, "How you doing?"

"I'm doing fine," I replied nonchalantly. "What about yourself?"

"I'm okay. You know, trying to do my job and catch a few criminals."

"Caught any today?"

"Not yet. But, I'm sure you can help me," he responded.

"I wish I could," I told him and then I looked down at the ground and kicked at a small rock by my feet.

Meanwhile, he threw the question I was expecting at me. "So, what brings you by here?"

"I was in the neighborhood," I lied.

"So, you just decided to stop and check out the scenery, huh?" he asked sarcastically.

"Yep, that about sums it up," I replied, giving him the exact same tone he gave me.

"Well, have you run across any evidence that we may have overlooked?"

Hearing this man ask me about evidence they may have overlooked got my stomach all messed up. The way he was looking at me as he waited for me to answer his question was intimidating like a muthafucker. I wished I could have just vanished right then because I honestly didn't know what to say, especially if he decided to search my handbag and found the diary. And if that happened, boy, would I be in a world of trouble! I mean, this man had the power to arrest me at any given moment, if he wanted to. So, I had to play it cool and act like I had some damn sense if I wanted to sleep in my own bed tonight. I began that process by saying, "No, I haven't. But, the way this investigation is going, I sure wish I had."

The detective hesitated a moment, I guess to study my body language as I responded to his question. He asked, "Hear anything on the streets?"

"Nope. I haven't heard a thing. But, as soon as I do, you gon' be the first person I call."

"I hope so," he replied skeptically.

"Oh, believe me, I would. But, let me ask you this."

"What is it?"

"How did you know I was here?"

"I didn't."

"So, what made you stop by?"

"Remember there's still an investigation going on and your cousin's place is the murder scene. So, I come here more often than I would like to. As a matter of fact, I know the neighbors around here are sick of me knocking on their doors and asking them the same questions over and over again. But hey, it's my job and I've got to do it."

"Well, do whatcha do. But, keep me posted on any new developments," I said to him as I opened my car door.

"You do the same," he insisted as he held my door open for me and closed it the moment I got into my car. "You still got my card, right?"

"Yeah, I do."

"Okay, good," he said.

Instead of making another comment I smiled and waved goodbye as I drove off.

And as I drove away, I watched him through my rearview mirror watching me until I was out of sight.

Cruising down Kempsville Road, I could think about nothing else but that conversation I just had with that detective. He really was creepy and I hated when I was around him. He made me feel like I was the one who pulled the trigger and killed Kira especially the way he kept questioning me. I just hoped he found the real killer soon because I just didn't know how much longer I was gonna be able to take this.

19

Getting My Weight Up

Syncere Speaks

This was my fifth time trying to call Nikki and she wasn't even home to accept my damn call. It was 9:30 at night, where the fuck was she at? She wasn't at the beauty salon because I had my peoples from the outside call there for me on three-way. When I had them call her cell phone, that shit went straight to voicemail on the first ring. The way I feel right now I am going to fuck her up the second I see her silly ass. That's my word!

"Thirty minutes until lockdown," said this ugly-ass female C.O. named Patterson. After she made her announcement, I stood there and watched her as she instructed one of these dumb-ass niggas in here to turn off the TV. When she turned out the cell lights from the switch on the outside of the block, I watched her closely as she walked off. What's so unbelievable about this whole scene is how unattractive this chick is. But there is one thing I can't take from her and that is how phat her ass is. Niggas in here be hollering at her all the time, trying to swell her head up, but she had to know that the top part of her was truly fucked up. I wouldn't fuck her if she paid me because I wouldn't be able to get over how ugly her face was. Fuck throwing a bag over her head and bending her over, 'cause that shit wouldn't work for me either. Instead of entertaining her ass like all the other cats here, I took a seat on the bench near the only two pay phones in the block and waited for one of these niggas to free the lines.

This one nigga, who everybody called Butch, was holding the phone up, crying to his girl, asking her all the questions cats normally asked their chicks while they were caught up in the trap. From the way he was acting, I could tell she was feeding him a whole lot of bullshit lies and whether he wanted to believe it or not, she was gonna do what the fuck she wanted to do regardless if he gave her permission or not. That's just how hoes were which is why I ain't gon' let myself get all fucked up in the head over a broad I left on the streets. She is either gonna do right or she ain't.

Now, don't get me wrong, I would cuss a bitch out if she tried my patience or neglected to take care of my business like she was supposed to. But, I would never put myself out there and question her about who she'd been fucking. Niggas won't admit it but information like that broke cats down behind these walls. And police wanted to know why there was a lot of domestic violence? Shit, I got the answer for 'em. Bitches just didn't want to act right after their man got bagged up. Don't string a nigga along and tell 'em you gon' be faithful and wait for them after they got hit in the head with a five-, ten- or fifteen-year sentence. Just be straight up! Tell 'em you ain't built for that type of ride and bounce. It ain't that hard to do.

While I continued to listen to this crybaby-ass nigga scream on his girl, this little frail-ass buster walked up to me and asked me if I was in line to use the phone. I nodded my head and told him yeah. He took a seat on the bench next to me and started some small talk.

"They been on the phone long?" he asked.

"Yeah. Both of 'em time should be almost up."

"Good, 'cause I need to make a quick call to my sister before one of them C.O.s cut the phones off. I gotta make sure somebody shows up to court for me tomorrow."

"Tomorrow's your sentencing day?"

"Yep, and I'm hoping the judge take it easy on me and let me walk out of here on time served."

"Whatcha in here for?"

"A parole violation."

"Whatcha do?"

"Dirty urine."

"How long you been on paper?"

"Three years but I got two more over my head."

"How long you been locked up?"

"Ten months."

"Whatcha P.O. say about it?"

"Man, that bitch is crazy! She told my lawyer that she's gon' recommend to the judge that he give me all my time back and send my ass back up the road."

"Damn, nigga! She's out to get you."

"Tell me about it. That's why if the judge fucks around and let me get out of here, I'mma see if I can get the Parole Office to switch me to another P.O."

"I wish you luck, home boy."

"Thanks because I'm gon' sure need it." Then he said, "Yo, it looks like Butch is about to hang up."

"Yeah, I see," I replied and stood up from the bench. After Butch cursed his girl out one last time, he slammed the pay phone down on the hook and walked away. I grabbed the phone and called Nikki's home telephone number again. I didn't know exactly how much time I had left to make this phone call, but I figured it couldn't be less than five minutes which was more than enough time for me to get some shit off of my chest.

The phone rang only two times before I was connected and when I heard Nikki say hello, I went into venting mode.

"Where the fuck you been at?" I asked her, gritting my teeth.

"Out trying to take care of your business."

"This time of the night?" I asked, getting more aggravated by the second.

"Yeah, I was talking to Quincy. I just left from up the car wash about an hour ago. Before I seen him, I had the two appointments with the attorneys."

"So, where did you go after you left Q?"

"I stopped by my grandmother's house," she told me.

"Yo, Nick, you know I don't like to keep calling you and can't getcha on the phone."

"I know that. That's why I told my grandmother I couldn't stay long."

"So, what was the two lawyers talking about?"

"Broccoletti said he'd charge you thirty-five hundred for the bail hearing and fifteen grand to pick up your case."

"What about the other lawyer?"

"Taliaferro said he'd charge you fifteen hundred to get you a bail hearing and ten grand to represent you. So, I was thinking we should go with him."

"What did Q say about it?"

"He was leaning toward Taliaferro but said it really didn't matter because it's what you want."

"A'ight, then." I paused and thought for a second. "Let's

go with that Taliaferro cat. Make sure you get with Q tomorrow morning so he can get you some dough. That way you can take it over to Taliaferro so he can get busy working on my shit."

"Okay."

"Oh yeah, and when you talk to him, ask him how quick he can get me the bond hearing."

"I already did."

"And what did he say?"

"He told me that if I got him some money in the next forty-eight hours, he could have you in front of a judge by the end of the week."

"A'ight, word! Don't forget to get with Q in the a.m. and make sure you get Taliaferro that dough by tomorrow evening."

"I'm on it."

"A'ight. So, is everything else okay?"

"Yes, everything's fine."

"Oh yeah, did you go up to the car wash and check up on how steady the business was?"

"Yeah.

"So, how was it?"

"Well, it was crowded up there when I went."

"What time did you go?"

"It was about one-thirty and I was only there for about thirty to forty minutes."

"Was Q there when you went?"

"He wasn't outside. But his car was there, so I'm assuming that he was on the inside."

"A'ight, that sounds good. I'm gon' call you tomorrow night about eight o'clock so be home."

"Okay."

"Oh yeah, I want you to keep looking out on my place if you don't mind."

"Nah, I don't mind."

"A'ight. Well, I'mma talk to you."

"Love you."

"Yeah, you better, or else I'll be wasting my time," I replied and hung up.

20

The Chopping Block

Nikki Speaks

After that slime ball-ass nigga hung up, I sat back in my chair and replayed the words, "Yeah, you better, or else I'll be wasting my time," in my head and got an instant attitude. This cat was acting like he really had it going the fuck on. But, he ain't got shit going on and I don't even love his ass! I only told him that to make him feel like something, wit' his insecure and controlling ass!

The nigga was a loser for real! And the only reason why I was fucking with him was because he had a little bit of dough. Love ain't have shit to do with it. Always trying to give me orders and tell me what to do. Then if I took my time or didn't perform the tasks to his expectations, the nigga went ballistic and acted really immature. It made me wonder how the hell his mama raised this know-it-all muthafucker. But, then again, he didn't even matter because his simple ass would be all right. As soon as I got enough information on him about these murders, I was gon' deliver that bastard to the police on a silver platter! Mark my words!

* * *

I got an early-morning phone call from Rhonda telling me to meet her at the salon by eight o'clock. The tone of her voice was urgent so I asked her what was going on but she refused to go into details over the phone. I wanted to demand that she tell me but before our conversation ended, I conceded by telling her I would be there. It only took me forty minutes to shower and get dressed. Before I realized it, I had twenty-five minutes to get to the shop so I grabbed my car keys and handbag and headed outside to my car.

I arrived at the salon a couple of minutes before eight and when I appeared at the front door, Rhonda gave me this funny look. Immediately after I unlocked the door and walked in I asked, "What's wrong with you?"

"We gotta talk," she said.

"Yeah, I know that. But, what about?"

"It's about you putting everybody in this shop in danger."

"What the fuck are you talking about?" I asked, about to snap on her.

"Nikki, I know you snitched on Ricky and his crew to get out of jail and I also know that Kira helped you do it."

"And so what?" I asked defensively. "Those niggas had it coming to them. Him and that no-good-ass Brian left me downtown in that jail to fucking rot. They didn't give a fuck about me. They turned their backs on me the second they found out I was locked up. What was I supposed to do? Just sit there like I'm some damn fool? No ma'am, I think not! And as far as Kira was concerned, she was against it when I first ran everything down to her. When she finally realized how grimy her husband was and that he really didn't give a fuck about her, she came around and paid his good-for-nothing ass back."

"She may have been against it in the beginning, but she sure changed her mind very quickly. And look where it got her."

"That shit that happened with my case had nothing to do with Kira's murder. Whether you know it or not, Ricky got killed way before Kira did so how could he have had something to do with her murder?"

"Brian and the rest of his home boys aren't dead."

"Okay, you're right. but dem niggas are clowns. They ain't got no clout; what kind of strings could they pull behind bars?"

"Don't be surprised if they pulled something. I truly believe with all my heart that they're gonna come after you next. That's the real reason why I'm worried about you being here."

"Well, that's too damn bad because I ain't going nowhere!"

"Come on, Nikki, let's not take it there."

"I'm sorry, Rhonda, but it's too fucking late for that! Because on some real shit, you're standing there trying to play me like I'm some ol' gullible ass bitch! And it ain't that type of party with me."

"I'm not trying to play you. I just don't want to get caught up in the crossfire if a whole bunch of niggas decide they wanna run up in here."

"Well you know what, Rhonda? It ain't gon' happen so get over it."

"You don't know that for sure."

"Look, I don't know what else to tell you. But, I will tell you that I'm not going nowhere, so deal with it." I threw my right hand over my hip and dared her to say some smart shit.

"You need to wake up," Rhonda retorted.

"And what the fuck does that mean?"

"Nikki, you are not Kira and you will never be. So, stop walking around here trying to fill her shoes."

"You are such a hater, Rhonda, and that is not cool!"

"Call me whatcha like. But, at least I'm not fucking running around here snitching on everybody and their mama to get out of doing hard time."

"Oh bitch, please! Save that shit for somebody who wants to hear it. Trust me, if the shoe was put on the other foot, your ass would've sung like a bird too."

"No, I wouldn't have. I've got more sense than that."

"Okay, where were your senses when you let Tony come up here, kick your ass and disrespect you in front of everybody?"

"That's nothing you need to concern yourself with. What you need to worry about is that nigga you're fucking with."

"Oh, trust me, he's fine."

"That ain't what Kira said in her diary. She thinks he's a fucking nut case. She also didn't trust him because she believed he had something to do with her and Mark getting shot outside her apartment."

Surprised by Rhonda's comments, my mouth dropped open and my heart fell into the pit of my stomach.

"You sneaky bitch," I yelled. "You did have Kira's diary that night I called you but you sat right there and lied to me. You read every word she wrote, witcha nosey ass!"

"Get out of my face Nikki."

"Bitch, I ain't in your face yet."

"Trust me, Nikki, you don't want none of me."

"Nah bitch, you don't want none of me," I warned her. "You got one more muthafucking time to fuck with my shit. Then, I'm gon' crack you upside your head and then I'm gon' put your ass out the shop!"

"Don't wait until I go through your shit again. Do it now," Rhonda dared me.

When I looked into her face, I realized that this bitch was serious. If I didn't go upside her muthafucking head, she was going to go behind my back and tell every bitch in this shop she punk'd me out! I couldn't let that happen, because if I did ain't nobody in this place gonna respect me. Without thinking about it any longer, I lunged and hit her dead in her right eye, catching her dumb ass off guard. Before she realized what I did it was too late. Her eye swelled up and closed shut on her that instant.

"Bitch, you hit me in my muthafucking eye," she screamed and immediately retaliated.

She could only see through one eye and that was her left one so when she swung on me, I blocked the blow and managed to grab the bitch by her shirt. With both hands I pushed her back up against the cabinet top of her station as hard as I could. Curling irons, flat irons and spritz bottles started falling all over the place.

"Get the fuck off me, bitch," Rhonda roared as she threw a combination of punches back at me.

We were tagging each other like we were in a boxing ring. At one point, it seemed she was getting the best of me because this hoe got one of her bumpers and started hitting me in my head with it. That shit was hurting so badly, I got an instant headache. Then my head began to ring like a damn bell. I was barely functioning but I mustered enough strength to grab the curling irons out of her hand. Believe me when I say that the moment I got them in my hand, I struck that bitch back as hard as I could.

When they landed across the bridge of her nose, she went crazy.

"Oh bitch, I'm gon' kill you now," she snapped, twisting my arm so I could drop the curlers.

I held on to them for dear life and just kept swinging. When she realized that I wasn't going to let them go, she kicked me dead in my crotch and the pain from that blow had every nerve in my body screaming out. My knees buckled under the weight of my body and in slow motion I fell to the floor. Rhonda immediately jumped down on top of me.

"Yeah bitch, I gotcha now," she screamed as she stood over me and threw a barrage of punches.

Her fists were coming from the left and right. All I could do was lay in the fetal position with one hand covering my head and the other one holding my crotch. I was helpless as hell and for a few seconds I couldn't defend myself. Then, as the pain in my pussy started subsiding, I turned over on my back and started throwing more blows. The front door to the shop swung open and Tabitha was standing there with her mouth wide open.

"Oh my God! What are you doing?" Tabitha yelled and she rushed over to where we were fighting.

Winded by all the physical contact, Rhonda managed to say, "This bitch hit me first so I'm teaching her a mutha-fucking lesson!"

"Them weak-ass punches you throwing at me ain't shit you fucking hoe!"

"Look, I know y'all upset but y'all are gonna have to break this shit up before one of our customers comes in here," Tabitha told Rhonda as she attempted to pull her off me.

"Get off me, Tabitha," Rhonda warned her.

"Nah, 'cause y'all need to stop this crazy-ass shit," Tabitha continued as she latched on to Rhonda's arm.

I don't know if it was Tabitha's strength or Rhonda's willingness to give in, but she allowed Tabitha to pull her off me. As soon as she got up and turned her back, I got up on my feet and kicked that bitch dead in her ass. Believe me, she wasn't prepared for that one because she stumbled a little bit and lost her balance. It was just enough for me to bounce back and go toe to toe with her ass again. As I reached over to tag her stinky ass again, Tabitha jumped in the middle and the punch I threw landed on her.

"Wait a minute, you hit me," Tabitha yelled.

"My bad," I said, as I stepped back a few feet. "But, I was trying to hit that bitch!" I pointed in the direction of Rhonda.

"Oh, so you ain't had enough?"

"Nah, bitch! I didn't have enough, so what's up?" I stood back with a smirk on my face.

Of course, nothing jumped off. Tabitha grabbed Rhonda's arm again and pulled her in the opposite direction toward the back office. Rhonda told me that she was quitting and when she left, she was taking all the customers with her. I said, "I don't give a fuck! Take all dem' hoes with you! Trust me, they ain't gon' make or break this muthafucking shop!"

"Yeah, we'll see," Rhonda said.

"So, when you leaving?"

"As soon as I get all my shit out of here."

"Well, that ain't quick enough," I told her. "So, how 'bout you have your ass out of here by tomorrow."

"I'mma tell you now that I ain't gon' be out of here by tomorrow. So, you might as well cancel that."

"Oh yes, the hell you are," I yelled.

"Yeah, whatever! 'Cause you ain't making no kind of sense."

"I guess I can show you better than I can tell you," I told her as I grabbed my handbag from off the floor and head toward the front door.

"I guess we'll see then."

"Fuck you, you ol' poor ass bitch," I screamed, walking out the door. Right before the door slammed behind me, Rhonda said something to Tabitha but whatever she uttered wasn't loud enough for me to hear. I just let that one go over my head. Since I was already en route to my car, I totally ignored her and kept it moving.

* * *

Still shocked about what had just went down between Rhonda and me, I tried to pull myself together and gather my thoughts cruising down Virginia Beach Boulevard toward Norfolk. I grabbed my cell phone and dialed up my grandmother while I took a quick assessment of my battle wounds in my rearview mirror. From the looks of things, my face was scratched up pretty badly. But, it wasn't bad enough that I needed medical attention. I figured I would be all right.

Since I had some time on my hands I made a trip back home to clean myself up because I was looking real rough. As soon as I got in the door, I headed straight to my bathroom, pulled out a first aid kit and went to work. When that was done, I grabbed my big bag of Sun Chips out of my pantry, a cold bottle of spring water out of my refrigerator and took my butt into my living room to watch television. I tuned to a couple of old movies and, surprisingly, I enjoyed them. When I checked time it was a little after one in the afternoon and I remembered that I needed to get Quincy on the phone.

He was unavailable when I called the car wash but he did leave word with the parking attendant for me to meet him there by two o'clock. About thirty seconds after I pulled up into the parking lot, I saw Quincy driving into the service area located at the back of the car wash, talking to a chick.

I couldn't see exactly how she looked because her back was facing me but I was able to see her entire backside along with everybody standing out there. Oh yeah, home girl had an audience and a half watching her as she made small talk with Quincy. Before I exited my vehicle, I threw on my sunshades to hide my battle scars and made my way over to where they were standing.

"I see punctuality is one of your strong suits," I commented the moment I walked up on him.

"Not all the time," he replied. Before he had a chance to continue what he was about to say, home girl turned toward me and when I saw who it was, I just stood there in shock. I couldn't stop my mouth from moving.

"Oh my God, Sunshine," I said as my heart dropped.

In return, she gave me one of her cheesy smiles and asked, "What's up Nikki?"

Shocked, Quincy asked, "Damn, how y'all know each other?"

"She use to do hair at Kira's shop," I told him as the blood flowing through my veins started boiling. Feelings I had buried inside of me for this chick resurfaced in that instant. All I could think about was that Sunshine went behind Kira's back and fucked Ricky while she was working for her. Now, tell me how grimy is that? Well, they say you reap what you sow. Right after Ricky got Sunshine her own shop, the Feds rushed in on her and locked her dumb ass up for affiliating with him. I couldn't believe that this hoe was standing right in front of me acting like we was cool or something. So, in a nice way, I asked her how the hell she got out of jail.

"I won my appeal," she told me.

"When did you get out?"

"I've been home about a week now."

"So, where you at?"

"Whatcha mean?"

"Ay, y'all, excuse me for a minute. I gotta go into my office and do something right quick," Quincy interjected.

"A'ight," Sunshine said.

I just gave him the okay by nodding my head. Immediately after he rushed off, I turned my attention back on Sunshine. "Now what was I saying?"

"You was asking me where was I at?"

"Oh yeah, I wanted to know where you were working?"

"Oh, I'm not doing anything right now but I plan to get back in the swing of things as soon as I get other things in order."

"Well, I wish you the best 'cause it's real hard out here."

"Too late 'cause I'm already feeling it. But, I'm a smart girl so I'll be all right."

"Yeah, you will," I said with certainty. "But, hey, I gotta go holler at Q for a minute. I'll talk to you later." As I was about to walk off, she said, "Hey Nikki."

I turned back around and Sunshine said, "Look, I know you don't like me on the strength of your cousin. But, I gotta say that I am truly sorry to hear about what happened to her."

"You don't have to be sorry."

"I know I don't but I just had to say it. Not only that, I know what I did with her husband was foul but, believe me, I'm paying for it now. I can't sleep at night because my conscience is killing me. My family is shitting on me and I really ain't got nowhere to go. If I could turn that clock back and get some of this bad karma off me, I would do it. Kira didn't deserve none of that shit I took her through."

"I appreciate you saying all of that, Sunshine, but it wasn't all your fault. Ricky got what he deserved, too."

"Yeah, I know but I just had to get that off my chest. You know what's so crazy? If I would not have seen you today, I was gon' take a trip up to the shop so I could tell you exactly what I'm saying right now."

"Well, you would've sure been wasting you time going up to the shop," I commented nonchalantly.

"Why? Y'all closed down?"

"Nah, there's just a whole bunch of phony ass bitches that work there is all."

"Are Rhonda and Tabitha still there?"

"Oh yeah, but not for long," I replied sarcastically.

"Why? I mean, what y'all got beef with each other now?"

"Yep, we sure do."

"Damn, I thought y'all were cool?"

"I thought we were too but I found out different. I just tried to take her fucking head off!"

Utterly surprised by what I was saying, she placed her hand over her mouth and said, "Wait, y'all were fighting?"

"We sure was."

Sunshine chuckled a bit and said, "Damn! I just can't believe that."

"Well, believe it," I told her. "But, I ain't gon' worry about it 'cause she ain't gon' be doing hair in there much longer."

"I'm sorry that you're going through all that drama."

"Shit, don't feel sorry for me, 'cause I'm all right," I assured her. "To hear you say that to me really shows me that jail sure has changed you."

"It did. But you know what? I didn't think I was all that bad when I was out there."

"Shiid, you could've fooled me," I commented sarcastically, "because you were the biggest bitch in town. No one liked you 'cause they knew you would go after their man if he had some dough."

"Yeah, you're right. I can't argue with that. Let me set the record straight and say that Ricky pursued me. It wasn't the other way around."

"Okay, he probably did but that still didn't make it right. I mean, where was your conscience?"

"I guess I didn't have one."

"Damn right you didn't! The fact that you worked for Kira, laughed in her face and was her husband's mistress was a bit much!"

"Shit! I wasn't the only chick he was fucking with."

"Everybody knew that. But, I need to know why you did it?"

"It wasn't like me and Kira was the best of friends and Ricky was kicking out a lot of fucking money. I mean, he use to give me anything I asked for. He didn't care about prices plus his personality was addictive. I swear, it seemed like every time me and him got together and hung out, I couldn't get enough of him."

"Oh really."

"Yes, that's why I didn't want to give him up."

"But he wasn't yours to have."

"Yeah, I know all that but when he was with me, it felt like he was mine."

"Did he ever tell you that he was going to leave Kira?"

"Nope, he sure didn't. What's crazy is that I use to threaten to break off our relationship if he didn't leave Kira."

"And what would he say?"

"He told me I could do whatever but he was not leaving his wife."

Surprised by her answer, I said, "Oh, so the nigga had a heart, huh?"

"Nikki, you may not believe it but Ricky had a heart of gold. He was so sweet it was ridiculous. The fact that he would sit back with me and tell me about shit that bothered him also showed me that he had a sensitive side."

"Girl, please, that nigga ain't have shit! He was an asshole just like the rest of these ballers out here that think they got a little bit of power."

"Nah, Nikki, Ricky wasn't like that."

"Yeah, whatever. I know first hand about all the shit that nigga use to take my cousin through. I ain't gon' lie, when I first found out that you was fucking him, I wanted to take a trip over to that new shop Ricky put you in and rip your head off."

"So, what stopped you?" Sunshine asked nonchalantly.

"Kira stopped me," I told her. "She told me not to worry

about it 'cause you were going to get back everything you did to her. And she was right."

"Yep, she sure was. I ain't gon' lie to you when I say that when them damn Feds ran up in my shop and arrested me for dealing with Ricky, I was no more good. I was sick as a dog."

"I'm sure you was. But, if you could do it all over again, would you fuck around with him?"

"After all that time the judge wanted me to do, hell nah! I would've left that nigga right where he was."

I laughed at the way Sunshine expressed herself and said, "I'm glad you learned a lesson from all of this and it was good talking to you. I gotta run in here and talk to Quincy right quick. I'll see you again."

"A'ight, you take care."

"I will. You do the same," I told her with much sincerity.

Actually, after talking with home girl, I kind of saw her in a different light. She seemed to have developed some morals and I applauded her efforts to be honest and apologetic about what she did to Kira. I just hoped, for her sake, that she learned something from all of this. If she hadn't, she was gonna always be in that slump. Maybe the next time shit hit the fan it would be too late.

Quincy was about to walk back outside when I opened up the door to go in. He stopped in his tracks and said, "Come on in."

I followed him into his office, took a seat in one of his office chairs and asked, "So, you trying to hook up with Sunshine, huh?"

He chuckled and said, "Nah, not really. But, if she wanna give me some pussy, then I'll take it."

I laughed back at him. "You are so crazy!"

"Nah, I ain't crazy. Trust me, I got plenty of sense."

"You know she used to fuck around with Ricky while she was working for Kira?"

"Nah, man, I don't believe that."

"Well, believe it 'cause I ain't gon' lie about some shit like that."

"So, why you ain't whip her ass?" He asked in a joking manner.

"She wasn't fucking my man!"

"So, what was y'all talking?"

"She was just apologizing to me for what she did to Kira."

"And what did you say?"

"I told her it was okay." I switched the subject. "Hey, enough about your peoples. We need to talk about the lawyer for Syncere."

"Did he say which one he wanted to represent him?"

"Yeah, he told me to hire Taliaferro."

"I kind of figured he would."

"Wait. You haven't talked to him?"

"Nope, not since that time you called me on three-way."

"He sent me up here to get the money so I can take it to the lawyer."

"How much you need?" He asked, getting straight to the point.

"Fifteen hundred."

"That's for the bail hearing, right?"

"Yeah."

"A'ight, here you go." He peeled a handful of fifty-dollar bills from a stack of dough he pulled out of his pants pocket.

"Think I can get some gas money out of that knot you're toting?" I asked, smiling.

"Oh, you know you're good for it." He peeled off three more fifty-dollar bills and handed them to me.

"Thank you," I replied as I stuffed the money away in my handbag.

"What time you got to see the lawyer?"

"I've got no specific time but I'm gonna go by his office as soon as I leave here."

"So, when is he gon' be able to get Syncere in court?"

"He told me he'd be able to do it by the end of the week."

"Ahhh damn, that's what's up! Look, I wantcha' to hook me up wit somebody."

"Hook you up with who?"

"With one of your home girls. 'Cause, check it out, I just moved in my new place a couple of days ago so I'm looking for somebody I can chill with tonight."

"You don't need me to hook you up when you got Sunshine waiting patiently for you outside."

He smiled and commented by saying, "I don't want her. I mean, let's be real. What can I do with a chick just coming from the joint? Nothing but give me some of that phat ass she got."

"Damn Q, you are so grimy."

"No, I'm not. 'Cause, she's looking for somebody to take care of her and I ain't in the business of doing shit like that."

"I heard that," I commented sarcastically and then I smiled.

"So, whatcha gon' do? You gon' hook me up or what?"

I stood up from the chair and said, "Quincy, I gotta go."

Giving me a disappointed look, he asked, "So, you ain't gon' look out for me?"

"You don't need my help," I assured him.

"Yes, I do."

"No, you don't. And anyway, I don't have any friends."

"What about dem chicks you work with at the salon?"

"Oh, trust me, you don't want none of them Section-8 bitches that work up in there."

"Shit, I ain't looking for a wifey. I just want somebody to chill with."

"And you got ol' Sunshine outside."

"Come on, stop playing with me."

"I'm not playing."

"Well, whatcha doing later?"

"I'm going to see the lawyer first and then I'm going home."

"Okay. Why don't you do me a favor later on?"

"What kind of favor?"

"Come 'round my crib and help me fix up my bathroom with this new stuff I just bought. I got some hot pictures for my walls, too, that I'm gon' need help putting up. You know what I'm saying, give it a woman's touch."

"Yeah, sure, I'll do that for you. Wait a minute; I just remembered that I'm gonna need to be home at a certain time so I can get Syncere's call."

"Why don'tcha just forward your calls to your cell phone?"

"Oh, damn, you're right! I can do that."

"Does that mean you're gonna come?"

"Yeah, I'm coming. What time?"

"I'mma close this joint down at six o'clock. Call me around six-thirty and I'll give you the directions to my spot."

"Where do you live?"

"Out the beach."

"Oh, all right. I'll call you later," I assured him as I began to make my way out of his office.

"A'ight, do that," he replied and then we said our goodbyes.

21

The Fake Bitches

Rhonda Speaks

Word about me and Nikki fighting spread around like a bad virus. Every stylist working here cornered me in the lunchroom area wanting the juicy details about how Nikki reacted after I whipped her ass.

"So, tell us what happened," April said.

Penny and Tabitha, my other stylists, didn't say anything. Instead, they both stood with their backs against the wall, arms folded, waiting for me to speak.

Finally, I took a deep breath and said, "I really don't want to go into that long and drawn-out argument we had that led up to the fight. But, I will tell you that I went the fuck off."

"What did she say?" April asked.

"Girl, we would be in here all day if I tell you all the shit she said."

"Did she get in your face?"

"She tried, but I stopped her right in her tracks," I told her, lying through my teeth. "As soon as she ran up on me,

I swung at her and popped her right dead in the face. From there, we started throwing blows."

"Who won?" Penny asked.

"Come on, now. What kind of question is that?"

"Oh, so you won?" April asked.

"I tore her ass up," I bragged.

"For real?" April asked, with excitement.

"Yep, she sure did," Tabitha added.

"So, what gonna happen between y'all now?" April asked.

"I'm leaving the shop. If y'all wanna follow me then come on."

"Hell yeah, I'll follow you," Penny blurted out. "Because there's no way in hell I'm gon' stay here and work for that hoe."

"Me either," Tabitha and April said in unison.

"All right. Just give me a couple of days to find us a shop and then we can take it from there."

"A'ight," everyone said simultaneously.

"Oh yeah, Rhonda, did you tell Nikki you knew about her snitching on Ricky and his crew to get out of jail?" Tabitha asked me.

"Damn! That bitch is a snitch?" April asked.

"Yep, she sure is. That's why Rhonda and her got into it," Tabitha added.

"I wonder what Kira would've done about her snitching ass if she was still alive?" Penny wondered out loud.

"She wouldn't have done shit because she snitched on Ricky her damn self."

"What!" Penny shouted in disbelief.

"Girl, you don't know the half of it," I commented, looking directly at Penny.

"All I wanna know is how you got wind of all this info," April said.

"From Kira's diary."

"What other kind of juicy stuff was in there?" Penny asked.

"Just some shit about her stealing Ricky's stash money and then getting robbed by that cat she was fucking around with named Russ."

"Wait, I know you ain't talking about that dark-skinned guy who came up here to get his hair washed by her that one time," April eagerly asked.

"Yep, that was him," I assured her.

"Did her diary say how he robbed her?" April asked.

"Yeah, it said that she had met him at a hotel so they could leave town together and live happily-ever-after. But instead of jumping on the road right then, he talked her into giving him some pussy. After he fucked the shit out of her, she dozed off for a while and when she woke up she was tied to the bed. That's when he talked shit to her and took her dough."

"Damn, that was cold! I can't believe she fell for that shit," Penny commented.

"Yeah well, she did. The funny thing about it is that she came back to work the very next day and didn't say anything about it. She just said that she decided not to leave town and that instead of me giving her the shop back, we could become partners. So, I went along with it."

"She probably was too embarrassed to say anything about it. I know I would've been," Tabitha concluded.

"Shit, I thought I was her best friend," I said.

"Well, I guess Kira didn't see it that way," Tabitha continued.

"You're probably right," I said and then noticed two unfamiliar women walking through the front door. They had to be walk-ins, so I immediately broke up the party and ordered everybody back to work.

"Gotta get that money," I said and everybody scattered.

* * *

Tony was sitting in the living room on the sofa ,watching the NBA playoffs and eating pizza he ordered from Pizza Hut when I walked into the house. I knew he didn't like to be bothered when he was into the game so instead of saying hello and asking him where my kids were, I waved at him, grabbed a slice and headed into the direction of my children's rooms. Both of them where in bed, so I gave 'em kisses and headed back into the living room. When I returned, Tony was watching a commercial so I knew he would have time to say a few words until the game came back on.

"That pizza is good, huh?" he asked.

"It sure is."

"The kids fucked it up, too."

"How long they been sleep?" I asked him.

"Probably for about twenty minutes now."

"They looked like they were tired as hell."

"They probably was."

"Did you go out and look for a job today?"

"Yeah, I put a few applications in at a couple of spots."

"I hope you ain't lying."

"What do I have to lie for? Shit, I ain't on trial."

"I didn't say that."

"Yeah and you ain't said whether or not you stepped to Nikki at work today either."

"For your information, I did. I'm surprised you haven't noticed my eye all scratched and swollen up."

"Yeah, I was getting ready to ask you about that. What happened?"

"I confronted her and told her that I knew she and Kira snitched on Ricky and that she needed to go. She got mad, started talking shit to me and then she ran up on me. From there shit got really ugly."

"Oh so, she thinks she go hard, huh?"

"She sure does."

"So, who won?" he asked, smiling.

"Boy, don't play. You know I ain't no joke when it comes to these hands."

"Yeah, I know cause, you be acting like you can whip my ass too," he commented. "So, what's gon' happen now?"

"I'm gonna leave."

"But why? That's your shop too."

"Yeah, I know. But, I ain't trying to be up in there when them niggas decide they want to take out revenge on her ass. I'm gonna get my own shop."

"Where you gon' get one at?"

"I don't know but I'm sure I'll find a spot in the next couple of days."

"Well what did she say, when you told her you was leaving?"

"She just started talking stupid, saying I needed to leave out of there by tomorrow. Shiid, I told her to make me."

"And what did she say?"

"I don't know what she said, because I tuned her ass out. Not too long after that, she carried her ass."

"Do you think she's going to do something underhanded since you ain't gonna be out of there by tomorrow?"

"I wish she would try it. Because if she knows like I do, I could fuck her world up right now. And she wouldn't be able to do shit about it."

"How?"

"By calling her probation officer."

"And whatcha gon' do when you get 'em on the phone?"

"I'd tell 'em she was fucking around with a drug dealer and that she was trying to bail him out of jail from a gun charge."

"Nah. Nah. You sound like a fucking snitch! Just let me handle it."

"Whatcha gon' do?"

"I'mma get word to Syncere about what kind of bitch he's fucking with."

"How are you going to do that?"

"Remember, I got peoples doing time in Norfolk, so it ain't gon' be hard. As a matter of fact, my boy Bam just made trustee and he would love to get that kite to Syncere."

"And whatcha think that's gonna do?"

"Real niggas don't fuck with hoes they know snitch for a living. And what I heard about Syncere on the streets, that nigga is a straight killer. He's not gon' have her around after he gets word."

"I betcha he wouldn't mind knowing Kira wrote in her diary that she believed he had something to do with her and Mark getting shot outside her apartment."

"She put that in her diary?"

"Yeah, and she said she didn't trust him because he was too sneaky. She wrote that when she found out he had something to do with Mark's murder, he was going to pay big time."

"Word?"

I nodded my head.

"Do you still have her diary?"

"Nope, Nikki got it back."

"Why did you give it back to her?"

"I didn't. I stuck it back in the drawer above her station before she came to work.

Tony sucked his teeth and said, "It's all good! 'Cause we still got her stupid ass under the gun."

"Look, whatever you do, just be careful. And don't get caught up in the middle."

"Don't worry. I got this," he assured me and went back to looking at his game.

22

Blinded

Nikki Speaks

The meeting with Mr. Taliaferro didn't take long once I handed him his dough. He did reassure me that he would pay Syncere a visit tomorrow and have him in court within the next couple of days. He also stated that I would have to appear at the bail hearing and take full responsibility for Syncere to make every court appearance, if he was granted a bond. I told Mr. Taliaferro I fully understood the terms.

Later that evening, Quincy gave me the directions to his spot and I met him shortly thereafter. Actually, he lived in an exclusive community right off Shore Drive, deep in Virginia Beach. His townhouse overlooked the beach and it was nice as hell! The best part was that you wouldn't be able to find it if you didn't know exactly where you were going. You could only see his house from the beach and not while you were driving down Shore Drive. That's what you called a hide-a-way.

From the bare rooms you could tell that he had just moved in. You could smell the fresh new paint. There was no living room suite, no dining room table or chairs and a few appliances to operate inside the kitchen area. He only had minimal necessities like a breakfast table and chairs, a refrigerator and a dishwasher. A few decorative items were thrown around the floor in the dining area and most had price tags still stuck to them, waiting for a chance to find their permanent place in the home. The master bedroom and bathroom were furnished, while the guest room remained bare.

"Whatcha think?" Quincy asked me as we stood in the hallway looking into his bedroom.

"It's really nice in here and it's spacious too."

"I know, that's why I love it."

"How much you pay a month?"

"Two grand."

"Damn! That's a lot of money."

"Yeah, but it's worth it," he commented. "Come on, let's go back into the kitchen."

As we re-entered into the kitchen area, he asked me if I wanted something to drink.

"Whatcha got?" I asked.

"I got orange juice, a little bit of cranberry juice, bottled water and some other type of shit if you're up for it."

"What is it?"

"I've got a bottle of Grey Goose, some Southern Comfort and half a bottle of Rémy Red."

"I'll take a glass of the Rémy Red," I said.

Minutes later, I had my drink of choice nestled in the palm of my hand and watched Quincy pour himself a shot of Southern Comfort.

"So, did you take care of the thing with the lawyer today?" he asked after we both took a seat at the breakfast table.

"Yes. He's going to pay Syncere a visit at the jail tomorrow."

"Is he going to still be able to get him in court by the end of the week?"

"Yep, he said he's going to get him on the court's docket in the next couple of days."

"How do you feel about that?"

"What do you mean? Is that a trick question?"

"Nah. I was just wondering if you were happy about it?"

"Of course I am."

"You ain't got to front with me, Shorty."

"What makes you think I'm fronting?"

"Because I know how he treats you."

"And how is that?" I asked defensively.

"Look, we ain't gotta go into all that. Just know I've heard him scream on you over the telephone more than a few times. And personally, I didn't think it was cool at all."

"So, if you didn't think it was cool, why didn't you step to him and tell 'em?"

"Because, it wasn't my place to do that. That's y'all's personal life. Not only that, Syncere isn't the type of cat you can sit down and talk to on that level."

"I see you've made that observation as well."

"Shiiid, I had seen that part of him a long time ago."

"So, if you knew this about him then why did you go into business with him?"

"Because of the many benefits."

"Explain yourself."

"Yo, check it out. I'm on paper and when you're on paper, you got to have a steady job. I ain't the type of cat who's into that manual labor bullshit. I'm just not built for it. One day I happened to run into Syncere and he told me he was looking to take this car wash off this other cat's hands but he needed a silent partner to go in half with him.

Since I had a little bit of dough I said let's do it. We got a real accountant who does our bookkeeping and our payroll. So, I'm paid with a real check, which was all I wanted. The rest of my dough from the business is paid to me under the table. Then I got my hustle, so I'm straight."

"It sure sounds like you've got everything under control."

"Not everything. But I will."

"Care to share?" I asked and then took another sip of my drink. Before he could answer the question my cellular phone started ringing. I looked down at the caller I.D. and saw it was Syncere trying to get through, so I said, "Hold that thought. It's Syncere."

"Look, please don't tell him we're together," he insisted.

I was puzzled by Quincy's request. But after a few seconds, I shrugged and proceeded to answer Syncere's call.

"Hello."

"Hey, you a'ight?"

"Yeah, I'm straight."

"Did you take care of that thing with Q this morning?"

"Yeah, we met up."

"So, he gave you the dough?"

"Yeah and I took it straight to the lawyer afterwards."

"And what did he say?"

"He said he was going to come and have a talk with you tomorrow."

"And what about the bail hearing?"

"Nothing's changed. He said he's going to get you on the court's docket within the next couple of days."

"A'ight. That's what's up," Syncere replied, pleased with my answer.

"So, is everything all right on your end?"

"Oh yeah, you know me."

"Have you been able to order any commissary yet?"

"Yeah, I put my order in the very next day."

"You haven't had any run-ins with any of those guys in there, have you?"

"Yo, let me tell you something about me: Niggas all over this joint either know me or heard about me on the streets. They know I got plenty of dough and soldiers who would go to war for me at any second. So, if there is some bitch-ass haters roaming 'round here who got it out for me, they ain't gon' act on it 'cause they ain't got enough heart. Believe me, they gon' keep their feelings buried under their chest."

"I hear you," I said nonchalantly.

"You better 'cause this shit here ain't no joke."

"You telling me," I mumbled.

"What cha' say?"

"I was talking to myself."

"Oh yeah, before I forget, what time did you get up with Q today? Because, I tried to call him around 3 o'clock."

"I don't remember exactly what time it was," I lied. "But, I do remember it being late in the evening."

"Was he at the car wash when you got there?"

"Nope, he came around later. As soon as he gave me the money, he went right back out."

"Yo, what's up with that nigga? Shit, I ain't been able to holla at him since that time you called him on the three-way."

"Maybe he's trying to take care of all your business."

"It ain't that much business in the muthafucking world. I think he's ducking me 'cause he ain't never stayed away from the car wash this much."

"Why would he be ducking you?"

"Never mind, 'cause it sounds like you're trying to get deep in my business."

"No, I wasn't. I was just trying to make conversation."

"Don't fucking lie to me!"

"I'm not," I said, trying to convince him.

"Yo, Nikki, I ain't trying to hear that shit right now. Just get word to Q and let 'em know that I'm gon' call up to the car wash at one o'clock on the nose. So, I'm gon' need for him to be there."

"No problem."

"Well a'ight, I'mma holler back at you tomorrow."

"What time?"

"What time you getting off work?"

"I don't know. Rhonda is leaving so I'm gonna be really busy until I can get shit on a system around there. Just call me about the same time you did tonight."

"Yeah, a'ight, I'mma holler at you tomorrow then."

"Yeah, okay," I responded, unenthused, because it was becoming pretty apparent that this nigga was starting to turn on me. He never appreciated anything I did for his crab ass. But, it was cool though because I had a trick for his ass!

Disgusted by my conversation with Syncere, I put my phone away and took another sip from my glass.

"You okay?" Quincy asked me.

"I was until I got that phone call."

"What he say?"

"Nothing worth repeating."

"What did he say about me?"

"He just wanted to know what time I met up with you today. He said every time he tries to call you, you ain't never around."

"That's it?"

"Well, he thinks that you're ducking him for some reason."

"I ain't ducking him!"

"That's what I tried to tell him. But he told me to mind my fucking business!"

"Yo, that nigga is bugging out! He's too fucking paranoid for me."

"That's your partner."

"Yeah, sometimes I wonder about that, too," he commented as he poured himself another shot of liquor.

"Can I ask you something?"

"What's up?"

"Why didn't you want me to tell Syncere that I was over your crib?"

"Because first of all, I knew he was going to want to talk to me and I ain't in the mood for that right now. And secondly, he would not have understood that you were chilling at my house while he was in jail."

"I see your point now. Let me ask you question, though."

"Go ahead."

"Have you and him ever had to go head to head with each other since y'all started working together?"

Quincy hesitated and looked at me really weird. To make him feel a little more at ease, I said, "It's okay, Q. I promise I won't ever mention this conversation to him."

"You sure?"

"After that dumb shit he just said to me over the phone, he'd be lucky if I make another trip downtown. I damned sure don't feel like signing my name on the line to bail his selfish ass out!"

"Oh, you just talking. 'Cause as soon as that nigga tell you to jump, you gon' ask him how high."

"That's what you think."

"Nah, Shorty, that's what I know. I see your type every day: The nice, pretty type who doesn't know shit about the streets. So, as soon as she gets a little taste of a hood nigga, she gets all blinded and let 'em take complete control over her life."

"Is that so?"

Quincy nodded his head.

"Well, I sure hate to break this to you, but I'm far from being the type you just described."

"I hope you're not in denial."

"No, not at all. But, I do know one thing."

"What's that?"

"You're trying to avoid my question."

"What question was that?" he knew which question it was though.

"The question was about whether or not you and Syncere ever had run-ins since y'all been working together?"

"Yeah, we have."

"How many times?"

"A couple."

"How did y'all settle the dispute?"

"I don't remember how. We just did. I mean, men do things different from women. We just let shit be what it is supposed to be, because the most important thing is the money that needs to be made. All that other bullshit is put on the back burner."

"How is y'all's relationship now?"

"It used to be all good until recently."

"What happened?"

"Nothing major. Everything's cool," Quincy replied, giving me a feeling he was trying to brush me off. I respected the fact he was the type of man who wasn't into running his mouth like a gossiping-ass chick and left the subject alone.

"That's good. Now, tell me whatcha got in here to snack on 'cause I'm getting kind of hungry right now."

"I got a can of Pringles over there on top of the refrigerator, but that's it."

"Oh, that's cool. Can't say that I won't eat the whole can," I warned him with a smile as I got up from the chair to retrieve the can.

"Do your thing, Nikki."

Meanwhile, his Blackberry started ringing and he answered it. I remained quiet because I didn't want to cause any problems, just in case it was one of his lady friends on the other end. I had too much drama already. About two minutes later he said, "Yo, I'mma handle it. Just give me a couple of days." And then he hung up.

"Want to take a trip with me tomorrow?" he asked.

"Where to?"

"D.C."

"Yeah, I'll go. But, whatcha gotta' go there for?"

"I got to take care of some business."

"I hope you ain't trying to make a pick up," I said to him with caution.

"Oh, nah, I don't make trips like that. But, I do have to see somebody very important."

"So, why do you want me to go?"

"Because I wouldn't mind having some company."

"When are you coming back?"

"Right after we get there, I'm gonna turn around and come on back down the road."

"Okay then, I'm down," I assured him.

"Yo, you're tearing them chips up."

"I told you I was starving."

"Want me to order a pizza?"

"Yeah, do that. Make sure they add extra cheese to it."

"No, problem. I got it covered."

After we ordered the pizza, the time flew by and before we knew it, we were diving into it. The pizza was cooked exactly the way I wanted it, not to mention it was even tastier than it looked. With the constant flow of Rémy Red,

I was beginning to feel the effects of it. I believed Quincy was feeling the effects of his liquor as well because he started asking me some really weird questions.

"You sure you really want to be with that nigga?"

"Who? Syncere?"

"Yeah, who else?"

"Why you asking me that?" I asked.

"Because you don't seem like you're happy."

"That's because I'm not."

"So, why you still fucking with him?"

"I don't know."

"Are you lonely or something?"

"Nah, I ain't lonely."

"Well, get it together, then. 'Cause, to be perfectly honest with you, I seriously don't think you're emotionally or mentally built for the type of nigga he is."

"And what type of nigga is that?"

"Do you really want to know?"

"Yeah, of course."

He took another sip of his drink and said, "Yo, Syncere is a fucking mad man and he don't give a fuck about nobody but himself."

Sensing that the alcohol was speaking through him, I saw an opportunity to get more information out of him and seized the moment.

"If you feel like that, then why are you still in business with him?"

"Oh, don't worry. This shit I'm doing with him is only temporary. Believe me, I got a plan."

"What kind of plan you got going on?"

"Oh, you'll see. And it won't be very long."

"So, whatcha gon' do after that?"

"I've got some other shit lined up."

"Does Syncere know about this house?"

"Oh, hell nah! And you can't ever tell him about it either!" he said urgently.

"I won't," I assured him. "But, let me ask you this: How close were you to Mark?"

"You talking about Syncere's peoples?"

"Yeah, him."

"Oh yeah, he was cool as shit. But, we wasn't that close. I mean, he used to come by the car wash and gamble with us every now and then but that was it. I mean, he used to mainly fuck with Syncere. They used to do a lot of business together. So, he would come by like twice a week to pick up the dough Syncere owed him."

"Why was Syncere owing him money?"

"Because Syncere use to cop his shit from him. And sometimes Mark would just front it to him because they was cool like that. But, I remember one time at a dice game when Mark stepped up to Syncere and asked him about a rumor he heard . . ."

"What was the rumor?" I asked, cutting Quincy off in mid sentence.

"There was a whole bunch of Mark's peoples was complaining about Syncere stepping on the dope and selling them garbage. And the same people also got word to Mark that Syncere was getting high."

"You are fucking kidding me," I blurted out immediately after listening to what Quincy had just said.

"No, I'm not. So anyway, when Mark approached him at the dice game, he asked Syncere was he smoking that shit! When he did it, he kind of screamed on him in front of everybody. And by doing that, Syncere felt like Mark had disrespected him. So, shit got real heated! And it almost looked like I was about to be in the middle of a blood bath, but somehow niggas got in between them and was able to cool things down."

"So, Syncere was getting high?"

"Hell yeah, that nigga was getting high. But, Mark didn't know it until some other nigga hipped him to it."

"What was he getting high off of?"

"That nigga did everything from snorting coke, to lacing his weed."

"Do you think he's doing it now?"

"How can he and he's in jail?" Quincy asked and then he laughed. "But, as soon as he becomes a free man, all hell is gon' break loose!"

"Do you think he had something to do with Mark getting killed?" I boldly asked, not even expecting a response.

"Hell yeah! I know he did."

Hearing Quincy utter those words out of his mouth made my heart sink to the pit of my stomach. He actually admitted Syncere had something to do with Mark's murder. This was fucking unbelievable! But, my question to him was, how the hell did he know all of this? And before I could ask him he continued by saying, "Shit, everybody in his crew knows he knocked Mark off. Syncere had it set up to look like a robbery, so the heat wouldn't come back on him."

"But why? I mean, what in the hell could Mark have done to make Syncere put a hit out on him?"

"With Syncere, it was a matter of control. And if he couldn't get it, then he was going to eliminate the problem that was preventing that from happening."

"Did you know that Kira lost her baby after she got shot that night?" I asked with anger.

"Yo, she was pregnant?"

"Yeah, she sure was," I replied as water filled my eyes.

"Damn! I'm sorry to hear that."

"I swear to God, I ain't gon' lift a finger to do another fucking thing for that bastard! And you know what? I hope that muthafucka rot in that jail cell.

"Well, whatcha' gon' do when it's time for him to go to court?"

"I ain't gon' do shit! I ain't even gon' accept anymore of his collect calls."

"Yo, baby you better be careful. 'Cause if that nigga knows you know about that shit that went down with your cousin and Mark, he'll have somebody kill you. So, you gon' have to play it very easy."

"I know I'm dealing with a fucking psycho! That's why I'm gon' get his ass before he gets mine."

"And how the fuck you gon' do that?"

"I don't know. But, I'll find a way."

"Now, you know you can't go to the police with this shit! 'Cause, who the fuck gon' admit to pulling the trigger for that shit? Nobody. So, it's going to be your word against his. And then, once he finds out that you went to the police with that shit, you gon' fuck around and come up missing for sure!"

My heart started pounding rapidly when he told me about the repercussions I would endure if I went to the police about Mark's murder, so what was I going to do?

"My life is one big mess," I commented and sighed.

"Yo', you gon' be a'ight. Just hold your head up."

"How can I do that, when I know I'm fucking with a nigga who's a killer?"

"I wish I could answer that, but I can't. I mean, all I can tell you is that you gon' have to find a way to leave him alone."

"How?"

"I don't know."

"Well, tell me why you decided to tell me all of this?"

"Yo, let me explain something to you."

"I'm listening."

"Nikki, in spite of what transpired in my past relationship with Kira, I still got mad love for her because she was a cool chick. So, when I heard about her getting shot behind some beef Syncere had with Mark, I was mad heated. I honestly wanted to put a bullet in that nigga's head myself. But when I found out she was all right, I kind of pushed my emotions to the side."

"Kira told me why y'all broke up. But I want to hear it from you."

"What she said was probably true. I mean, what can I say other than the fact that I was cheating on her?"

"But, why?"

"I really don't know why. I just did it."

"But, you had to have a reason."

"Men don't necessarily have to have a reason to cheat. We just do it, if the opportunity presents itself. I mean, every man I know gets excited about finding out how new pussy feels. Especially if the chick was nice with a thick phat ass. Yo, niggas love that shit."

"So, I've heard. But, tell me something."

"What is it?"

"Why don't you have a girl?"

Quincy smiled and said, "Because chicks play too many games. And plus, they're too needy. Always want you to be up under them all the time. And then they're too damn moody."

"Not all of us."

"Shiid, that's a lie. Because every chick I fucked with got all the same characteristics."

"Not me."

"Yeah, right."

"No, I'm serious. Because I'm not needy and I am definitely not into a man being up under me all the time. Shit, I like my space. That's why I encouraged Syncere to keep his place out Newport News."

"Well, you know what? You are among the few."

"Stop fucking with them chicken heads and you wouldn't have those problems."

"Thanks for the advice," he commented and then he took the last sip of his drink.

The night started to wind down while Quincy and I were engrossed in our conversation. And once I realized how late it was and that I was too intoxicated to drive anywhere, I asked Quincy if I could stay the night. He happily obliged and boy, was I happy about that!

He and I ended up sharing his bed. I slept down one end and he down the other. I was kind of shocked that he didn't try any funny stuff. I'm guessing it was because he dozed off and fell asleep on me first. Too bad though, because I would've given him some and felt bad about it later.

23

The Next Morning

Nikki Speaks

Quincy woke me up around nine o'clock this morning and we jumped on the road. We made a pit stop to my apartment, so I could take a quick shower and change into some clean attire. It only took about thirty minutes to do everything and then I was out the door. On our way up I-95, we made another stop at a Hardee's restaurant and ordered a couple of combos and back on the road it was again.

"Ummm, this is good," I told Quincy, making reference to my sandwich.

"Yeah, this Philly burger I got ain't that bad either," he replied between chews as if he was trying to savor every last bite.

"You better slow down before your ass gets choked up," I commented and laughed, but he paid me no attention. Instead of an episode of clowning me, he continued to devour his sandwich.

We finally reached D.C. around twelve thirty in the afternoon and it seemed like the closer we got to his destination, the more familiar this area looked to me. And as soon as Quincy drove by the same West Indian Restaurant Kira had that run-in with Russell at, I knew exactly where I was.

"I ate there before," I announced to Quincy.

"Whatcha know about Jamaican food?"

"I know a lot about Jamaican food," I assured him.

Minutes later, we pulled up in front of a grocery store that looked exactly like the one Kira and I came to so she could meet with Papí.

"Wait, does a Spanish guy named Papí own this store?"

"Yeah. How you know him?" Quincy asked me while turning the car ignition off.

"Well, I've actually never seen him before. But, I took a trip up here with Kira about two months ago."

Shocked by my response, he asked, "She came up here to see Papí?"

"Yeah. She said she had to take care of some business regarding Ricky. I stayed back in the car while she went in there to talk to him."

"Damn, Kira's ass was gangsta as shit, huh?"

"I don't know about all of that. But, I will say that she knew how to handle her fucking business!"

"Well, I'm about to do the same thing. So, hold tight and I'll be right back."

"All right," I told him and then he walked away.

After he disappeared inside of Papí's store, I turned back around in my seat and used the lever on the side of my chair to recline it. I leaned my head back against the head rest and closed my eyes to the music coming from the CD player. I began to meditate about everything Quincy and I had talked about the night before. Running everything back through my head was kind of mind-boggling. I mean, who would have ever thought Quincy would volunteer and give me the whole rundown about Syncere? If you asked me, the shit with him was scary. I honestly couldn't believe I was screwing around with a fucking lunatic. But, I should've known something wasn't right with him when he jumped on me and tried to choke the breath out of me for asking him questions about the shooting. He was acting suspect then but the naïve side of me just wouldn't allow me to see right through it. Was it denial or what? But I did know this: He was going to pay for the shit he put me and my family through. I just had to figure out exactly how I was going to make him suffer.

While my mind was in overdrive, I heard two people talking within a couple of feet from the car, so I looked up to see who those voices belonged to. Quincy was the first person I saw, standing alongside a Hispanic guy who had his back facing me. His position changed when Quincy looked over at me and realized that I was looking in their direction.

"I thought you were sleeping." Quincy said aloud as he approached my side of the car. The Hispanic guy followed behind Quincy.

Instead of responding, I smiled and rolled down the window because it was evident that he wanted to introduce me to his friend.

"Carlos, meet Nikki, the young lady I was telling you and Papí about," Quincy continued as he leaned over to peer into the car.

"*Hola*, Nikki," Carlos said as he peered into the car alongside Quincy.

"Hi," I said, smiling. Then my facial expression changed as I held a stare directly at this man's face.

"Are you all right?" Carlos asked me, giving me a suspicious look.

"Yeah, are you okay?" Quincy interjected. "Because you look like you know this man."

Feeling my heart race at the speed of light, I rearranged

my expression by smiling. And then I looked over at Quincy saying, "Yes, I'm fine. I just thought I recognized this gentleman from somewhere," I lied with the most sincerity.

"Where you thought you recognized me from?" Carlos asked.

"At this nightclub that plays salsa music," I lied once again, looking back in his direction.

"Where?" Carlos was looking at me like he was trying to place my face.

"Well, it's been a little over a year now, so I don't exactly remember the name of it."

"Was it here in D.C.?"

"Yeah," I replied nodding my head, the lies continuing to pour out of my mouth.

"Well, I haven't been to any nightclubs around here in a couple of years. You sure it wasn't some other place?"

"Well, maybe I got you mixed up with somebody else." I was trying to play it off and pretend that I was confused about knowing him.

"It's a possibility," he commented and then he gave me a sly smirk.

Wanting to join in on the conversation, Quincy said, "Hey Nikki, I was just in the store telling Carlos that you're Kira's cousin."

"Oh, yeah," I said, not at all pleased with his gesture to volunteer information about me to this fucking killer. But I remained cool because this guy was watching my body language like a hawk.

"Yeah, Carlos and his uncle knew Kira and Ricky real good," Quincy boasted.

"Is that right?" I commented nonchalantly.

"Yes, and we're sorry to hear about her passing," Carlos said as he searched my face for any sign of nervousness and fear.

"Thank you very much," I replied and then I purposely looked down at my watch.

"Got somewhere to be?" Carlos asked, watching me closely.

Just as I was about to answer him, Quincy looked down at his watch as well and said, "We gotta go 'cause time is creeping up on us. Gotta beat that traffic back down the Highway 95. It gets crazy when you're driving through the Richmond area."

"You sure ain't lying about that," I added as I looked into Quincy's face with a sigh of relief.

"Why don't you two stay here for the night? My uncle and I can show you guys around town and put you up in a nice hotel, so you can rest up and leave in the morning," Carlos insisted.

"Mr. Carlos, that offer sounds so tempting but I help to take care of my grandmother at night so I've got to get home ASAP."

"Well, at least stay a while for a drink," he continued, adding in a little persuasion.

"I wish I could, but maybe next time," I replied, sticking to my guns.

"Yeah, we can do it another time," Quincy told Carlos as he extended his hand for a shake.

While Carlos reached out to shake Quincy's already awaiting hand, I turned back around in my seat and looked straight forward. I began to pray silently, asking God to allow me and Quincy a chance to get out of this situation we were in alive.

When I heard Quincy tell Carlos he'd talk to him later, I knew my prayers were being answered.

"See you soon, Ms. Nikki," Carlos said, as Quincy turned the car ignition.

"Okay," I replied and waved my hand goodbye as I

forced a smile on my face. Luckily, Quincy had started driving away before Carlos saw my smile fade.

About a half a block up the street, I turned around in my seat and looked through the back window of Quincy's car. I was curious to see if Carlos had jumped in a car to follow us. Plus, I knew my life depended upon it.

"You a'ight?" Quincy asked me.

"Can you please just get me back to Virginia," I pleaded and then I let out a long sigh.

"That's what I'm doing."

"Could you drive a little faster?" I asked desperately as fear began to consume my entire body.

"What, you want me to get a ticket or something?"

"No, I just want to get home."

"Okay. I'll have you there in a couple of hours, so just relax and enjoy the ride."

But I couldn't relax. I leaned forward and buried my face into the palm of my hands as all kinds of crazy thoughts began to ring in my head.

"Yo, Nikki, you sure you're all right?"

I looked up from my hands and as I was about to tell him about his friend Carlos, his cell phone rang. At that instant, I froze and I honestly couldn't move a limb on my body. My heart and the gas bubbles in my stomach made up for my lack of movement.

As soon as he answered the phone, I went into full alert, watching his facial expressions and listening for any signs that there would be trouble in paradise.

"I'm about to get on the highway now so it's gon' be hard to turn back around," I heard him say.

Hearing Quincy's response to the caller's question sent me into a state of paranoia. At that point, I knew I couldn't hold back. I nudged him in his arm with my left hand and my eyes began to tear. I whispered, "Please don't turn around. They're gonna kill me!"

Shocked by my words, Quincy pulled his phone away from his ear, pressed down on the mute button and said, "Kill you! What the fuck are you talking about?"

Completely ignoring his question, I asked him, "Who is that on the phone?"

"It's Papí's other nephew, Juan."

"Why does he want you to turn around?" Suspicion began to build in my body.

"What? Hold up," he told me and then went back to his call, which lasted about another ten seconds.

"Why does he want you to turn around?"

"He said that Papí had a proposition for me but that I had to come back to the store to discuss it."

"What did you tell 'em?"

"You heard me tell 'em I had a call on the other line and that I'd call him back."

"Listen to me," I urged him as I leaned over toward him. "Under no circumstances can you take me back over there."

"What's going on?" Quincy asked.

"Remember when I told you I walked right by this Hispanic-looking guy coming from the direction of Kira's apartment on the day she got murdered?"

"Yeah, I remember that."

"Well, Carlos was that guy!"

"Ahhh, man! Now, I get it."

"Get what?" I asked anxiously.

"When I told them I had Ricky's wife's cousin waiting outside in the car and that you had taken a ride up here to the store with Kira about two months ago to discuss some business concerning Ricky, they got real interested in who you were. When I was about to leave, Papí suggested to Carlos that he come outside to meet you. I thought it was kind of odd 'cause Papí could care less about meeting new people especially because of the type of business he's in."

"Is that a dope spot?"

"I'd doubt it. He wouldn't ever sell dope out of his store. That's just a drop-off station for money."

"So, whatcha think is gonna happen now?"

"I don't know," Quincy said as he took the 295 South Exit.

Seeing familiar signs gave me a temporary sense of relief. Just knowing I was moving farther away from Papí and his men gave me a false feeling of hope. Why had Carlos killed Kira? The thoughts that were running through my mind weren't quite adding up. I looked back at Quincy and said, "What could Kira have done that would make them kill her in cold blood like that?"

"Maybe Ricky owed Papí some dough."

"But I don't think he did."

"Why did Kira come up here to have a meeting with Papí, then?"

"I'm not sure but after Ricky started feeling the pressure about all that time the Feds gave him, he called Kira and told her he needed her help to set up a drug buy from Papí. If everything went according to plan, he could get a big-time cut. When Kira told him no, he threatened her. She reached out to Papí, hoping that when she provided that information about Ricky's plans he would, in turn, provide her with some protection."

"Did she tell you what he said?"

"Yeah, she told me he said he was going to take care of everything and before she left he handed her an envelope filled with twenty-five grand in cash."

"Did she take it?"

"Hell yeah, she took it! He told her to take a vacation with it."

"Ahhh, man!" Quincy said, squinting his eyes as if he had felt a sharp pain in his head.

"What's wrong?"

"They killed her because she took the money."

"But, he offered it to her. What was wrong with taking the money?"

"Nikki, you cannot accept money in this game from a man like Papí for information that's gon' have a nigga killed. That's not how it works."

"Why did he offer the money to her then?"

"Because it was a test."

"That's not fair; Papí set her up!"

"I guess he felt that since she was married to Ricky she should've known the rules."

Absorbing every word Quincy uttered, I began to feel sick to my stomach and begged him to pull the car over on the side of the highway. Once he pulled over, I immediately forced opened the passenger side door and leaned over into the grass. Two seconds later, I was puking my guts up. I felt Quincy rubbing my back in a circular motion as I purged myself of all my anxiety. He wasn't really making me feel any better but knowing that he was there felt a little reassuring. As I was leaning back into the car, Quincy's cell phone started ringing again.

"Oh my God, I betcha that's him again," I said fearfully.

Quincy looked down at his phone and said, "Yeah, it is."

"Wait. Please, don't answer it."

Unsure of how he should handle the situation, Quincy fumbled with his phone until it stopped ringing. When he realized what he had just done, he sighed heavily and said, "Man, I can't believe I just did that."

"Quincy, please, get me out of here," I told him as I pulled the passenger door shut.

Quincy pulled back onto the highway and we rode in

silence for about three miles. He broke the silence by saying, "I just fucked up!"

"Why, because you didn't answer your cell phone?"

"It's more than that."

"Then what is it?"

"I'm supposed to make another trip back up here in a couple of days to pick my product up from one of Papí's peoples. When I do that, I'm gon' have to explain to Papí why I didn't answer his nephew's call and why I didn't show up."

"Then don't go."

"Are you fucking crazy? I can't just let him keep fifty grand of my dough."

"What's more important, your life or that fifty grand?"

"Papí wouldn't kill me over that shit."

"Then, what are you worried about?"

"I'm not sure but I'm starting to get this funny feeling."

"You know what?"

"What?"

"If you would not have gone in his store running your mouth about Kira's cousin sitting in the car then none of this shit would have happened."

"Who the fuck knew Papí was the one who had Kira killed?" Quincy asked, getting defensive.

"Come on now, let's not do this. What's done is done. We just got to figure out what we're gonna do."

"Nikki, Carlos is a very smart man and he probably knows you remember seeing him leave Kira's apartment building that day. So, if he'll ride all the way down to Virginia Beach to knock off Kira, then he's gonna come after you next."

"Oh my God! Please don't tell me anymore."

"I'm sorry, but you gotta know that these men are professional killers. They will hunt you down until you're dead."

"Whatcha think I should do?"

"You could hide out for a while and see if this shit boils over."

"Hide out where?"

"Maybe at a relative's house or out of town somewhere."

"What if I go to the police?"

"The police ain't gon' help you! Did they help Ricky stay alive?"

I refused to answer Quincy's question because it was a no-brainer. Papí was a very powerful man with a lot of money so if he wanted you dead, he'd get you. Which was the point he made when he had men go into the jail as U.S. Marshals with authentic identification. Now, if that wasn't some serious shit, then I don't know what is. Going to the cops was definitely out of the question. I wouldn't even live long enough to testify on the stand. My main focus, right now, was to stay alive, since my mission to find Kira's killer was accomplished. The only difference now is that there's no way of making these muthafuckers pay. They were too powerful and I want no parts of them. I'm just hoping Kira will forgive me for going back on my word.

For the rest of the trip Quincy and I opted to remain quiet. When the ride was over we went back to his place, since that's where I left my car. When I grabbed my car keys from my handbag I hesitated and looked at Quincy. He saw my sudden stop in movement and turned around.

"Are you okay?" he asked.

"I'm scared to go home."

"Stay here then."

"Are you sure?"

"Yeah, I'm sure. It's the least I can do."

"But, what if Papí sends Carlos here to look for me?"

"I just moved here. He doesn't know about this spot."

"I'm sure he could find out."

"Calm down Nikki," he said, grabbing my hands. "This place is in a good friend's name so he ain't gon' be able to find me."

I hesitated, searching his face for some assurance. His look told me that he would protect me and my eyes began to fill with tears. I immediately said, "All right."

After accepting Quincy's invitation to stay the night at his place we settled down in his bedroom. He offered me a drink, but of course I declined because I needed a clear head tonight and because of the circumstances. He grabbed himself a glass of Rémy.

"You sure you don't want anything to drink?" he asked again.

"Yeah, I'm sure."

"Want something to sleep in?"

"Yes," I said and sat on the edge of his bed.

"Well here, take this," he said, handing me an oversized T-shirt.

I took the T-shirt, headed into the nearby bathroom and changed. When I returned, Quincy was lying in his bed shirtless. He was staring up at the ceiling and it was evident that he was in deep thought. I asked, "Are you all right?"

Turning his attention to me, he said, "Oh yeah, I'm straight."

"What were you thinking about?" I asked, sitting on the bed.

"About my life."

"What about it?"

"I'm just wondering if I'll ever get out of the game and settle down and have kids."

"You don't have kids?"

Quincy smiled. "Nope, I sure don't."

"Would you like to have some?"

"Yeah, one day," he answered and took a sip of his drink.

"Is it good?"

"Yeah, it's a'ight but I would be better if you would drink it with me."

"Nah, I'm cool."

"Come on," he insisted, crawling over to the other side of the bed. "Here, just take one sip." He ushered the glass up to my mouth.

I turned my head away from the glass so Quincy grabbed my chin. "If you don't take a drink, you're gonna have to give me a kiss."

Shocked as hell by his forwardness, my heart fluttered. But, I didn't let on how I felt. Instead, I looked at him like he was crazy. "Give you a kiss?"

Quincy smiled. "You heard me."

"Come on now, you know I can't do that."

"Why not?"

"Because I fuck with your boy and you use to mess with my cousin."

"True, but we're two adults trying to find true love. We might be meant for each other."

"I doubt it," I replied and stood up from the bed.

"Hey, where you going?" Quincy grabbed my arm and pulled me back down to the bed.

The gentle force of his touch gave my body the chills so I gave into his advances. Once he took me into his arms, he buried his head in my neck and started kissing me. Oh my God! This man's lips were soft as hell and the way that he was massaging my ass and thighs underneath this T-shirt was making my pussy drip like a faucet. Shit, I had enough of this feeling, touching thing and I was ready for this nigga to rip my panties off and give me what I'd been looking for. To move this thing along, I grabbed his right hand from off my ass and place it inside my panties. "I want you to feel how wet you're making me," I told him.

Excited by the touch of the juices from my pussy, he pulled his hand from out of my panties, swirled me around, pushed me on my back and the rest was history. Yeah, the nigga tore me up. He had me in the scissors position and on all fours. I was shocked as hell when he was fucking me from the back real hard, then pulled his dick out and started eating my pussy. That was truly some hot shit. Syncere or my old boyfriend, Brian, ain't never fucked me like that before. It was a shame but these days you never get the total package. After we both came, we collapsed onto the bed beside one another and dozed off.

The next morning Quincy woke me up with a hot plate of blueberry pancakes and a glass of orange juice. "Good morning," he said as he handed me the plate.

I wiped my eyes to get better focus. After I realized he was standing before me with a plate of breakfast, I was at a loss for words. I mean, I honestly thought this nigga was going to try and act like nothing happened last night but I guess I was wrong. I took the plate and asked him if he cooked this himself.

"Yeah, I cooked them. Did you think I couldn't cook?"

"I honestly never even thought about it," I replied, placing the plate on my lap. I took a sip of the orange juice.

"So, whatcha gon' do today?" he asked, sitting on the bed next to me.

"I'm not sure. I wanna go by my apartment so I can get a few things and take 'em over my grandmother's house but I am scared to death to go there by myself."

"I'll go with you."

"For real?"

"Yeah, I'm for real. What time you wanna go? Because I got a lot of shit I got to do today."

"I'm ready whenever you are."

"Okay, well I'mma make a quick run downtown and when I come back we can go, a'ight?"

"All right."

Pulling a key from his keychain, he handed it to me and said, "Oh yeah, and if you decide that you wanna go somewhere, here's an extra key to my house."

I took the key.

We didn't discuss what happened last night, which was fine with me. I probably would've felt awkward if he brought it up. We did, however, get the chance to talk about my situation with Syncere. His only advice was for me to leave that nigga alone before some tragic shit happened. I assured him that I would.

24

The Bounty

Rhonda Speaks

I got up and took a long, hot shower before I left to go to the shop. It had been four days since I last talked to Nikki, so you know I was wondering what kind of schemes she had under her sleeve. While I was getting dressed, Tony turned around in the bed to see what I was doing. His ugly ass needed to be on somebody's construction job site.

"What time is it?" he asked.

"Quarter 'til nine. Why, you gotta be somewhere?"

"Nah," he replied and then he let out a long yawn.

"What time did you get in last night?"

"It was a little after one."

"What kept you out 'til one in the morning?"

"I was trying to make some moves. I got this nigga whose gon' look out for me and front me some good shit as soon as he gets it in his hands."

"Please spare me the details," I replied sarcastically.

"Ay yo, guess what?" Tony said, changing the subject.

"What?" I asked, nonchalantly.

"I talked to my boy Travis last night over his girl's crib and he told me that he got word to Syncere the very next day."

"So, did Syncere have anything to say about it?"

"I asked Travis that same question, but all he said was that Syncere was like, 'Good looking out, dog' and gave him a handshake."

"Whatcha' think is gon' happen now?"

"I guess we gon' just have to wait and see," Tony told me and then turned his unemployed ass back over to get some more z's.

"I sure wish you would go and get a real fucking job!"

"Yeah, yeah, yeah," he said and threw the covers over his head.

I threw a shoe at his lazy ass. I mean, come on, he needed to wake the fuck up and smell the coffee. It was time to go out into the world and get some real money. When was he gon' realize that? Probably never. My mother always said that if a man wasn't doing what he was supposed to do for his family in the beginning of the relationship, then he was never gon' do it. She right about that.

25

Suicide Mission

Nikki Speaks

Quincy helped me get a few things out of my apartment and followed me over to my grandmother's house to make sure I got there safely. Right before I went in the house he gave me a chrome .380 handgun for my protection. He also showed me how to take off the safety and fire it. I wasn't too happy to have this piece of iron in my possession for obvious reasons—being on probation would be number one on my list—but I had to consider my safety first. I decided to chill at my grandmother's house for a while or at least until I figured out what I wanted do with my life.

My grandmother was folding clothes in the laundry area next to the kitchen when I walked in the house. I dropped all my things in the foyer and went to see if she needed some help. Of course, she insisted that she was fine. I took a seat in a chair and started asking questions.

"How you doing grandma?"

"I'm fine, baby. How are you?"

"I'm okay."

"What's going on with that beauty salon?"

"I'm just waiting for Rhonda to leave."

"Did she say when she was going?"

"No ma'am. I went up there early this morning before everybody got there and placed a note on her station letting her know that I was going to give her a few more days before getting the authorities involved."

"Do you think the other beauticians will follow her?"

"There's no telling because all of them are sometime."

"How is your boyfriend doing?"

"Who are you talking about?"

"I'm talking about that Syncere fellow."

"Grandma, I thought I told you that we're not together anymore."

"Did you? Well I don't remember," she replied in deep thought. "But don'tcha think you should give him another chance? 'Cause he seemed like he was a nice fellow," she commented.

Nice fellow my ass, I wanted to say but was interrupted by the doorbell.

"Nikki answer that. It might be the mailman and I'm waiting for an express package," she stated. I rushed to the front door and without even asking who it was, I opened the door and got the surprise of my life.

"Going somewhere, bitch?" Syncere asked as he stood before me.

I tried to remain calm but it wasn't working. "Syncere, when did you get out?"

"Don't worry about it," he said and then pushed me backward into the house.

"Whatchu doing? Why are you pushing me?"

"Just shut the fuck up!" He whipped out his gun and pointed it directly at me. I realized that this psycho-ass nigga was holding a .45-caliber semi-automatic weapon. I was about to ask him why he was pointing a gun in my face but before I could say a word, my grandmother walked up in the foyer behind me.

"Nikki, what is going on here?"

"Grandma, please, go sit down," I demanded.

"Chile, tell me why he's got a gun pointed at you?"

"You better listen to her Granny, before you get hurt," Syncere interjected.

"Young man, are you threatening me?" my grandmother asked Syncere, giving him a stern look.

"Grandma, please, go in the living room!"

"Nah! Both of y'all are going in the living room. Now, move!" Syncere demanded.

The tone of Syncere's voice triggered something inside of me and I knew that if I was going to keep us alive, I would have to work fast. I followed his instructions and pulled my grandmother into the living room.

My grandmother and I immediately took a seat on the living room sofa next to each other. However, Syncere disapproved of the seating arrangements and ordered me to stand up.

"Get the fuck up, you rat!" he shouted with the gun still pointed directly at me.

"What are you talking about?" I asked, though I knew exactly what he was referring to.

"Oh bitch, you know what I'm talking about. Yeah, I heard about your snitching ass when I was on lock. Niggas is down in Norfolk blasting your name all over that joint talking about how you snitched on your cousin's husband so you could get your stank ass out of doing a bid. Here I am, fucking with you, and your ass is the Feds!"

"Don't believe that! They lying on me!" I replied, trying to convince him that I was telling the truth but he wasn't buying a word I was saying. In the blink of an eye, he smacked me directly across my face. The force of his blow knocked me down on my knees. As I grabbed the side of my face, I saw my grandmother attempt to leap toward him but I jumped up and intervened.

"Grandma, don't worry, it's gonna be all right. He's gonna leave soon. He won't hurt you," I whispered a promise I didn't even believe. The look of fear in her eyes broke my heart.

"Syncere, why are you doing this? Put the gun down 'cause you're scaring my grandmother."

I breathed a sigh of relief when Syncere lowered his gun and tucked it back in his waist. Before I could react he hauled off and punched me in my jaw so hard it felt like my bones shattered. I screamed out in agony as my legs wobbled then buckled.

"I'mma beat you to death with my bare hands," he growled.

Seeing how psychotic this nigga had become, I knew that it was a matter of time before he unleashed his wrath on me. A voice in my head kept saying I was gonna die.

Not tonight, I thought. And if I do it'll be fighting!

"Help-p-p-p!" My grandmother began to yell. "Somebody help us—"

Syncere turned his back on me to silence my grandmother. I seized the opportunity, while his back was turned, to reach inside my purse and grab the pistol Quincy had given me. With shaky hands both firmly clasping the gun, I aimed at his back, closed my eyes and fired once.

Boom!

It sounded like a canon exploded. My eyes flew open just in time to watch Syncere hit the floor. I fired three more times out of fear. I *needed* for him to be dead.

"Nikki . . . oh, Nikki," my grandmother wept in anguish.

I rushed to her side and told her not to move while I called the police. I think she was in shock.

"Don't leave me," she said, grabbing my arm tightly.

"Grandma, he can't hurt you. Everything's all right," I assured her. "Let me get the police over here to help us."

Once I calmed her down, I got on the telephone and called the police. Within minutes, flashing red and white lights, emergency sirens and homicide detectives littered the block. The crime scene was taped off and I was cornered inside my grandmother's kitchen for three hours under intense questioning. It never occurred to me that the homicide detectives would question my self-defense theory. They almost tripped me up when they asked where I had gotten the gun to kill Syncere. Luckily, I was thinking on my feet and said that he'd brought it with him and dropped it during our struggle.

"Ms. Simpson, would you mind coming down to the station? We have more questions to ask," one of the detectives stated.

"Tonight?"

"Yes, Ma'am."

"Look, I'm exhausted, I have to get my grandmother out of here and we both need to get some sleep. I'm sure whatever you need to ask me can wait."

"When forensics come back you may need a lawyer," the detective threatened.

"How 'bout I lawyer up now! This interview is over."

I hope they didn't start any bullshit and try to harass my ass over Syncere. On my way out I overheard one of the detectives running down my arrest jacket. He was talking about me as if I was some drug-trafficking, gun wielding, gangsta bitch!

I knew it was really my cue to get the fuck outta dodge.

* * *

After I settled down in the guest room of my parents house, I took out Kira's diary and wrote down everything that transpired over the last few days. I wrote every single detail and even jotted down my conversation with Quincy about why Syncere had Mark murdered. The diary as a way to communicate with Kira and fill in the blanks to all the questions she had before her life was taken. Too bad I couldn't do anything about Papí and Carlos for killing her because she took fucking money from them. But, knowing how karma works, they would get what was coming to them. Fucking bastards!

26

The Unexpected

Rhonda Speaks

Today was a very busy day for the shop. We had clients sitting all around the salon waiting to be serviced and it was packed. I was tending to a client when Tabitha burst through the front door of the salon late, bringing attention to herself.

"Rhonda, girl, did you see the news this morning?"

I looked up from my client's hair and said, "Nah, who was on it?"

"Your girl Nikki was up there."

Shocked at Tabitha's response, I asked, "For what?"

"For killing her ex-boyfriend."

"What! When did this happen?"

"She told the police that when she was about to leave her grandmother's house to go to the grocery store, her ex-boyfriend, who had just got out of jail, was standing at the front door when she opened it. She said he forced her back into the house and threatened to kill her and her grandmother if she didn't do what he said. So, she cooperated with him until he struck her in the back of her head with the butt of his gun."

"Oh my God, Syncere pistol-whipped her?"

"He sure did. After he did that she somehow managed to get one of his guns from him and shot him."

"You bullshitting me!"

"No, I'm not," Tabitha assured me and then she turned around to walk over to her station. "Turn to the news channel. They'll probably show it again at twelve o'clock."

"Did they say how her grandmother was doing? She must have been so scared. That lady has been through enough. First Kira now this."

"Yeah, they said she was doing fine and Nikki had only suffered minor injuries."

"So, did they say if Nikki was going to be facing a murder charge?"

"Shit! You know she ain't being as though he was the one that intruded in on them with a whole bunch of fucking guns, threatening to kill 'em. Trust me, self-defense is written all over that one."

"You sure got a point there," I commented and tried desperately to pick up from where I left off with my client's hair. As soon as I was done and my client paid for my services, I picked up my cell phone and rushed to the back office for some privacy. I dialed my house number and waited patiently for Tony to answer. He answered on the third ring.

"Have you seen the news?"

"Nah, what happened?"

"Syncere got shot and killed," I whispered loud enough for him to hear me.

"Who did it?"

"Nikki."

"What! Nah, I don't believe that."

"It's true. They showed it on the news earlier."

"So, what did the news people say?"

"They just went into the spiel about how he ran up in Nikki's grandmother's house. Then after he went in there, he smacked Nikki on the floor and terrorized her and her grandmother."

"Goddamn! That nigga Syncere wasn't playing, huh?"

"He may not have been but he sure fucked up when he let his guard down. Because Nikki said that as soon as he turned his back she tricked him up and got his gun."

"Boy, she's one lucky bitch," Tony commented.

"You sure ain't lying about that."

"Hey, do you think Syncere told her that I reached out to him while he was on lock and blew the whistle on her?"

"I don't know," I said with hesitation. Then I changed my tone in an effort to make Tony feel a little easy and said, "But, knowing the type of nigga he was, I don't believe he would even run his mouth like that."

"Well, I hope not, 'cause I ain't trying to get caught up in no attempted murder charges on her and her grandmother."

"Shit! Me neither!"

"Well, keep your mouth closed just in case one of dem crackers come rolling up to the shop and start asking you questions," he instructed.

"A'ight."

"I mean, don't tell 'em shit! Just act like you don't know a damn thang. And that goes for them tramps you got working in there too."

"Come on now, you know I don't fuck with my stylists like that. Them hoes talk entirely too much for me."

"Yeah, whatever," he said. "All y'all just alike. Couldn't hold a muthafucking cup of water if it killed cha'!"

"Boy, I ain't trying to hear that mess you talking."

"Good, 'cause I'm about to hop in the shower."

"Hey, wait, do me a favor."

"What?"

"Take out a pack of hamburger so it thaws by the time I get off."

"Whatcha gon' cook?"

"Spaghetti."

"What time you coming home?"

"It's going to be kind of late, because I've got a shop packed with clients today."

"Well, don't worry about it. I'll fix the spaghetti."

"Thank you, baby."

"A'ight," he replied and then we ended the call.

Finally my day had come to an end and, as usual, I was the last one to leave the shop. I didn't mind though because my pockets were filled with a stack of greenbacks and all of them happened to be my favorite presidents. After I set the alarm and shut off all the lights, I let myself out of the door. The parking lot was heavily lit, so I wasn't worried when I leaned over to lock the door with my key. But, before I could turn around to leave, a man dressed in all black rushed up behind me. Before I could scream for help, he covered my mouth with a damp cloth filled with liquid chloroform. I tried to put up a fight but this stuff started working on me in seconds and before I knew it, my body went completely numb and I lost consciousness.

"I only ask you once," he said in his thick native tongue, "Where she live?"

"Who are you?"

I sat handcuffed to a chair in a dark warehouse looking at a Hispanic man I'd never seen before.

The three-inch hunting knife with the jagged blade tore into my knee and I screamed out in agony, "Nooooooo!" My life flashed before me as my bottom lip trembled. I tried reasoning with him, "I'll tell you what you need to know just promise me that you'll let me live. I have a family."

"I promise only one thing, *mami*. You tell me what I need—your death will be painless . . . If not, you'll die slow!"

27

Now Or Never

Nikki Speaks

Because of Syncere's death and the attempt on my life my mom and dad convinced me to go out of town to live with relatives for a while, at least until all of this blew over. They made a good point concerning all the media attention but most importantly regarding my life. I didn't fight the issue. Once all the proper paperwork was cleared through my probation officer, my dad made time to run me over to my apartment to gather several things that I needed for this trip. It didn't take me long at all to pack everything I needed so my impatient daddy loved it.

My scheduled flight out of Virginia was at two-thirty in the afternoon and I managed to pack all of my things with my mother's help, of course. I was ready to go.

Once I placed all of my luggage down in the hallway by the front door, I took a seat in the den area to catch my breath. My grandmother was watching the news when I walked into the room.

"Are you ready to leave for the airport?" she asked.

"Not yet but I will be in about three more hours."

"How do you feel?"

"I'm fine, Grandma. What about you? Are you still getting headaches?"

"No, baby. God has truly brought me through this ordeal."

"I'm glad."

"What about you? Do you still think that there isn't a need for you to go and see a psychiatrist, after all that you've suffered?"

"I don't need to talk to a shrink, Grandma. All I need is your prayers."

"Well, you done already got them," she assured me. "So, what time is your dad gon' leave to take you to the airport?"

"I'm not sure. But before I go, I'm gonna take a ride out to Kira's grave and sit out there for a while and talk to her."

"Yeah, that might do you some good."

We talked for a few more minutes until I grew restless of her continuous, unwanted advice. I know that she's what you would call a wise old lady and I also know she meant well, but when I've had enough, I've had enough.

Before I left the house, I realized that both of my parents had stepped out, so I left them a note telling them I was going to visit Kira's grave and that I would be back within the hour. On my way to the grave, I made a call to Quincy's cell phone, but I didn't get an answer. So I called the car wash next and a woman picked up the phone.

"Sparkle's Carwash and Detailing," she said.

"Hi, can I speak to Quincy?"

"Honey, Quincy ain't here."

"Do you know what time he's coming in?"

"Honey, ain't nobody seen Quincy in a couple of days. Who is this?"

"Just a friend. Who is this?" I said.

"I'm the other owner's mother."

"Is this Syncere's mother?"

"Yes, this is she. Who is this?"

"When you finally see Quincy, could you tell him Sabrina called?"

"All right," she said. And then I quickly hung up.

After my conversation with Syncere's mother, I had to pull my car over to the side of the road because my heart started beating uncontrollably.

I also got an uneasy feeling in the pit of my stomach. Before I could even catch my breath, my cell phone started ringing off the damn hook. I looked down at the caller ID and saw the word *private*; I elected not to answer it. I figured that whoever it may have been really could not have wanted to talk to me, especially by blocking their phone number. So, I said to hell with 'em.

It took me about ten minutes to get myself back together to make this drive. As I merged back onto the road, I began to wonder about Quincy. I couldn't believe that no one had seen him at the spot in a couple of days. That wasn't his typical behavior especially not when it came to his money. I flipped my phone open and re-dialed his number, but his voicemail came on the first ring once again. I started to leave him a voicemail, but at the last minute I decided not to. However, I did elect to make a quick detour to his house to see if I saw his car parked outside.

Quincy's car wasn't parked outside of his place, so I decided to write him a little note and leave it in his mailbox. That way, when he returned home, he'd know that I was there and to hit me up as soon as he got the chance. I completed the three-line note, folded it in half, stepped out of my car and headed toward the mailbox mounted on the wall next to his front door. But before I could barely get onto his front porch I heard a noise coming from the inside of the house, so I stopped in my tracks and stood very still.

I realized that it was a television I was hearing. "Oh shoot, he might be in the house after all," I commented out loud and proceeded up the stairs. Instead of sticking the note down in the mailbox, I knocked on the door and waited for Quincy to come to the door. But after making several attempts to see if he was indeed in the house, it had become apparent that he wasn't, so I reached over and stuck the note into his mailbox.

As I made my way back off the front porch, something told me to take a quick peep through his living room window since the curtain was slightly open. Unfortunately, I wasn't able to see much. And even though the curtains were slightly ajar, the only thing I could see was the back of the television and half of his leather sofa. I gave up and walked away from the window. Before I could make it down the stairs, a voice from out of nowhere said, "Are you looking for the young man who lives there?"

Startled by the sudden outburst, I looked up in the direction of the voice and saw this short, old, white lady peeping over her brown wooden fence. Judging from the gray hair slightly covered by a fashionable straw hat, she looked every bit of sixty years old.

When I got down by my car, I answered her by saying, "Yes, I am. Have you seen him today?"

"No, I'm afraid not," the elderly woman replied in a low whisper. "But, I did see him when he came in late last night with some woman."

"Do you remember about what time that was?"

"Well, the eleven o'clock news had just went off, so I'm assuming it was a little after eleven-thirty. They didn't stay long at all and about an hour later, I heard the woman scream to the top of her voice. I quickly climbed out of my bed to see if I could help but by the time I got to my bedroom window, I saw his BMW flying out of here like a bat out of hell."

"Did you see who was driving?"

"No, I didn't. It was too dark."

"So, you're saying you haven't seen him since?"

"No," the woman replied.

"What about the young lady he was with?"

"No, I haven't seen her either."

"Has anyway else been here?"

"No."

"Well, do you think that they could've been fighting?"

"It's hard to say, because I only heard her scream that one time."

"Well, have you ever heard him getting into any fights with a woman?"

"No. He's a pretty quiet neighbor," she started off. "I only hear him when he comes and goes. So, it kind of shocked me when I heard the commotion, which is why I called the police. But when they arrived and knocked on his door, no one answered, so, of course, they had no other choice but to leave. I talked to them before they left and told them exactly what I heard, so they advised me to give them a call back if the commotion started up again. But, it didn't so I went back to bed."

Tickled by this lady's ability and willingness to play private eye, I smiled at her and said, "I know your neighbors really appreciate you."

She smiled back and said, "Oh, they most certainly do."

"Well, I'm quite sure Quincy does too."

"Oh, is that his name?"

"Yes, ma' am. And I promise you that the next time I talk to him, I'm going to let him know how fortunate he is to have you as his next door neighbor."

"Oh, you don't have to do that," she said and smiled.

"Oh, no. I insist," I replied and took two steps backward in an effort to get the hell away from this talking-ass woman.

"You getting ready to leave?" she asked.

"Yes, ma'am. I gotta go."

"Well, what's your name?"

"Nicole. But, everybody calls me Nikki."

"Well, it's nice meeting you, Nicole. And my name is Mrs. Bentley. But, my friends call me Rose."

"Nice meeting you too, Ms. Rose," I told her and continued to take several steps backward. "Oh and if you happen to see my friend, could you please tell him that I came by?"

"I most certainly will."

"Thank you."

"You're welcome, sweetie," she replied in the most sincere manner, walked away from the fence and headed back into her house.

I jumped back into my car and took one last look at Quincy's crib before I put my car in reverse and rolled out of there for good. I looked back one more time and my attention focused on something that looked like a silhouette of a person's body standing a few feet back from the upstairs bedroom window. When I saw this image, my heart dropped. I figured that my eyes had to be playing tricks on me because I didn't remember seeing it when I first pulled up. And if it was there, then how did I miss it? It was kind of weird but I wasn't gon' jump to conclusions if I was seeing things. I closed my eyes and when I opened them again, I hoped the shadow or whatever the hell was behind that window would be gone. But, as soon as I opened my eyes and glanced back up at the window, that image was still there. My gut feeling told me to carry my ass because something just didn't seem right.

That nosey ass little bird in the back of my mind told me

to get out of the car and find out who was in the bedroom watching my every move. And guess what? My crazy ass listened to that little bird and I could have sworn that shadow looked like the woman he brought home last night. Of course that shit doesn't sit right with me. I mean, how dare that bastard bring another chick home? Hadn't we just shared something special the other night? If he wanted some companionship, he could've called me. But since he hadn't, I was gonna use the spare key he gave me and see what the hell was going on? Shit, I needed to know how serious they were. I wasn't gon' go off on her.

I was just gonna ask her a few questions because my feelings were hurt. I really felt betrayed so somebody was gon' tell me something.

It didn't take me long to get in the house because I was really anxious to see what she looked like. And right after I closed the front door behind me, I stormed right upstairs. The hardwood floor tile Quincy had throughout his entire home, including on this staircase, made a lot of *squeaking* noise when you walked on top of it. But, I didn't care because I kept right on moving.

After all that *squeaking* noise, I finally made it to the top of the staircase, walked straight to the door on my right, grabbed the doorknob and forced the door open. And when the door hit the wall behind it, my heart collapsed and my mouth flew wide open.

"Oh shit!" I said, and dropped my cellular phone to the floor.

One part of me wanted to run like hell, but then the other part of me told me not to. I took a deep breath and listened to the part of me that told me to stick around. I got the courage to move a couple steps forward and my entire body was instantly filled with anxiety. But, I couldn't let the anxiety consume me because I needed to figure out how Quincy and this woman died.

Before I entered into the bedroom completely, I glanced around the entire room from top to bottom and wondered to myself how and when their deaths took place. Quincy was sitting upright in the chair before the window, which explained the shadow I saw from my car. He seemed to have gotten the worst of it and as I began to walk closer to him, the black eye and bruises all over his face became more visible. His arms, legs and mouth were wrapped up in gray electrical tape, he was stripped naked and had a single gun shot wound to his head. The chick he was laid up with was none other than Sunshine.

My heart went out to her that instant and when I looked closer, I realized that she escaped the beating and got two gunshot wounds to the chest. The cat who ran up in here had obviously caught them both off guard, because the way she was positioned indicated that she was killed instantly. She probably died right after Mrs. Rose said she heard her scream. Quincy, on the other hand, looked like he was forced to get out of the bed. I tried to figure out why somebody would torture and kill 'em like this? I mean, he was a cool guy and mad niggas respected him, so what the hell could he have done to make somebody want to take his life?

Then it came to me: Carlos had been here. This had his name written all over it.

How did he find the house? This place was not even in Quincy's name. But then, I forgot who I was talking about. Papí had connects across the country with unlimited access to people's personal information. I had to get out of the house before he came back and tried to kill me too. Before I left I searched his entire bedroom for a safe.

I knew that if I found one it would be filled with a lot of dough. After going through everything with a fine tooth comb, I ran across a fireproof lockbox stored in his bottom dresser drawer underneath a pile of T-shirts and boxer shorts. The metal box was locked , but there wasn't a key in sight. I picked the box up anyway because I figured I could find a way to break into it later.

On my way out of Quincy's house, I retraced all my steps and made sure I wiped down every doorknob I touched. I even wiped my footprint off the door to Quincy's bedroom. Didn't want the homicide detectives thinking that I was a jealous girlfriend and killed them out of rage. No can do. Couldn't let that happen. After I closed the front door behind myself, I immediately wiped off the knob and crept back down the back steps. While I was making my way back to my car, I made sure I checked out my surroundings. Fortunately for me, no one was standing outside or looking out of their windows. I was relieved once I got back into my car and hopped back onto the highway.

I honestly didn't know if I was coming or going. My heart was beating like crazy and my adrenaline was pumping out of control. I knew that Carlos was somewhere in the area but I didn't know where. The best thing for me to do was get the hell out of town, fast.

On my way back to my grandmother's house, I thought about how the police were going to be swarming all over Quincy's place real soon. And the most important factor was that I wasn't gonna be involved in that investigation. God knows I'd had my share of police asking me questions. Damn it, I just remembered that I left Quincy a note in his mailbox telling him to call me. Ahhh, shit! The police were going to be all over me and wanting to know how I knew this guy. If it was the same investigator on Kira's case, I knew he was gonna wonder why everybody

I came in contact with got murdered. It was, of course, a damn good question. I just couldn't answer the question at that moment. Time would tell, though. In the meantime, I had to get out of town before I ran across somebody else's dead body.

After finding Quincy and Sunshine's dead bodies, I was in no shape to go out to the graveyard to say goodbye to Kira. Instead, I headed straight to my grandmother's house.

Still shook up about all the shit that was going on, I felt myself falling into an emotional slump. And the only way I knew that I could get through this was if I talked to someone. But, who? I mean, I couldn't go to the police because I'd be sucked in another freaking investigation. Besides, I didn't need that type of heat on me. My probation officer was already breathing down my neck about the Kira, Mark and Syncere murders. I couldn't have her sending the U.S. Marshals down on my trail because I was in the wrong place at the wrong time. No way!

Upon my arrival, I drove straight into the garage. On my way out of the car, I grabbed the lockbox off the seat next to me and headed into the house. When I walked through the kitchen I realized that I was alone from the note my grandmother left on the kitchen table. The note said that she was out running errands with my mom and that she would be back soon. I sat the lockbox down on the table next to the note so I could find something to pry it open with. My first thought was to get a screwdriver and a hammer and try to break open the safe. I grabbed the tools out of the utility closet next to the kitchen and started working on the lock. The curiosity of knowing how much Q had stashed in here was killing the hell out of me so I started banging the box harder. I noticed that the lock was giving way and I started getting excited. But, all that came to an abrupt end when I looked up and realized that I was not alone after all. Standing at the doorway of the entrance to the kitchen was my grandmother and she looked distraught. I stood up from the chair and asked, "Grandma are you all right?"

She didn't answer so I walked over to ask her again and Carlos came right up from behind her. As soon as he stepped away from her she fell down to the floor with her eyes still open. I knew she was dead and the thought just killed me.

"Why did you have to kill her?" I screamed, taking huge steps backward.

Carlos had his gun, with a silencer screwed into the end of the barrel, pointed directly at me. I knew my life was about to end. I guess I had run long enough. "Why did you have to kill my grandmother?"

"I kill any and everything that stands in my way."

"Is that why you killed Quincy and that woman in his bed?"

"He got what he deserved and so did Rhonda."

"Rhonda!" I replied, as if I was shocked to hear her name.

"Yes, Rhonda. She told me where you lived and where your grandmother and parents lived. Yeah, she gave you up before I put her to sleep as well." He took two steps toward me. "She even told me that Ricky caught his federal case because of you and how you and Kira snitched on him so you could get out of jail."

Instead of responding, I just stood there and started praying silently. Carlos pulled back on the chamber to place a bullet into position, so I abruptly shut my eyes. When I heard the first bullet igniting from the chamber, I reacted on impulse and ducked down. I threw both of my hands across my head to stop the inevitable.

Pow! Pow! I heard the shots exploding from the barrel. The shots were followed by a loud thud, so I removed both of my hands from above my head and opened my eyes slowly. When my eyes focused and I saw what was before me, my mind completely shut down. I felt a sense of *relief* and the speed of my heartbeat began to decline.

"Are you all right?" It was the same Caucasian detective who'd been investigating both Kira and Syncere's murders.

With a distraught expression on my face, I managed to nod my head. I said, "Oh my, God! I thought I would never say this to you in a million years, but I am so glad to see you."

"I'm sure you are," he replied, as he took precautionary measures to make sure we were safe. He began this task by kneeling down over Carlos's body to see if he had a pulse.

"Is he dead?" I asked, taking a few steps backward.

"Yes, he is," he assured me as he retrieved Carlos's handgun from the kitchen floor. He got on his radio and called for backup, along with a forensics team.

I ran over to my grandmother's side and started bawling my eyes out. The detective left me alone until backup came. When the coroners came in to take her body away, I really went ballistic. I tried to hold on to her for dear life, but they pried my arms from around her neck. "Please don't take her away," I begged.

"I'm sorry for your loss Nicole but you're gonna have to calm down," the detective told me.

"Calm down," I screamed. "How the fuck am I going to do that, when everybody around me is dying like flies."

"Nicole, you're gonna need to have a seat." He pointed directly at one of the kitchen chairs.

As soon as I sat down, a female police officer came over and told me to get up and follow them outside. When I got outside, the officer escorted me over to a patrol car and asked me to stand next to it, so I could give a full statement about everything that transpired. I didn't hold shit back. I broke everything down to her about how I found Quincy and Sunshine's bodies inside his house right before I came home. I even explained to her why he was killed and that Sunshine was just at the wrong place at the wrong time. Before I could give her in-depth information about why Kira was murdered, two more police vehicles and one unmarked car drove up. Every officer in uniform got out of their cars and started walking in our direction. For some reason, the officer in the unmarked car stayed behind. He was acting pretty weird to me so I watched him closely as he got out of his car, retrieved a bulletproof vest from his trunk and walked back toward his car door. It was even more strange when he opened up the back door and tossed the jacket inside. I was thinking to myself, *what the hell is he doing?* A woman started getting out of the car and when she stepped completely out of the car my mouth fell open as my heart began to race.

"Oh my God, Kira!" I screamed with mixed emotions as I sprinted toward her.

Hearing me scream her name, Kira smiled back at me and continued to walk in my direction, with the officer escorting her. When we were finally face to face, tears poured from my eyes and all I wanted to do was hold her in my arms. While I was holding her, I pulled my head back and asked, "Why did they tell me that you were dead?"

"Because this was the only way they could tie Papí to all the murders."

"So, you used me as bait?" I asked in confusion.

"Believe me, it wasn't really like that," she began to explain. "They were protecting you the whole time. While I was in the Witness Protection Program, I inquired about you every step of the way. If they didn't have anything positive to tell me about how the investigation was progressing, I went off."

"That's bull, Kira!" I snapped. "Because if they were on their game then Grandma wouldn't have gotten killed."

"Grandma is dead?"

"What? They didn't tell you," I snapped.

"Oh my God! Where is she?"

"She's gone. They took her body out of the house right before you came up."

In a panic, Kira grabbed my arms. "What happened?"

"That same muthafucker who shot you and left you for dead in your bathroom shower came up in here and killed her trying to get to me." Bawling her eyes out, Kira just stood there and said nothing. "And before he took Grandma out, that bastard killed Rhonda, Quincy, and Sunshine."

"Sunshine," she uttered with an expression of confusion.

"Yeah, Sunshine," I said, my face turning sour. "The one that used to work for you."

"But, I thought she was in jail."

"She was until about a week and a half ago."

"How did she get out?" Kira asked.

"She said she won her appeal," I responded, still aggravated. I said, "Look, I don't wanna talk about her. I wanna know why y'all used me like that?"

Feeling my pain of betrayal, Kira grabbed both of my hands and held them. "Listen, I know you're upset. But, after being shot two times, I was under a lot of stress. When the Feds came at me while I was in the hospital and told me that they could help me if I went into a Witness Protection Program, I gave in and said okay."

"Kira, we were in this shit together! Why did you leave me out of the loop?"

"They said it would be better that way."

"They don't know what's best for you. All they care about is using niggas to get other muthafuckers locked up," I yelled, snatching my hands from hers.

"Would you feel any better if I told you that Grandma knew about the whole thing?"

"She what?"

"Don't be mad, because they told her she couldn't utter a word."

"I'm not mad about that. I'm mad because y'all used her as a pawn and now she's gone," I said and then stormed toward the garage.

Kira came running behind me. "I need to keep a visual on you," the detective escorting her said, as he followed her.

"Okay." When she caught up with me, she cornered me and said, "Please Nikki, don't be mad at me."

"Kira, I'm not trying to hear that. A lot of people got killed behind this bogus shit you and the Feds conjured up."

Kira continued crying. "I know and I'm sorry. But, after I gave them the green light, I pretty much didn't have any say. If I would've known that it was gonna turn out like this I wouldn't have done it."

"So, what's gonna happen now?" I asked, looking at her escort.

"Now that we've got Carlos, we can link him to the big guy in D.C."

"Why couldn't you do it before?" I asked him. "You had Kira as a witness."

"Yeah, we did. But, she couldn't tell us who the guy was. All she could give us was his description and tell us he worked for Papí. We sent a surveillance team out there to see if we could gather any information on who he was or catch him at the location. We never had any luck until the day you and Quincy stopped by. That day was the very first time we got a glimpse of who he was. When he realized that you knew who he was, we knew that he was going to try to get rid of you. We elected to have around-the-clock surveillance on your place, as well as your grandmother's place."

Angered by his explanation, I said, "Why didn't y'all have surveillance on Carlos's ass?"

"We did. But somehow, he got wind of it and found a way to do a disappearing act."

"Well, where was the surveillance team when Quincy got killed? I mean, why couldn't y'all have prevented he and Sunshine from getting murdered?"

"Yeah, we could've. But, since we didn't deem him to be an important asset to this investigation, we didn't ask for the funding."

"Damn! That's fucked up," I yelled. "Whatcha do, just toy with people's lives?"

"Calm down, Nikki," Kira said to me as she pulled me back into her arms. "I know you're upset about Quincy. But, this investigation had to go this way, or we would have gotten killed, too."

"Look, are y'all through with questioning me? Because I'm ready to get out of town," I said and sighed heavily as I began to wipe the tears away from my face.

"I know you are but, unfortunately, we're gonna have to escort you down to the precinct first. We need to ask you some more questions," the same detective said.

Kira and I began to walk back in the direction of the police cars. When we sat down in the backseat, she looked over at me and said, "I promise I'm gonna make this up to you."

"Try bringing Grandma back."

"Come on now, Nikki. You know that's not fair."

"Well, what else do you want me to say?"

"I want you to say that you forgive me so that we can move forward and mourn the loss of Grandma together."

I refused to reply to Kira. She put her arms around my neck and hugged me. "I ain't gon' lie, Nikki. I missed you more than anything in this world." She began to cry as she held me. "And as soon as all this mess is over with, I'm gon' get out of that Witness Protection Program and start my life over. It would mean a lot to me, if you would come with me."

"Where are you going?"

"I'm not sure and it really doesn't matter as long as it's somewhere away from here. So, will you come?"

"I don't know," I said, 'cause I really wasn't interested.

"Well, I know you'll decide when the time is right," Kira stated.

The detective put the car in drive and sped off. I looked back at the entire scene of detectives and forensic specialists parading around my grandmother's property. My mind was in a complete uproar. I couldn't picture how my life was going to play out from this point on. I was also having mixed feelings about Kira's motives for going into the Witness Protection Program. I know she loved me and meant well, but I couldn't just let her come back in my life like everything was all fine and dandy. Hell nah! All this anger I got built up in me ain't gon' just go away like that.

After a couple of weeks, I finally accepted Kira's apology and afterward we were fine. The Feds finally dragged Papí and the rest of his crew to jail. After Kira and I testified for the grand jury and during their trials, they all got life sentences, except Papí. He got the death penalty. You should've seen his face when Kira and I stood on the stand to testify against him. He had the look of death on his face. Immediately after his sentencing, we got the hell out of town. We found a cozy spot in Houston, Texas, and now we're having a ball. Cats over here are different breed compared to those from D.C. and New Jersey. And they love to spend money too. Shit, if this *Southern Hospitality* keeps up, I might fuck around and become one of these niggas' *wifey*.

Want more Kiki Swinson?

Catch a preview of Kiki Swinson's novella,
"Keeping My Enemies Close"
from *Sleeping With the Enemy*

Available now at your local bookstore!

Chapter 1

Men aren't worth shit

"He better be gone when I get home. I put up with a lot of his shit, and this was the last straw," I mumbled out loud as I waited for the traffic light to turn green. The woman in the next car probably thought I was losing my mind. I was so preoccupied with my ongoing conversation I could not have cared less what she thought. And as soon as the light turned green, I left her in the dust and was immediately reminded that I was less than two blocks away from my apartment.

A huge knot formed in the pit of my stomach the instant I pulled into my apartment complex. The thick summer air smacked me in the face the moment I opened up my car door. As we all know, the summer brings out the freaks, so the parking lot behind my apartment building was crawling with people. Right after I locked my car door and began to walk toward my building, all the so-called hustlers lined up alongside their vehicles and started whistling at me, but I couldn't be bothered. *Been there done that, got the T-shirt and the hat. I'd rather work for mine. It's time for me to rise to the top and stand on my own two feet*, I reminded myself.

One guy in particular kept making comments about how he would love to take me out to dinner and get to know me better. When I continued to ignore him, his true colors came out.

"Oh, bitch, you ain't all that just because you're pretty with long hair and a fat ass. I fuck with hoes that look better than you!" he screamed.

But again, I refused to entertain any of their bullshit. Every last one of those lame-ass niggas had at least three baby mamas, drove a pimped-out Chevy or an Oldsmobile with 20-inch rims, and had an IQ of 105. They were immature as hell, and as soon as they ran across a half-Indian and black chick with a college degree and some class such as myself, they got all intimidated and started showing their asses. So the way I handled them was by ignoring them and keeping it moving. I sure wish I would have done the same thing with the nigga I spent damn near four years with.

When I met Todd, so-called man, I thought that he could change the world. Yes, I knew he was a hustler from Young's Park, but what did I care; he gave the money and excitement I was looking for. Not to mention he was F-I-N-E. He had a body to die for, which I later found out came from having nothing to do but work out during a five-year bid in Indian Creek State Penitentiary.

At first, blinded by Gucci bags and Jimmy Choo shoes, I overlooked his blatant infidelity. But after six trips to my primary care physician for antibiotics to cure my dripping pussy, I had had enough. The last time he cheated, I warned him that I would not take it anymore, but what did this motherfucker do? He pushed the envelope, tested the waters, and started fucking with a nineteen-year-old chick named Rema that lived right around the block from me. And to make matters worse, I heard the bitch was three months pregnant. Now what kind of shit was that? But you know what? It's okay. She can have his grimey ass because I am done with his bullshit once and for all.

Now, as soon as I stepped into my apartment, I immediately knew something was amiss. I was overwhelmed by a strong odor; it smelled like Clorox mixed with ammonia. I began coughing and gagging. "What the hell?" I said out loud as I continued down the short hallway toward my bedroom. The smell got stronger the farther I went. And when I entered my bedroom, I found that my closet door was gaping wide open. Upon further review, I noticed that every stitch of my clothes were gone. "Wait, now I know this nigga didn't steal all my damn clothes," I said to myself, confused. By now I had my hands covering my mouth and nose because the fumes were so strong. I closed the closet door, noticing that the sheets were missing from my bed, and the mattress had been sliced and diced, with cotton spilling out of it like a gutted animal. I began to get nervous. I ran into the bathroom, which was adjacent to the bedroom. There I noticed that my medicine cabinet hung open and was empty; the cabinet under the sink was also empty of my toiletries and smell-good essentials. The mirror on the medicine cabinet was smashed, and the glass lay in the small sink below it. Even my cushioned toilet seat had been sliced up, which would have made taking a shit impossible at that moment, although the nervous knot in my stomach was forcing me to feel the urge. Nevertheless, nothing prepared me for what I found next. Amidst all of the coughing, gagging, and eye tearing, I managed to pull back the shower curtain. "OH NO THE FUCK HE DIDN'T!" I screamed, incensed.

Todd had filled the tub with water, bleach, ammonia, Mr. Clean, laundry detergent, and any other household cleaner he could find, and put everything I owned—my clothes, toiletries, shoes, boots, expensive handbags, my mink jacket, contact lenses, bed sheets, towels, and face cloths—in the solution. All of my shit was ruined; there was no saving it. The bleach and ammonia together could make a bomb, so by mixing it, it had eaten away most of the material that comprised my belongings. Smoke was rising from the bathtub, and I was scared that if I touched anything, it would explode. I left the bathroom in shock, I ran into the kitchen to survey if he had done any other damage, and yes, he'd struck again. I found all my dishes broken and in the sink. The glasses were broken into shards so small it appeared that he must have taken his time with a spoon or a hammer to smash them. I could not even get the glass out of the drain; that's just how small the pieces were. By this time, I was hysterical. I walked into the living room expecting disaster, and once again Todd didn't disappoint me. He had sliced up the leather sofa and the love seat. The DVD player and Sony surround sound system lay in shambles. I pressed the power button on the television, and sparks started flying out of the back. Seeing this sent me running. The TV didn't explode, but I later found out that he had poured water into the back of it. I stood outside the front door of my apartment and fumbled through my handbag for my cell phone. When I finally found it through all the junk I had scattered inside, I grabbed it and immediately dialed my best friend Tenisha's number.

"Hello," she answered with a hoarse voice, pretending to be asleep.

"You sleep?" I asked, my voice quivering.

"Yeah," Tenisha breathed into the receiver.

"Well, get up! You ain't gonna believe what this nigga did to me!" I screamed.

"Mmmmm," she moaned, hoping that if she sounded like she was out of it, I would tell her I'd call her later.

"Come on, Tee, I know that fake sleep act. Now, get up

and stop being selfish all of your life! I need to talk to you!" I yelled, on the brink of tears.

"Okay . . . what happened now?" she asked, reluctantly. I knew she was tired of all my Todd stories, especially after all I'd been through with him and always managed to give him the benefit of the doubt and go running back to him with open arms. But this time it was different—he was gone for good this time. So I needed her shoulder to lean on.

"Girl, he destroyed everything I owned. He put all my shit in the tub and poured bleach, ammonia, and whatever else he could find in it." I began to cry. Then ten seconds later, I broke down.

"Why did he do that?" she asked nonchalantly.

"Because I told his ass to get out."

"Well, this ain't the first time you told him to get out, so there must be something you're not telling me."

"I just found out that bitch Rema is pregnant."

"You mean that young chick he was fucking around with?"

"Yes, and she's parading around here telling everybody, too."

"Oh, now *that's* serious."

"I know. And that's why I couldn't let that one slide."

"You did right by putting his no-good ass out. But I think I would've done it a different way, like change the locks or something so he would not have gotten in to mess your shit up."

"Well, it's too late for that," I replied between sobs.

"So, what are you going to do now?"

"I don't know. But I can't stay here while the place is like this."

"Wait there, I'm gonna come by and see you," she said.

"Okay, I'll be standing outside waiting for you," I told her, and then we hung up.

Turn the page for a preview of Kiki Swinson's
Wifey
and
I'm Still Wifey

Available now at your local bookstore!

From WIFEY

Tired of the Drama

It's 4:30 a.m. in the morning and I've been pacing back and forth from my bed to my bedroom window, which overlooked the driveway of my six-hundred-thousand-dollar house, waiting for my husband Ricky to bring dat ass home. Who cared about all the plucks he had to make every other night? I kept telling him, all money ain't good money! But he didn't listen. Not to mention, I had to deal with all his hoes on a daily basis. We've been married for seven years now, and since then I've had to spend a whole lot of nights alone in this gorgeous five-bedroom home he got for us two years ago. That's how his three children came into play. All of them were by different chickenheads who lived in the projects. But one of them had a Section Eight crib somewhere in D.C. and she was ghetto as hell. Just like the other two, who lived not too far from here.

Now, Ricky didn't have enough sense to go out and donate his sperm to women with some class. Every last one of them were high school dropouts, holding eighth-grade educations and an ass full of drama. They figured since Ricky had a baby by them, that he was gonna leave me to be with their nasty tails. Oh, but trust me! It won't happen! Not in *this* lifetime. Because all they could offer him was pussy. And the last time I checked, pussy wasn't in high demand these days like them hoes thought. That's why I could say with much confidence—that *Ricky needed me*. I kept his hot-headed ass straight. And not only that, I've got assets. I'm light-skinned and very pretty with a banging ass body! Niggas in the street said I reminded them of the rapper Trina because both of us favored each other and we had small waists and big asses. And to complement all that, I knew how to play most of the games on the street, as well as the ins and outs of running the hair salon I opened a few years back. Not to mention, Ricky gave me the dough to make it happen. Now you see, he was good for something other than screwing other chicks behind my back. This was why I was always trying to find reasons not to leave his ass.

So, after pacing back and forth a few more times, Mr. Good Dick finally pulled his sedan into the driveway. I made my way on downstairs to greet his butt at the front door. "What you doing up?" he asked as soon as he saw me standing in the foyer.

"Ricky, don't ask me no stupid-ass questions!" I told him with much attitude. Then I moved backward two steps, giving him enough room to shut the front door.

"What you upset for?" he responded with uncertainty.

I'm standing dead smack in front of my husband, who is, by the way, very, very handsome with a set of six packs out of this world. I'm wearing one of my newest Victoria's Secret lingerie pieces, looking extra sexy; and all he could do was stand there looking stupid and ask me what I'm upset for? I wanted so badly to smack the hell outta him; but I decided to remain a lady and continue to get him where it hurts, which is his pockets. This dummy had no clue whatsoever that I was robbing his ass blind.

Every time he put some of his dough away in his stash I was right behind him, trimming the fat around the edges.

"Kira, baby don't give me that look," Ricky continued.

"You know I'm out on the grind every night for me and you."

"Ricky, I don't wanna hear your lies," I tell him and walk to the kitchen.

And like I knew he would, he followed in my footsteps.

"Baby!" he started pleading. "Look what I gotcha!"

I knew it. He's always pulling something out of his hat when I'm about to put his ass on the hot seat. He knows I'm a sucker for gifts. "Whatever you got for me, you can take your ass right back out in the streets, find all your babies' mamas, play Spin the Bottle and whoever the fuck wins, just give it to them." I fronted like I wasn't interested.

"Shit, them hoes wouldn't ever be able to get me to cop a bracelet like this for them!" Ricky tells me.

"They weren't hoes when you were screwing 'em."

"Look Kira, I didn't come home to argue wit' you. All I wanna do right now is see how this joint looks on your wrist."

Curious as to how iced out this bracelet was, I turned around with a grit on my face from hell. "You look so sexy when you're mad," he told me.

Hearing him tell me how sexy I looked made me want to smile real bad, but I couldn't put my guard down. I had to show this clown I wasn't playing with his ass and was truly tired of his bullshit. All his baby mama drama, the other hoes he was seeing and the many trips he took out of town, acting like he was taking care of business. Shit, I wasn't stupid! I knew all them trips he took weren't solely for business. But it's all lovely. While he thinks he's playing me, I'm straight playing his ass, too.

"Where you get this from?" I asked, continuing to front like I wasn't at all excited about this H series diamond watch by Chopard.

"Don't worry 'bout that," Ricky told me as he fastened the hook on it. "You like it?"

Trying to be modest, I told him, "Yeah." And then I looked him straight in his eyes with the saddest expression I could muster. I immediately thought about how I lost my mother to a plane crash just hours before I graduated from high school. I tried talking her into taking an earlier flight from her vacation in Venezuela, but she refused to leave her third husband out there alone and wanted to guard him from walking off with one of those young and beautiful women roaming around the beaches. So once again, she allowed her obsession for wealth to dictate her way of life. I hated to admit it but over the years, I had become the spitting image of her. I wanted nothing to do with a man who couldn't give me all the fine things in life. And since my mother had not been married to her third husband long enough, I got stiffed when his will was read. The only two choices I had was to either move in with my uncle and his family or my grandmother Clara, who were my only living relatives. So, guess what? I chose neither. I did this because I just felt like I didn't belong with any of them. I mean, come on. Who wanted to live in a house that always smelled like mothballs? Who wanted to live with an uncle who forced you to be in church every Sunday? Plus, you had to abide by his rules. And he didn't care how old you were, either. So, it had to be fate when Ricky came into my life.

He got me my own apartment not even a week after we met. The fact that he loved to spend his dough on me made it even sweeter. He tried really hard to make sure I got everything I needed, and I let him. Hell yeah! That's why most of the time when I'm upset, I can make him feel really guilty about how he's been treating me lately.

"Why do you keep taking me through all these changes?" I asked as I forced myself to cry.

"What you talkin' 'bout, Kira? What changes?"

"The constant lies and drama!"

"Tell me what you talkin' 'bout, Ma!"

"I'm talking about you coming in this house two, three, and four o'clock in the morning, every damn night, like you got it like that! I'm just plain sick of it!"

"Come off that, baby," Ricky said as he pulled me into his arms. "You know those hours are the best time for me to work. I make mo' money and get less police."

"Who cares about all of that? I just want it to stop!"

"It will."

"But when? I mean, come on, Ricky. You got plenty of dough put away. And I've got some good, consistent money coming in my salon every week. So, we ain't gon' need for nothing."

"Look, I'll tell you what? Let me finish the rest of my pack and make one last run down to Florida, then I'll take a long vacation."

"What you mean, vacation?!" I raised my voice because I needed some clarity.

"It means I'mma chill out for a while."

"What's a while?"

"Shit, Kira! I don't know! Maybe six months. A year."

"You promise?" I asked, giving him my famous pout.

"Yeah. I promise," he told me in a low whisper as he began to kiss my neck and tug on my earlobe.

That instant, my panties got wet. Ricky pulled me closer to him. He cupped both of my ass cheeks in his hands, gripping 'em hard while he ground his dick up against my kitty cat. I couldn't resist the feelings that were coming over me. So when he picked me up I wrapped my legs around his waist, only leaving him enough room to slide his huge black dick inside my world of passion. I'm so glad I had on my crotchless panties because if I had had to wait another second for him to pull my thong off, I probably would have exploded.

"Hmmm, baby fuck me harder!" I begged him as I used the kitchen sink to help support my weight. His thrusts got harder and more intense.

"You like it when we fuss and make up, huh?" Ricky whispered each word between kisses. But of course, I declined to answer him. Swelling his head up about how I like making love after we have an argument, was not what I deemed to be a solution to our problems. After we got our rocks off, he and I both decided to lay back in our king-sized bed until we both dozed off.

Around 12:30 in the afternoon is about the time Ricky and I woke up. I hopped into the shower and about two minutes later, he hopped in right behind me. I knew what he wanted when he walked in the bathroom. It's not often that he and I take showers together, unless he wants to bend me over so he can hit it from the back. He knows I love giving it to him from the back, especially in the shower. The slapping noise our bodies make together in the water, as he's working himself in and out of me, turns me on.

After Ricky got his rocks off, he left the shower and returned to our bedroom to get dressed. "What you gon' do today?" I asked him as I entered into our bedroom, wrapped in a towel.

"Well, I'mma run by the spot out Norfolk and see why Eric and them can't get my dough straight."

"Please, don't go out there and scream on them like you got something to prove."

"I'm not. I'mma be cool 'til one of them niggas step out of pocket."

"See, that's one of the reasons I want your ass to stop hustling!" I pointed my finger at him.

"Won't you stop stressing yourself? Believe me, most niggas out there got nothing but respect for me."

"What about the one who don't?" I continued with my questions as I started to lotion my body down.

"I've got plenty of soldiers out there that'll outweigh that problem."

"Yeah, yeah, yeah!" was my response, hoping he'd catch the hint and shut up.

Unfortunately this wasn't the case. Ricky kept yapping on and on about how good his product was, and how the fiends were loving it. Once I had gotten enough of hearing about his street life, I grabbed a sweatsuit and a pair of Air Force Ones that matched my outfit and threw them both on. I scooped up my car keys and my Chanel handbag, and headed out the front door.

When I pulled up in front of my salon, it was packed. I knew I had at least four, if not five, of my clients waiting on me already. I know they were mad as hell, too, considering I was supposed to have been here three hours ago. My first appointment was at ten o'clock. Hell! I couldn't get up. After waiting up all night for my trifling-assed husband to come home and then after all the fussing I did, I still let him con me outta my drawz. As I made my way through the salon doors, I greeted everyone and told my ten o'clock client to go and sit at the washbowl. "Tasha, girl, please don't be mad wit' me," I began to explain as I threw the cape around her neck.

"Oh, it's alright. I ain't been waiting that long," Tasha replied.

"What you getting?"

"Just a hard wrap. I got two packs of sixteen-inch hair I wantcha to hookup."

"Did you bring a stocking cap?"

"Yep."

"A'ight. Well, lay back so I can get started."

Within the next two hours, I had all four of my clients situated. They were either under the dryer or on their way out the door. Seven more of my clients showed up, but three cancelled. I thanked God for that because I wouldn't be getting out of this shop until around ten or eleven o'clock tonight. That couldn't happen. I had to get home and wash those two loads of clothes I had packed up top of my hamper before I heard Ricky's mouth about it.

He loved for his house to be cleaned at any cost. If his ass wasn't so unfaithful, we could have had a housemaid, because nothing must be out of place. This fetish for absolute cleanliness got on my nerves sometimes. I mean, shit, ain't nothing wrong with leaving a damn dirty glass or a plate and a fork in the sink every now and then. As for certain garments in his wardrobe, I was forbidden to throw them in the washing machine. I was always reminded to read the label instructions for every piece of clothing he had. If it said "Dry Clean Only," then that's where it was going. I got a headache just thinking about it, so, I made a rule to put a big *"H"* on my chest and handle it.

A few more hours flew by and my other stylists' clients started falling out the door, one by one. This meant our time to go home was coming.

"Rhonda," I called out to one of my hair stylists, who happened to be one of the hottest beauticians in the Tidewater area.

"Yeah," she replied.

"You feel like giving me a roller set after I put my last client under the dryer?"

"Girl, you know I don't mind," Rhonda replied as she bopped her head to Lloyd Bank's single, "On Fire."

Rhonda's good people. I knew she was going to tell me yeah, before I attempted to even ask her. That's just her personality. She'd been working with me ever since I opened the doors to this shop four years ago. From day one, she's showed me nothing but love, even through all the drama her kid's father had been giving her. Her kid's father, Tony, is also a ladies' man; just like Ricky. I keep telling Rhonda to get him like I get my husband. Stick him where it hurts: either steal his money or his pack. It can't get any simpler than that. But nah, she ain't hearing me. That's why them hoes Tony's messing with was laughing at her, 'cause she was letting that nigga play her.

Now my other stylist, Sunshine, was working her game *entirely* different. She was your average-looking chick with ghetto-assed booty. Niggas loved her. Every time I turned around she had somebody else's man walking through my salon doors, bringing her shit.

Sunshine was strictly hustler bound. No other kind of man would attract her. You had to be driving a whip, estimating thirty Gs or better. And his dough had to be long. I'm talking like, from V.A. to the state of Rhode Island, to mess with that chick.

Oh, and Sunshine's wardrobe was tight, too. She wasn't gonna wear none of that fake-assed, knock-off Prada and Chanel that these hoes were getting from the Chinese people at the hair stores. No way. Sunshine was a known customer at Saks Fifth Avenue and Macy's.

I've seen the receipts. Sometimes I thought she was trying to be in competition with me, considering I was like a regular at those stores and all. But there can be no contest because when it's all said and done, I am and will always be the baddest bitch.

Since the day had almost come to an end, I sat back in Rhonda's station as she did her magic on my hair. We were in a deep conversation about her man Tony, when Ricky walked through the door. "Good evening," he said.

"What's up, Ricky!" Rhonda greeted him.

"Nothing much," he responded.

"Where you just coming from?" I wanted to know.

"From the crib."

"Our house?"

"Yeah."

"So, what's up?"

"I need to switch cars witcha," he said as he took a seat in one of the booth chairs across from me.

Something must be getting ready to go down. And he wasn't gonna spill the beans while Rhonda sitting up in here with me. I let her finish my hair and in the meantime, Ricky and I made idle conversation until she left. After she finished my hair, it only took her about ten minutes to clean up her station. Then Rhonda said her goodbyes and left.

"So, what you need my car for this time?" I wasted no time asking Ricky the second Rhonda left out the door.

As I waited for him to respond, I knew he could do one of three things. He could either tell me the truth, which could probably hurt him in some way later down the line. Or he could tell me a lie, which would really piss me off. And then he could throw Rule #7 at me from the *Hustler's Manual*, which insisted that he tell me nothing. A hustler's reason for that was: "The less your girl knows, the better off ya'll be."

"I need it to make a run," he finally said.

"What kind of run?"

"You don't need to know all that!" Ricky snapped.

"Look, don't get no attitude with me because I wanna know where you're taking my car."

"And who bought you the LS 400?"

"I don't care who bought it! The fact remains, it's in my name. Just like the Benz and that cartoon character Hulk–painted, 1100 Ninja motorcycle you got parked in the garage."

"And your point?"

"Look, Ricky, just be careful. And please don't do nothing stupid."

"I'm not," he assured me with a kiss on my forehead.

"Don't have no bitch in my car," I yelled as he made his way out the door.

While he ignored me like I knew he would, I stood there and watched Ricky unlock my car door and drive off. At the same time, I wondered where he was goin'.

From I'M STILL WIFEY

It Ain't Over

Can you believe it? After all the planning I did to leave my husband Ricky to run off with Russ, it backfired on me. It has been two-and-a-half months since the whole thing went down. Now I'm sitting here all alone, in my hair shop, thinking about what I am going to do about this baby I'm carrying.

Rhonda and Nikki both didn't believe me when I told them that I was pregnant by Russ. But after I pulled out a calendar and counted back the days from the last time we were together, it finally registered through their thick skulls.

"So, what cha' gon' do about it?" Rhonda asked me the day I got the results from a pregnancy test about a month ago. The first thing that came out of her mouth was for me to get an abortion since I ain't gon' have a baby daddy. God knows where he is. But I told her that was the furthest thing from my mind because whether I had Russ in my life or not, I was gon' have this baby. And then she said, "Well, what would you do if he found out you're pregnant and wants to come back with a whole bunch of apologies and shit?"

I told her that shit ain't gon' happen because first of all, Russ ain't gon' find out I'm pregnant 'cause ain't nobody gon' know I'm pregnant by him. And second, after that stunt he pulled on me to rob me for my dough, I know he ain't gon' never show his face around this way ever again. He would be a fool to. I mean, he don't know if I told Ricky that he robbed me or not. So to play it cool, he's gon' do like any other greasy-ass nigga would do after they pull a stick-up move, and that is to disappear. And even though he thinks he got away with it, he hasn't. 'Cause whether Russ knows it or not, karma is coming for his ass. And what will give me much pleasure is to be able to see it hit 'em.

Hopefully my day will come very soon.

Back at my place, which is a step down from my ol' two-story house, I decided to pop myself a bag of popcorn and watch my favorite show, *America's Next Top Model*. Afterward, I began to straighten things up around my two bedroom, two-bath condo until my telephone started ringing.

"Hello," I said without looking at the caller ID.

"Whatcha doing?" Rhonda wanted to know.

"I was just dusting the mantel over my fireplace."

"Girl, sit your butt down. 'Cause if my memory serves me, I do remember you being on your feet all day today."

"I'm fine. But what I wanna know is, why you didn't come back to work today?"

Rhonda sighed heavily and said, "Kira, if I could kill Tony and get away with it, I would do it."

"What happened now?"

"Girl, I caught this nigga talking to some hoe named Letisha on his cell phone."

"Where was he at?"

"He was in the bathroom, sitting on the fucking toilet, taking a shit."

I laughed at Rhonda's comment and asked her what happened next.

"Well, before I busted in on him and smacked him upside his damn head with my shoe, I stood very quiet in the hallway right outside our bedroom and heard this bastard telling that hoe how much he missed her and that he was going to get his hair cut at the barbershop. And right after I heard him say that, that's when I went off."

"So, what did he do?"

"He couldn't do shit with his pants wrapped around his ankles. So, he just sat there and took all them blows I threw at his ass. And then when he dropped his cell phone, I hurried up and snatched it right off the floor and cussed that bitch out royally."

"And what did she say?"

"I ain't let her say shit. 'Cause after I told her who I was and that if I ever caught her in Tony's face, she was gonna get fucked up, I hung up."

"So, what was Tony doing while you was going off on that hoe?"

"Trying to hurry up and wipe his ass, so he can get up from the toilet and I guess take his phone back. But as soon as the bastard stood up to flush the stool, I threw his phone right up against the wall as hard as I could and broke that bad boy in about ten little pieces."

I laughed again and said, "Damn girl! That's some shit I used to do."

"Well, jackass didn't see it coming. So, it made it all the better."

"Where's he at now?"

"In the kitchen helping Ryan with his homework."

"So, did he ever go out and get his hair cut?"

"Hell nah. Shit, he knew better."

"Well, what kind of lies did he tell you about everything that happened?"

"Girl, that nigga ain't gon' volunteer no information. All he had to say was that I was crazy as hell. And then he went on about his damn business."

"Rhonda," I said before I sighed, "I know you're sick and tired of going through all that bullshit! Because I sure was when Ricky was on the streets."

"Hey wait," Rhonda interjected, "I forgot to tell you that he called the shop today while you was at lunch."

"Did you accept the call?"

"Yeah. But we only talked for a few minutes."

"What did he say?"

"He just wanted to know where you was and when was you coming in. So, I told him that you wasn't. And that's when he asked me to call you on three-way. But I told him the three-way call thing wasn't working."

"I bet he got real mad, didn't he?"

"Hell yeah!"

"So, what did he say after that?"

"Nothing but to tell you he called. And for me to tell you to come down to the county jail and see him before the U.S. Marshal picks him up and takes him off to the Federal Holding Facility in Oklahoma, because he has something very important to talk with you about."

"Well, he should already know that it ain't gon' happen. But, I am wondering what he's got so important to talk to me about."

"Girl, he's just probably saying that so he can get you to come down and see him."

"Yeah. You probably right," I agreed.

"Well, are you going to ever tell him that you're pregnant by Russ?" Rhonda blurted out of the blue.

"Nope. It ain't none of his damn business. All he needs to focus on is signing those divorce papers my lawyer is getting ready to send his ass."

"So, you're serious about that, huh?"

"You damn right!" I commented and then I said, "I'm gonna get that nigga outta my life once and for all, so I can move on."

"Look, I understand all that. But I wouldn't let his ass get off that easy. Because the next time he calls the shop, I would make it my business to wreck his muthafucking ego and tell him, *'Yeah nigga, while you was running around behind my back with Sunshine's stinking ass, I was fucking your boy Russ right in your bed. And I just found out that I'm pregnant by him.'*"

"Oh my God! That'll kill him!"

"That's the idea," Rhonda told me.

I said, "Girl, that nigga gon' try and come through the phone after I tell him some shit like that."

"Well, no need to worry 'bout that. 'Cause it ain't gon' happen." Before I could comment, she told me to hold on because somebody was beeping in on her other line. When she clicked over, it got real quiet. But just like that, she was right back on the line and said, "Hey girl, one of Tony's homeboys is on the other end trying to holler at him. So, let me call you back."

"A'ight," I told her. Then we both hung up.